Hinterland

David Barnett

Stafford, England

This is a work of fiction. All the characters and events portrayed in this book are fictitious, and any resemblance to real people, or events, is purely coincidental.

Hinterland
by David Barnett

Cover by Gabriel Strange
Art Direction and Typesetting by Gabriel Strange
Editor: Donna Scott

Set in Footlight MT Light

First edition, Immanion Press, 2005

0 9 8 7 6 5 4 3 2 1

1st Immanion Press Edition
http://www.immanionpress.wox.org/
info@immanionpress.wox.org

http://www.davidbarnett.net

ISBN 1-9048-5319-6

Printed in the UK

Hinterland

To Claire.
For believing.

ONE
WEIRD SHIT HAPPENS

Town, then; with its brash neon and brittle laughter and forlornly-waved ten pound notes; its transactions and whispers and shouts; its harsh, bright lights which illuminate our surfaces just as they add inky, unfathomable depth to our shadows.

Through the heaving, liquid mass of people my eyes graze towards the mirrored wall behind the bar and the light bounces towards me the reflection of three guys plumped up in coats and scarves, boots stained with black slush and salt from the roads. They're arguing over the telling of a funny story, one of them waving his arms and saying loudly: "This is how it starts. *THIS IS HOW IT STARTS.*"

We don't hang around long enough to hear the rest of the joke because then we're off, up and moving.

Who says go? It isn't me, I'm fairly sure of that. Pete still has half a pint left. And Tony is half-watching some old movie on the muted TV screens in the bar, his lips silently synching with the actors'. A good night. A Saturday night. A normal night.

"Where are we going?" Tony asks as we bundle into the taxi outside the bar.

The driver turns and looks at us, his face in shadow, coolly appraising each of us in turn. "Club is it, lads?"

"Not Janeiro's again, please," mutters Pete.

"Or Fanny's," says Tony.

"Or Crunch," I add.

The driver's gaze burns through the darkness, lingers on me. "Something *special*? Something *different*?"

"We're not going to a strip joint," I say. "We can't afford it."

The driver laughs and suddenly we're lurching away, spiralling outwards from the town centre. The bright lights blur. We're going fast. Too fast. I feel a little sick.

"Weird shit happens in the suburbs," says the driver.

"What?" I say.

"Have you seen the rain-wet dogs barking at empty shop doorways?" he says. "The scraps of black polythene that hang scarecrow-ragged on barbed wire, the flocks of dark birds that loiter on telegraph wires and go suddenly quiet when you walk down the street?"

Tony looks at me, scared, no doubt remembering tales of unlicensed cabs that take the unwary to dark building sites on the other side of town. Pete frowns, and says: "What the *fuck* are you talking about, pal? And where the hell are we?"

I look out of the window. I don't recognise anything. We're right out in the sticks, among unfamiliar streets, lost in the anonymous estates.

"I have a theory," says our driver. "Do you want to hear it?"

For the first time, I notice there's no meter or radio in the car. We're paused at a set of traffic lights; I can see our reflection in a glass-fronted shop. There's no light or sign on top of the vehicle.

This isn't a cab.

Tony's realised as well. "*Fuck*," he says softly.

"I think," says the driver conversationally, "that because people work and socialise and generally *live* in city centres, there's this massive build up of, oh, call it what you will; psychic energy, perhaps. And it all just sort of sits there and throbs like a huge power station. But when you get away from that, into the fringes, the hinterland, well, the distinctions become blurred, the edges get frayed, the picture goes out of focus.

"Weird shit happens."

"It's a theory, I suppose," I say. We're still stalled at the traffic lights.

"Fucking nutter," says Pete. "Come on, we're getting out here."

Pete pulls the handle and the door opens. Tony scrambles over him to be first out, followed by Pete who cuffs him around the head.

The driver turns again and says from the shadows of the front seat: "It's okay. We're here, anyway."

"Where?" I say, trying to find some kind of form in the darkness.

There's a movement, a shrug. "Like I said. The hinterland."

I get out of the car and it immediately drives away, the driver not waiting for payment. I watch it disappear around a bend in the road. Strange. I look around to see Pete and Tony venturing down a dark alley, called by the siren allure of repetitive beats. I follow them and the next thing we're knee-deep in rubbish and outside a big, solid, wooden door. Overhead is a sign in flaking paint. *Arcadia.*

"Is this it?" says Tony. "Maybe we should get back..."

"Fuck that, I want a drink," says Pete, rapping on the door. A hatch opens and there are a pair of eyes staring at us, one as blue as a clear sky and the other as green as the sea.

The eyes regard Pete and Tony. “No,” says a deep voice.

“Let’s go…” says Tony again.

Then the eyes light upon me.

“Wait." A heartbeat, then the sound of bolts sliding back from their housings. "Okay.”

Then we’re in and suddenly I’ve lost an hour. I’m drinking a bottle of Red Mist, starting to sober up unpleasantly, realising that I’ve lost the others, and, somewhere along the way, the plot.

There are three women dressed as schoolgirls leaning on the cigarette machine. Then it occurs to me they aren’t dressed up. They really are schoolgirls. They wear the same ties and uniforms as Tony’s kid sister. One of them sees me staring and grabs her crotch, sticking her tongue out like, well, like a kid. One of the others is smoking what looks like a crack pipe. Jesus. I blush furiously and turn away.

The club is full of purple smoke, and it’s really getting to the back of my throat. To my left I’m vaguely aware of a small dance floor, and somewhere an unseen DJ is playing what sounds like the theme tune from an old TV show underlayed with an acid jazz beat. On The Buses. Or perhaps Bless This House. Shit, that’s going to bother me all night now. I’m a little freaked, alone in this smog, shapes picked out in grotesque, back-lit silhouette, but at least this place is something different, a change from up town where it’s all billykids whizzing their tits off and doomers with sandwich boards telling you the end of the world is nigh, office girls cackling in cowboy boots and mini skirts.

Through the strobe-shot haze I think I spot Tony, slumped on the bar and trying to catch the attention of the bored girl standing behind it. I lurch towards him.

He peers at me through Bryan Ferry eyes. “Thank

Christ. Thought I'd lost you. Do you want another?"

I shake the half-full Red Mist and nod.

"Make it three, love, and a pint of lager," Tony bellows at the girl. She's wearing a rhinestone-studded combat vest and perfect-white bloomers.

She looks at Tony in a bored, *you're dog-shit*, kind of way, blows a huge bubble-gum globe which pops with the smell of strawberry, and sighs: "I told you, you can't have a drink unless you have the password. Club rules."

Tony squints at me, his twenty-pound note flapping at half-mast. "I think she's serious. Do you know this password?"

I shrug. "How should I know it?"

"You've got a drink, haven't you?" he nods at my bottle. I look down at it, almost in surprise. I wonder where the drink did come from. I don't remember buying it.

I feel a hand clamp itself on my shoulder and warm, beery breath in my ear. It's Pete, and he's well pissed still. "Lads, lads," he grins. "Where have you been?"

Tony grabs the lapel of Pete's shirt when he notices the dregs of the pint swilling about in Pete's hand. "Where did you get that drink? What's the password?" He's almost hysterical now. Christ, calm down.

Pete shrugs Tony's hands off with a hint of annoyance and warning. "'*Et in Arcadia, Ego*'."

I think Tony is going to cry. "What? Is that French? What is this bloody password?"

"It's Latin," I supply, helpfully.

"That's *it*," snaps Pete, running a hand through his aggressively-cut, blond hair. "That's the fucking password. Lola told me, and I'm going back to her before some other chancer moves in."

Peter lurches off into the mist. The DJ is playing an easy listening Christmas tune. I pat Tony on the back and tell him to follow me when he's got the drinks. I want to see this woman that Pete's found in this godforsaken place. I stay around long enough to drain the Red Mist and hear Tony haltingly quoting pidgin Latin at the bar girl then dive into the purple smoke.

And suddenly I'm alone again; really truly alone. I know Pete and Tony are nearby - probably within touching distance - but I feel for an instant that I've left them behind, moved forward. But not quite far enough to connect with the people in this club. I'm stuck, somewhere in the middle, somewhere between worlds. Then I feel a gravitational pull to the familiar, and the mist clears and delivers me to Pete.

I find him in a dark corner, arm draped over the back of a leather Chesterfield settee, languidly stroking the shoulder of what is obviously a man in drag, and not very good drag at that. "Lola" evidently didn't bother to shave before turning out for the evening, and tufts of black hair poke from under the cascading curls of the blonde wig. I don't like to think about the fake breasts wrestling in the tight vest top and the hairy legs under fishnet tights. I say nothing, my face set in a grinning rictus as Tony slides in beside me with a tray of drinks. I like to think I'm the tolerant type, you know, up on transgender politics and all that. I wish I could say the same for Pete. I've seen him put a bar stool through a window because someone knocked his pint over.

Tony hasn't noticed, I realise with something approaching mild panic, as he hands the drinks round and points an unsteady finger first at my bottle of Red Mist and then at me, and slurs: "Nearly eighteen quid. That's the last round I buy in this place. Whose idea was this club, anyway?"

Pete takes a mouthful of Lola's Red Mist before sliding it across the table towards her, his eyes lingering on hers. His. Christ, I don't know. I feel all fidgety and still sit there, staring, that stupid grin on my face. This could get very ugly, and I've suddenly just realised I don't really know where the hell we are.

"Just what is this shite, anyway?" grimaces Pete as the drink goes down. He swiftly takes a draft of lager to wash away the taste.

Tony replies: "Guarana and alcohol and other stuff, herbs and things. It's supposed to be better for you than beer. And it improves your, you know..." he makes some kind of 'waa-haay' noise and shoves a fist up in the air.

Jesus Christ, Tony hasn't noticed either. My mouth's aching from smiling. I try to stare at Lola, try to telepathically communicate that she should get the hell out of Pete's way before he realises what's going on. Lola just winks at me. Pete takes another mouthful of beer and looks for a long time at Lola, saying: "I don't need a big girl's blouse of a drink for that, I can promise you."

That's it. Too much. I have to take control of this situation because although I don't really know what Pete will do when the realisation of what's going on penetrates his fogged-up brain, I can imagine. I stand up too sharply, knocking the table and coming so perilously close to spilling Pete's pint that he glances warningly over the rim of the glass at me. I grab Tony by his shirt and haul him into the mist.

"What's got into you-" he begins before I clamp a hand over his mouth and hiss: "Look at her, *she's a fucking bloke*, for God's sake! Pete's going to go ape-shit when he realises. Does this look like the kind of place we want Pete to go postal in? We've got to sort this now."

Tony pushes me off and leans forward a bit to see Pete playfully winding one of Lola's synthetic curls in his fingers. The mist in his head seems to clear. "Jesus Christ," he whispers, and then before I can stop his mouth again he says louder, "Jesus Christ!" Then he's practically shouting: "Jesus Christ, Pete, that's not a bird, it's a fella!"

Then the effluent punches the wind-making machine. Pete squares up to Tony, Tony makes a grab at Lola's head to prove his point and save himself a kicking, Lola jerks backwards a bit too hard, and the wig slips down over his face. Tony starts pissing himself laughing, Pete just stares incredulously, and Lola straightens his barnet, grabs his handbag, and flounces away from the table, tipping me a wink and blowing me a kiss as he passes.

And I just stand there with that stupid fucking grin hurting my face.

After that there's a long silence, which even the DJ seems to acknowledge with a break in the easy listening for several seconds. As Neil Sedaka starts to sing about a lonely man, Pete shakes his head, as though clearing it of cobwebs, glares malevolently at Tony, and says: "Come on, let's go for a kebab."

The big bouncer with odd-coloured eyes lets us out of Arcadia into the dark alley without a word. High above the steep, black walls of whatever buildings we're sandwiched between the sky is a deep blue. Dawn is on the way. At least it's Sunday tomorrow, and no work. I just wonder where the hell we are.

Pete sets off resolutely towards the main street at the far end of the alley. Something stirs among a pile of bursting black bin bags. Shit. I hate rats. Nonchalantly, I cough and stamp noisily after Pete, hoping everything I've been told is true and they really are more scared of me than I am of them.

None of us recognises the main drag. Sodium-yellow streetlights illuminate a quiet road with anonymous red-brick shops and shuttered businesses standing silent sentry on either side. Chip wrappers blow gently in the chill eddies of the morning. It's very quiet, and it's cold, very, very cold. We stop and my feet crack the sheen of ice forming on a small puddle.

"Ah, bollocks. We'll never get a taxi. Bollocks." Tony's blowing into his hands to warm them up. He sounds well pissed off. Then I remember he's supposed to be working at his Dad's petrol station at nine. Christ, better not let him know it's gone five. I spot an old-fashioned, red phone box a couple of hundred yards along the unfamiliar street.

"Come on," I decide. "Let's go get a cab."

The out-of-date BT poster inside the piss-stinking phone box features an inanely-grinning Busby announcing that it is situated on the corner of Fugue Street and Lethe Lane. I've never heard of either of them. At least there are a few taxi cards stuck there, although they do have outdated area code numbers. I ring one and give the girl our location, "Lethe Lane... Lethe Lane..." she ponders. "I should know that one. Give me a clue."

I confess sheepishly that I don't quite know where I am myself. She gives a telephonic shrug. "It's okay, the driver'll find it. Give us fifteen minutes."

I step back out on to Fugue Street, glad to be back in the fresh air. To the east the sky has a hint of blood red, the sun struggling to get up like everyone else on a Sunday morning. Christ, I wish I was in my bed.

Tony and Pete are sitting on a low brick wall outside a boarded up shop. Far away I hear the electric hum and brittle clink of a milk float. Pete looks up expectantly. "Is it sorted? I'm fucking freezing here."

"Fifteen minutes. Is he okay?"

Tony looks rough. I wouldn't fancy being in work in four hours' time. There's a wet patch on the front of his shirt.

"He's puked, hasn't he?" says Pete in disgust. "Splashed all over me new jeans. He'd better be in better shape for this lads' weekend in Amsterdam."

"Don't you worry about that," croaks Tony, wiping vomit from his mouth with the sleeve of his jacket. We've had this trip planned for months; we always like a couple of good blow-outs in European cities every year - Prague, Tallinn, Paris - usually following the football if we can tie it in, but this time just for the sheer enjoyment of it. Pete's right, though. I hope Tony's stamina improves, because it's not going to be a quiet weekend.

"Just don't be standing near me with puke all over your mouth when I'm chatting up the birds," warns Pete, playfully punching Tony in the shoulder.

"You'll be paying for them like you always do," says Tony, slapping him back. "That's unless they're blokes in disguise."

As they start to brawl, I turn away distractedly. This really is an odd road. I peer down what must be Lethe Lane, running at a right angle off Fugue Street. A set of traffic lights blinks unceasingly through its programme, though not a single car has negotiated the junction while we've been standing here. Tall buildings rear up along the length of Lethe Lane as far as I can see. Back the way we walked, Fugue Street curves around sharply, while in the other direction there seems to be a big church or school. The oddest thing about this part of town is the shops. They're all closed, obviously, but you get the feeling it's not just down to the time of day. Everything about this place seems... forgotten.

For example, halfway down the street on the other side there's a pub, and over the door there's one of those old illuminated signs, for Double Diamond lager, of all things. When's the last time you saw a pub serving Double Diamond? And something else. Outside the pub is an old-fashioned metal dustbin. It's been wheelie bins round here for years. There's a newsagents next door, and the billboard tacked to the wall holds a torn, flapping piece of paper headed The Daily Sketch. The Daily Sketch? When was that last published, the Sixties? Is this a joke? Some kind of student art project?

There's a liquid sound like a cat being choked, and Pete whines: "Oh for fuck's sake, he's off again!"

Tony is doubled up on the pavement, losing the night's beer together with what looks like a good portion of his large intestine splashing warmly on to the ground. I feel my own bile rising and look away, concentrating on an advertisement for Woodbine cigarettes outside one of the shops. Peter interrupts: "Where's this fucking taxi, Dave? It's been half a bloody hour."

He's right. In fact, it's been longer: my fake Tag Heuer tells me it's almost a quarter to six. Jesus, poor old Tony.

"That club was weird, though, eh?" I say, trying to distract Pete from Tony's coughing.

Pete looks up at me. "What?"

"That club. Arcadia. Weird."

Pete considers this for a moment. "What?" he says again.

I can feel myself getting annoyed. "Pete. The club. Arcadia. The place where we've just spent half the night. *That fucking club…*"

There's a sound, a faraway beep of a horn. Pete looks up. Thinking he's trying to take the piss out of me for some reason, all this pretending not to remember the club, I stalk off to the middle of the silent frosty road and jog round the bend a short way. I'm almost shocked to see a car with its headlights on, parked a hundred yards away. I can make out a light on top of the car as well. It's either our taxi or the police. Either would be equally welcome at the moment, so I jump up and down on the Tarmac and wave. A brief moment later the engine guns and the car heads towards me. It is our taxi, thank Christ. And a real one, as well. Not like that unlicensed weirdo who brought us here.

I ease into the front of the Nissan Sunny, letting the warmth envelop me, while Pete bundles Tony into the back. I hope he isn't going to puke again. The driver looks sheepish as we set off.

"Sorry I'm late, lads. I couldn't find this place for

the life of me. Couldn't place the street at all, and I don't know why because it's a main road."

"Haven't you got a map, then?" offers Pete aggressively from the back. He's totally lost his patience now. I silently pray for him to shut up because I don't want this guy to put us out here.

"That's the odd thing," muses the driver. "It's listed in the A-Z index, but when you get to the page and follow Segg Way, which it's supposed to run off, you get to the end of the page and turn over and it isn't there. Must be a printing error or something."

I'm horribly sober now, and cold. A hangover's beginning to take hold and I must look like shit. My boots are caked in crap, presumably from the alley where that club was. It's almost six, and it will be properly light soon. We turn on to Segg Way, and suddenly I'm on familiar ground. Cars appear from nowhere, and we pass houses with lights on. Civilisation at last.

I'm the last drop off, and after gratefully paying the taxi driver I stagger up the two flights of stairs to my flat, letting myself in and collapsing fully clothed on to my bed. After a couple of minutes it's obvious that sleep isn't going to come. Sighing, I slip on a CD of something chilled and sit at my desk in front of the big window, building a spliff to smoke while I watch my town yawn, stretch, and come to life.

I love my Saturday nights.

TWO
SCHRODINGER'S FRIDGE

I awake sharply, still sitting in the director's chair, the joint dead between my fingers, and gasp a single word: "Arcadia!"

I shake my head, clearing the last of the fog. It's something after eleven, and apart from a stiff neck I feel surprisingly rested and ready for Sunday afternoon. Just need a shower to feel human again. I wonder how poor old Tony's going on at the service station; I'll give him and Pete a call later on, see how they're shaping up. As I stand under the dribbling warm water I reflect on the previous night. Strange, but good. Good but strange.

By the time I've soaked myself thoroughly and washed away the real and imagined detritus of Saturday night it's almost midday and I'm famished. Naked and dripping soap and water everywhere I pad from the bathroom through the living room and to the kitchen, leaving soggy, perfect footprints on the carpet. Balking at the effort needed to cook something more complicated, I slam a few slices of stale-ish bread under the grill and take the top off a tin of Heinz beans before returning to the lounge and flopping, still wet, on to the sofa.

Flicking through the TV and simultaneously powering up the stereo, I settle on a random channel - it looks like an old Survivors re-run - and an upbeat music station on the radio. Satisfied with my multi-media stimulus, I head back into the kitchen to check on the toast.

Fed and dressed, I still have six hours before I can see Mags. I stare at myself in the mirror and try to decide who I am today. The Dave who goes on three-day drinking benders with his mates from way back? The Dave who trawls the counter-culture dives of his town, mind spinning from recreational drugs? Mags' Dave? The Dave I am at work? My Mum and Dad's Dave? Or the private, secret Dave who only I know?

Today I feel just like being myself, which is a little bit of all those mixed together. And the whole is greater than the sum of the parts, so when I'm being me, I'm dynamite, unstoppable. I flash the mirror a world-beating smile and head out into my town.

The day is crisp, chill and winter bright, just the way I like it. Leaves crunch under my boots and plumes of hot breath trail from my mouth and nostrils. The sky is clear but heavy with prospects. Snow, perhaps; it's been forecast for later in the week. It's going to be a good day.

My town is very much like any other. Far enough from the nearest city to retain its identity and have its own football team but close enough to visit for shops and big clubs on special occasions. Things here are on a more manageable scale, it's more difficult to get lost and be anonymous, there's still a sense of community and belonging.

I'm warm in my thick corduroy jacket and twill trousers. I walk to the end of my road without seeing a soul and then on to the ringway, busy with Sunday drivers and orbiting buses. I'm not quite sure where I'm headed, but a walk in the park seems a pleasant plan. I follow the ring road round for a while, then cut in behind St Boniface church and on to the desolate land that used to be the old council offices. Some kids are playing footy in the debris, and their battered ball comes winging towards me. I try to volley it back but the kick goes awry and the ball bounces awkwardly away. I've always had two left feet when it came to playing football. I shrug an embarrassed apology. One of the kids shouts: "Wanker!" and they all laugh.

They're just a bunch of kids, but for a second their glowering eyes light upon me, shining dully from dirty, feral faces. I falter and stumble on a broken house-brick, provoking more sniggers; low and menacing. I flush and alter my course off the patch of spare land. Their territory. They gather on it like animals, sniffing the air, trying to weigh me up, the hint of curled lips and yellow teeth hiding in the ingrained dirt of their faces. For God's sake, get a grip. They're just kids. But I can feel their eyes burning into my back as I walk, detouring down a narrow alley, unable to resist casting a glance over my shoulder as I turn the corner. But they're just normal kids again, kicking the ball at each other and exchanging easy obscenities.

The snicket is quiet, filled with lock-ups and dodgy looking car repair garages, and almost deserted. A big meathead with a spanner watches me with suspicion from the shadows of a garage doorway, and behind him I can make out the snuffling nose of an eager Alsatian. I keep my head down and walk on, until I come to a familiar road. Colin's street. Relieved to be on familiar ground once more, I decide to pay him a visit before heading on to the park.

A lot of people think Colin's weird. He must be knocking on fifty, and lives on his own in a big house that used to belong to his parents before they died.

Colin just took over the place after they were gone. It's still decorated as they must have left it, floral wallpaper and desperate furniture. It's full of unintentional kitsch, flying ducks on the kitchen wall, unidentifiable glass ornaments in brown and beige, even a few of those mass-produced paintings, the woman with the blue face and a huge swan. I suppose he is a bit weird, but not because he's fifty and lives on his own. Jostling for space with his parents' crappy legacies is Colin's own collection of tat; books and comics and odd magazines about crop circles and UFOs. He also has a healthy collection of porno mags, which I suppose is fair enough. My mates think there's something wrong with me, going to visit Colin, but he's okay. He's never come on to me, or anything. Well, he did once offer to give me a blow job while I was flicking through one of his Swedish mags, but he was joking. I think.

The green front door with the ghastly oval of coloured glass swings open when I knock on it. I sigh and step inside. I'm fed up of telling Colin he lives in a rough area and should really be more security conscious, but it never seems to penetrate. His mind's always on other things.

I walk into his kitchen and he's sitting cross-legged on the lino, surrounded by rusty tools and drawing with a marker pen and a set square on the door of his fridge, which he has unscrewed and removed from the juddering white Indesit in the corner. The kitchen is bathed in stark, yellow light from the fridge which reflects off Colin's spectacles in the gloomy room. He looks up without surprise when he sees me standing in the doorway.

"David, my boy, come in. Sorry about the mess," he says, then carries on musing over the square he's drawn on the door of the fridge.

"Colin, what are you doing?" I say, not meaning to sound as exasperated as I do.

He stops to scratch his beard and adjust his glasses,

then holds up a piece of plain glass, roughly the size of the square he's drawn on the white metal of the door. "Why, I'm putting a window in the fridge, of course."

I wait for him to go on, but he simply continues with his study of the door and absently picks dried egg yolk from his beard. Eventually I feel the need to ask: "Why?"

"Well, I've got to know, dear boy. It's been bothering me for years and I've decided to do something about it. Plus, it'll help when it comes to restocking the fridge."

"Got to know what, Colin?" I say calmly, but this is getting on my nerves. Sometimes he just talks in riddles for the hell of it.

"The light, David, the light. Does it stay on when you shut the refrigerator door? It's a puzzle that has been perplexing philosophers since, well, since the refrigerator was invented. And I intend to know."

Sighing, I tiptoe through the tools and crap to where the doorless fridge hums away quietly. Feeling along the rim where the door should be, I find what I'm looking for. "Look, Colin, see this little button here? When you shut the door it turns the light off, and when you open it the button pops out and the light comes on. I thought everyone knew that." To prove my theory, I press the button a couple of times and make the diffuse shadows in the kitchen dance.

"Ha!" barks Colin. "Don't blindly accept everything, my young lamb. Just because the light goes off when you press the button, it doesn't logically follow that it goes off when you close the door."

"Of course it does!"

"Not so. How can you possibly know that for a fact when you can't see inside the fridge? Don't presume."

I begin to argue but Colin holds up one hand to silence me. I shed my jacket, despite the coldness in the kitchen. I know I'm going to be here for some time.

"Now then," begins Colin, a bearded Buddha cross-legged amid the wreckage. "How familiar are you with Schrodinger's Cat?"

"Didn't it used to get chased by Pavlov's Dog in that old cartoon?"

"Different field altogether, David. Erwin Schrodinger postulated an interesting proposition, which I will simplify for you thus: take a cat, and put it in a box. Into this box you also put, say, a canister filled with poison gas. This canister has an exactly fifty per cent chance of releasing its fatal contents, and a fifty per cent chance of not doing so, on a count of ten. Close the box. After ten seconds, is the cat alive or dead?"

"There's no way of knowing while the box is closed."

"Exactly!" shouts Colin, startling me. I pull one of the battered chairs away from the table and perch on it.

He takes off his glasses and rubs dust off the lenses with the hem of his food-stained pullover. "Until you look into the box, you have no way of knowing whether the canister released its deadly load and killed the cat, or whether the poor pussy is alive and well. Therefore, according to Schrodinger, the cat is at once in both states: alive *and* dead, until the box is opened and we can make one of those states real in *our* sense of reality."

"All of which means..?"

"All of which means that the light in my fridge is both on and off when the door is shut, but because when I open the door a logical sequence of events comes into play, in that the light comes on because the door is open, Schrodinger's theory cannot be proved either way. A window in the door of the fridge will simulate the act of circumventing the opening of Schrodinger's box and I will at last be able to find out whether that bloody light stays on or goes off when the fridge door is shut."

"In the meantime, this chocolate mousse is melting.

Mind if I have some?"

"Be my guest," says Colin, standing stiffly, his quest for philosophical knowledge momentarily sidelined. "Have you seen The Justice League of America lately, by the way?"

While I spoon the mousse into my mouth we leaf through a stack of American comics on the table. Colin's the only person I know who can read psychological and sociological meaning into this stuff. Most of it's adolescent power fantasies and women in star-spangled knickers, but some of it's actually okay and looks like it might be written with normal adults in mind. Colin is midway through explaining how Captain America embodies the concept of the United States' assumed responsibility as world policeman and his place in the world post 9/11 when something occurs to me.

"Oh yeah, something really weird happened to me last night."

Colin suddenly loses interest in Spandex-clad, muscle-bound freaks. If there's anything guaranteed to pique his interest, it's use of the word 'weird'. He's practically a student of the weird and wonderful.

I recount to him our adventures in the dodgy club, Arcadia, and the deserted streets where time seemed to have stood still. How Pete seemed to have forgotten about Arcadia just minutes after we left it. "What did you say that road was called again?" he says.

"It was a junction. Lethe Road, or Lane, and Fugue Street."

"Interesting, interesting... Lethe is an easy one: the river in Greek mythology which was said to impart forgetfulness to anyone who drunk its waters. That would fit in with your evening, no? But fugue? A musical term for... although, hold on... wait here."

Colin stalks out of the kitchen, leaving me to finish off the chocolate mousse and to flip through a comic featuring lots of men with big guns and unlikely names. He wanders back in with a hardback copy of the Oxford English Dictionary and absently scratching his balls "Here it is: Fugue. As we thought, a musical term, but... aha! The second definition reads: 'Loss of awareness of one's self coupled with flight from one's usual environment'."

Colin looks over his glasses at me and a slight shiver runs down my spine. "Would that be anything like what you boys were experiencing last night?"

"Shit," I say slowly. "That really is... weird."

THREE
THE ISLAND OF LOST WOMEN

The day has become dull and overcast while I've been in Colin's. Sunday afternoon no longer has its crisp, wintry appeal, but I decide to carry on to the park. I rolled a couple of joints before I came out and I wouldn't mind sharing one with the ducks.

I like the park, especially late at night when there isn't a soul about and you have to climb over the wrought iron gates to get in. There's a bandstand and a hedge maze and in the summertime girls in skimpy clothing lounge on the grass reading Bronte novels and eating ice cream.

Today, old soldiers are ranked along the graffiti-etched benches, families propel prams along shining paths, kids knock a football about among the frozen flower beds. The cold snap threatening early this morning has settled in full force. Winter draws on. Somewhere, a tinny radio is shouting out a match report. I wander along the Tarmac in the direction of the pond, framed by stark, leafless trees, and jam cold fists into my trouser pockets.

I first met Mags in this park, on a gloriously hot July Sunday, the kind you rarely get now. She was reading The Tenant of Wildfell Hall and sucking a Fab lolly. I was having a kick around with Pete and Tony and a couple of others, and with my renowned footballing skills managed to kick the ball straight at her, knocking the Fab out of her hand. Naturally she was pissed off, she called me a dickhead, I bought her another lolly, and we ended up going out for a drink that night. When I was at school I never got any girlfriends because I was decidedly not fab at sport, but if I'd been good at football I would never have met Mags.

The pond is frozen over, the ducks have gone. Flown south for the winter, I suppose. I think of Holden Caulfield in Catcher in the Rye, hassling the taxi driver about where the ducks go in winter. It must be great to just take off and get away when things have gone shitty, just go to a better place. I take out one of the spliffs from my top pocket and spark it up with my Zippo, inhaling deeply.

The ice looks thick. I wonder if it's strong enough to take my weight? There's a bit of an island in the middle of the pond, and I vaguely remember building rafts and punting out to it when we were kids, if the park attendant didn't catch us. It's years since I've been out there.

I feel a bit giddy from the dope, probably because it's almost four o'clock and all I've had to eat is beans on toast. Stifling a giggle, I test the strength of the ice with my boot. It seems firm enough, so I put my whole weight on the one foot, eventually stepping on to the ice.

Finishing the joint, I flick the roach on to the ice and take another step forward. This is mad. The island is at least thirty yards from here, and this pond is deep in places. But something spurs me on. When we were kids, there was definitely a reason why we crept out to this island, something that was secret but scary as well. I haven't thought about that for years. With each step I take towards the island, memories surface unexpectedly. Strapping old plastic barrels together and floating precariously across the pond in the dead of night, I can't have been more than nine or ten. Giggling nervously in the dark with the pond water slapping warningly on the side of the makeshift raft. Pete was there, Tony as well.

I'm about halfway across now, and the ice suddenly feels much thinner. I risk a look back at the park; there's no-one in sight and voices seem distant over the slight rise of the landscaped grounds. Shit, I should go back.

"We should go back," says Tony.

"Shut it, soft lad," warns Pete, the same age as us but bigger and more threatening. I add diplomatically: "Look, we're halfway there now. It's the same if we carry on or go back."

"We're sinking!" moans Tony. He's right, as well; my trainers and the knees of my jeans are wet through. I'll catch it when I get home. Pete keeps paddling with the makeshift oar fashioned out of a tree branch and an old pan. "Look," he says through gritted teeth. "We're nearly there, all right?"

The island is bigger than it looks from the bank. As I half-walk, half-skate towards it, I can see it stretching back quite a way, hidden from the rest of the park. I didn't realise the pond was so wide, never mind the island.

We bump against mud and stop abruptly. Without waiting, all three of us scramble through the mire on to land. Far behind us the street lights beyond the park twinkle like distant stars, but here on the island it's as dark as it ever gets.

"What's supposed to be here?" I ask nervously. Pete shrugs, he doesn't know either. But everyone's talking about the island in whispers, about something on here. Or someone.

We start walking. The island seems to go on for miles and we're all terrified. Even Pete looks ready to go back when suddenly Tony says: "What was that?" He's practically shitting himself.

I grab hold of Pete and he doesn't shrug me off. "What was what?"

"A noise. Someone's coming."

Adrenaline rushes down to my legs and they start pumping, carrying me away, but Pete's holding on to me and won't let go, more from terror than anything else. "Get the fuck off," I whimper.

His grip relaxes. "Look," he says wonderingly. "It's a girl."

She's picking her way through the undergrowth in front of us, unafraid and as naked as the day she was born. Perhaps fifteen or sixteen, well developed, and smeared with what looks like years of mud and grime. She flashes a white-toothed smile at us and says: "Some more? You awfy young." Her accent isn't local, sort of odd and foreign. Then she tosses her long, matted hair back and calls over her shoulder: "There's more here."

From behind the girl there's movement, and then another emerges into the fine moonlight, equally naked and equally dirty. They look like sisters. Twins. "Come then, back to den," says the second in the same unusual dialect.

"The den?" whispers Pete. "What for?"

The first girl laughs harshly. "Wha' for? For what all laddies come over here for in middle night. Come on then, who first?"

And we're off and running, shouting and screaming and yelling back to the raft, not caring how much noise we make and just wanting to get off the island and back to the world we know.

I stand doubtfully on the ice, just a couple of steps from the island. In front of me there's a wide fissure, leaking pond water on to the frozen surface. I should make a move one way or the other soon. Odd how I'd forgotten that episode. As far as I recall, none of us ever talked about it again after that night. I wonder why?

With a standing leap I make it to the frozen mud of the island bank, glad to be off the unstable ice at last. All I've got to worry about now is getting back. But my curiosity's up now. The island looks like it hasn't been set foot upon for ages, but I can just make out a path through the frost-painted bramble bushes.

Suddenly I'm a kid again, pushing my way through the undergrowth, nervously anticipating what's going to be on the other side. Eventually I come to a clearing, which my memory matches with the place where the girls first appeared all those years ago. My palms are itching and my mouth feels dry. Come on, this is ridiculous. What am I expecting to find?

I'm vaguely aware that it's going to be dark soon, but I press on through the skeletal trees for what seems a mile but can't possibly be. When I'm just about to give up and head back to the frozen pond I stumble through bushes into another clearing.

There's a den in the centre, crudely constructed from old sheets of corrugated steel and cardboard boxes, covered in mud and dried leaves. At the doorway, where a tatty curtain hangs limply, there's the remains of a fireplace, ashes covered with a layer of frost. The roof of the den is clotted with duck shit.

Reminding myself to breathe, I pad down a slight incline and stand noiselessly a matter of yards from the hut. Just the home of a tramp, surely? But an insistent, nagging feeling tells me I'm on to something. Swallowing dryly, I step towards the hut and yank the curtain back sharply.

Empty. Looks like it hasn't been lived in for weeks at least. I step inside. Two makeshift beds, little more than packing crates pushed together and draped with dirty sheets. There's an awful smell of something rotting, and I almost yell out loud when I see the decaying corpses of two ducks hanging by a nail from the wall.

Dead ducks aside, it's almost quite cosy. The mud and leaves packed on the walls and roof insulate the den to some degree, and with that fire lit outside the door it could be habitable.

On the wall are two shelves, one packed with old coffee and jam jars and the other supporting, incongruously, books. The books draw me first, battered copies of the Bible, a few Reader's Digests, a couple of Arthur Haley and Jackie Collins blockbusters and several copies of Jane Eyre. Obviously the leftovers from absent-minded picnickers.

The same goes for the jars. Bits of food, packets of rancid butter, tea bags, salt and pepper sachets, crusts of bread with blue blossoms of mould. The remains from park bins. And there's a tin of money. Fivers, tenners, coins. I look at it thoughtfully. There's probably sixty quid. Whoever lives here must do a good trade in begging. Or something. I put the tin carefully back on the shelf.

I'm just about to leave, almost gagging at the smell, when something on the wall by the side of the ducks catches my eye. A yellowed newspaper cutting. Hurriedly snatching it from the hook it hangs from, I exit the den before my bile rises.

Outside in the cold air, it really is beginning to get dark. But I can't leave just yet. The cutting is from the Evening Post, and although it isn't dated I can tell from the typeface used that it must be thirty-odd years old.

FEARS GROW FOR PREGNANT WOMAN

Police today said they were very concerned for the safety of a pregnant young woman missing from a local mental hospital since Friday. Elsie Peters, 19, absconded from St Helena's during visiting hours in the afternoon. An inquiry has been launched into how the residential patient, who is expecting her child in November, managed to just walk out of the secure hospital. Meanwhile, a wide-ranging search has been underway for Miss Peters, who was wearing a hospital gown when she left St Helena's. Chief Inspector Michael Walker, leading the inquiry, said: "Unless Miss Peters has been taken in by someone she has now spent three nights out in the open, which can't be good for someone in her condition." If she is being sheltered by someone, then they are doing her no favours. She is a very sick woman."

Odd. If this is some tramp's hideout, why pin up a thirty-year-old newspaper cutting? Then I spot something else, which sends that old shiver racing up and down my spine again. To the edge of the clearing, almost hidden in the undergrowth, is what looks very much like a crude grave marker. Still clutching the newspaper I hesitantly cross the few feet to the unmistakable mound in the cracked earth and the clumsy cross inscribed with a single, scratch word: *mam.*

Then I'm looking at the den again, and down at the cutting, and thinking about a frightened, pregnant teenager hiding on an island in the middle of a pond in the middle of a town, and the twin daughters she brought up on foraged scraps and stolen food and eventually left to fend for themselves when she died. And I'm thinking about the unspoken secret of the town's menfolk who visited those girls in the dead of night, and that tin of money. A good living from begging. Or something.

And suddenly I'm nine years old again, running down an icy, overgrown path as fast as my terrified body will carry me, skidding and skating haphazardly across the frozen lake without a thought for the ice cracking beneath my feet until I'm safe and sound in the rest of the world.

As night falls, I stand for a long time on the shore of the duck pond, shakily sucking on my final joint to calm my nerves. The ice glows luminous in the night, making the island seem darker in the pond's middle. I still have the newspaper cutting crumpled in my fist. Christ, how long did they live there alone? I'm sure people would have heard about it if they had been found any time over the past ten years. They couldn't hush something like that up.

Good God, perhaps they're still both alive. The hut looked in a fairly good state of repair, there was food in those jars. But where are they now? Never mind about the ducks, Holden Caulfield, where do the lost women go when the pond freezes over?

FOUR
MAGS AND EMMA

Mags is waiting in my flat when I get home, lounging on the sofa and surfing through the digital channels. She's early but that's okay. I throw off the jacket and flop down on the sofa beside her.

We throw our arms around each and when we come up for air, Mags asks: "So what have you been up to today?"

Colin's fridge makes her laugh. Then something unusual happens. I remember walking in the park, and something to do with the duck pond, but not what, exactly. I puzzle for a moment, but Mags grabs me again until I break off to ask: "How long?"

Mags sighs and runs a hand through her short cropped hair. "Not as long as we thought. I have to meet Stephen at nine."

I pout and fold my arms across my chest. "Mags, you said you'd be free all Sunday night. What's his problem this time?"

"There's no problem," she says, stroking the nape of my neck. "This guy's coming up from London who

Stephen has to keep an eye on until tomorrow morning, as you know, but now this other fella's decided to bring his wife so it's sort of expected for me to be there for drinks. I'm sorry, Dave. Honestly."

"I know," I relent. "It's just... sometimes I wish..."

Mags silences me with a painted finger on my lips. I know she doesn't want to hear stuff like this, that we're just supposed to be having fun, but I think I'm really tumbling for her in a big way. Shit. Trying my best to shed my mood, I move her finger from my lips and plant a wet kiss on her mouth. She returns the pressure and soon we're tugging at each other's clothes. As she loosens my belt I whisper: "Do you want to go to the bedroom?"

"No," she manages between kisses. "Here."

I lie back and Mags climbs on top of me, and I'm aware of something uncomfortable in the small of my back. As the TV begins to flick through the channels at a crazy rate I realise I'm lying on the remote control. I shift slightly and must ease off the button, because the box settles on VH1. The video's Kate Bush, The Sensual World, best shagging song ever recorded. I reach a hand behind me to kill the lamp, then return it to the small of Mags' naked back as she slowly begins to lay a trail of kisses down my neck and chest.

Later, we're lying entwined on the sofa, the throw-over I brought back from Thailand wrapped around our bodies for warmth, flicking disinterestedly through the digital channels and talking in low voices. There's a thoughtful silence for a few minutes, and I can tell she's dying to twist round and look at the clock, but doesn't want to. She's grateful when I point out it's eight-thirty and say: "Do you want to use the shower before you meet Stephen?"

Mags is quiet while she towels herself off, and I know she's troubled, uneasy. Happens every time. She swings between wanting to be with me all the time and feeling incredibly bad because she's cheating on Stephen. I can't help her with that. She knows I'm here for her now, but she's terrified that I'm going to get fed up and go find someone I can be with all the time. At the moment, the situation suits me, I'm in control. But for how long?

Fifteen minutes later she's at the door of my flat, planting urgent kisses on my lips. "Call you tomorrow at work," she promises, then hurries down the stairs. As she turns into the next flight she looks up at me and smiles. I stand at the cool doorway until I hear the rattle of her car engine, then go back inside and ponder what to do for the rest of Sunday night.

As I'm gathering my clothes from the floor, a scrap of paper falls from the pocket of my jacket. It's an old newspaper cutting about a missing woman. Where did that come from? It's annoyingly familiar, niggling at the back of my mind, but I can't place it. How odd. Stuffing it back in my jacket pocket, I head into the bathroom to shower and think about Mags. I wish she was single, I really do, but she's been living with Stephen for years and they'll probably get married. I need to do something to take my mind off her.

I need Steam.

At nine-thirty I walk into Steam, the heat wrapping me like a warm blanket after the cold of the night. The DJ's dropping some hard tunes and sweat already hangs in the rafters like the beginnings of a rain-cloud. Sunday night's okay in Steam, nothing too packed or heavy, fairly busy yet relaxed. It's an old converted steam laundry out on the edge of town, run by two brothers, Mick and Mark, and the place where I come to get my head together - guaranteed no fucking technobilly, or billykids speeding and chewing. Maybe I'm just getting old, but I can't stand that hybrid of drum and bass and rockabilly that's everywhere you go this winter.

Steam's a fairly underground kind of vibe, Tony

and Pete for instance wouldn't be seen dead in here. I have a whole different set of friends at Steam, and most of them are probably in tonight, not being fans of Sunday night feel-good TV. Monty spies me as I ponder a drink at the bar, and strides over. "Dave, you okay, mate?" I take Monty's outstretched hand and give it a firm shake.

"Hiya, Monty. Who's in?"

He scratches his shaved head and tugs the bolt in his lip. At six feet three he's a pretty fearsome sight, but he's as soft as a puppy dog playing with a bog roll, really. "Most people. Emma."

I settle on a bottle of Red Mist, get a gin and tonic for Emma, and stand Monty to a Newky Brown because he's always skint, before following him over to one of the shadowy booths ranged along the far wall. I nod at Kex, John, Fi and Mark, one of the co-owners, before sliding in beside Emma. She pinches my waist and says: "Hi, stranger."

I wink at her and turn my attention to Kex, who's telling some story about a girl in Steam last night who collapsed after dropping three pills of indeterminate origin. I groan inwardly, because I know they're going to put me on this the minute I walk into work tomorrow morning. "Who was she?" I butt in.

Mark starts to protest about his club's no-drugs policy but everyone shouts him down and Kex looks at me in annoyance: "That's right, typical fucking journalist. Not 'how is she', but 'who is she, how old is she, where does she live, what does she do?'"

"You forgot 'how big are her tits?'" adds Fi, winking at me to show she's winding Kex up. I hold up my hands in mock surrender. "Okay, okay, point taken. I'm off duty tonight. Just trying to save myself some time in the morning."

"Hacks like you are never off duty," says Kex, relaxing a little. "As you asked, she's fine. It wasn't E. Someone had sold her fish tank purification tablets.

Made her sick as a rat. That's why she collapsed."

"Bollocks, Kex," I challenge, relieved I won't be spending Monday morning door-stepping some mother who's lost her daughter in a drugs death. "That old chestnut's been doing the rounds for years, man. No-one would be stupid enough to buy fish tank tablets for E; it's just an urban myth. You know, like the one about the phantom hitch-hiker, or-"

John comes to life at last. He's a bit of an old acid casualty and tends to wander off into his own little galaxies for hours at a time. "No way, man, that's straight up," he says, rubbing his red-rimmed eyes. Must have been burning two candles at both ends recently, but now he's as awake as I've ever seen him, and warming to his subject: "A friend of my bro had that same fucking experience, man, on the coast road a couple of summers back. He was driving on his own, really late at night, and it was so shitty, man, rain coming down and winds blowing up a gale. Then he sees this guy by the side of the road. I mean he doesn't want to pick him up, it's after midnight and this guy's a fairly straight sort of bloke, if it's the friend I think it is, but he thinks, hey, it's a shitty night, he can't leave him here in the middle of nowhere. So he picks him up and they get talking and it turns out the guy's crashed his car and needs to get to a garage so this other guy says okay and takes him to this petrol station a couple of miles down the road and when he gets out he swears that the guy just disappears *right before his fucking eyes*, man!"

"Wow," whispers Emma, as John collapses into his chair and remembers to breathe. She seems impressed and this vaguely annoys me. John summons the strength to continue: "But that's not the fucking worst thing, man, you know what is?"

"I bet I do," I sigh. "The next day he gets a paper and sees a report of an accident at the spot where he picked up the hitch-hiker the night before. There's a picture of the driver who was killed and it's the same guy your brother's mate give a lift to."

John looks at me in awe. "Exactly fucking right, man. Shit, I told you it was true."

"Aw, bollocks, John, you old hippy bastard," I laugh. "Come on, that story goes all over the country all year round and was never, ever true. This mate of your brother, what's his name?"

"Er, I dunno, Dave, but I can ask my bro," says John uncertainly.

"Go and ask him then," I say triumphantly. "He won't know who it was, or if he does it won't be his friend, but a friend of a friend. Phantom hitch-hikers, fish tank Es. Urban myths, folks, that's all they are."

Everyone starts excitedly relating their own friend-of-a-friend stories. I turn to Emma and she says: "I thought you weren't coming out tonight?"

I shrug. "Change of plan."

"Mags let you down, then?" she asks quietly, not looking at me. I pause. People here know about Mags, but not much. They know she's someone I'm close to, but not that she's living with some other guy. I've brought her here a couple of times and she's really into it, and most people seem to like her, but they can't really work out what's going on.

I think Emma's sort of sweet on me. We've kissed a few times, but nothing heavy. I like her, but just as a mate. I don't think I fancy her, but I don't know if the situation with Mags is clouding my judgement. If Mags wasn't on the scene perhaps I could fancy Emma more, I don't know. It's all a fucking mess.

"Do you want to go for a drive or something?" suggests Emma. I look at my Tag. Last orders in half an hour, but Mark and Mick will do afters for a select few when the doors are locked.

"Yeah, sure," I say, draining the Red Mist.

As we stand to leave, Kex nudges Fi and stage-whispers: "There they go again."

I get a bit annoyed, because I don't want everyone assuming there's something going on between me and Emma for her sake. Fi nudges Kex back and tells him to leave it. She's sort of the only one I've opened up to about the whole business. I give her a grateful smile as Emma climbs into her big coat and we head for the door.

We walk down the street close together, shoulders touching. It's nice, pleasant, I just wish I didn't feel it meant more to Emma than to me. The night feels a couple of degrees warmer, but Emma's Fiesta is still iced up. As we scrape frost off the windscreen together, she says: "Where do you fancy going?"

I don't know. What I really fancy is an early night, but I'm not going to let Emma down now I've made the effort to come out. "How about up Beacon Hill?"

From the top of Beacon Hill you can see the entire county. Two hundred and fifty years ago Royalist troops managed to spot Cromwell's New Model Army marching on our town a hundred miles away, and by the time they arrived the roundheads were walking into a bloody rout. These days you can drive more or less to the top, thanks to some new access roads put in by the council. We park on a wide, gravelled plateau and look down on the lights of the town, surrounded by the blackness of fields and moors and connected to other distant clusters of street-light stars by glowing, snaking roads. It's almost romantic. I wish Mags weas here.

Me and Emma talk, and laugh, and generally have a good time. I tell her about Saturday night, the dodgy club, getting lost in the streets that time forgot. She wants to go and look for Fugue Street, but I can't remember how to get there again. Instead I pluck a joint from the pocket of my jacket and we spark up, passing it between us in meditative silence.

"It's my birthday in two weeks," I say.

"I know," replies Emma, letting the smoke drift out

of her mouth and up her nose. "You'll be twenty-six. Old man. Anything planned?"

"Don't know, really. Mark and Mick reckon we should have a bit of a thrash at Steam. You know, Saturday night, say, after last orders keep the place open for a private party."

Emma perks up. "Yeah, we could get Delta to DJ. It would be really ace."

We both ponder the aceness of it all, staring through the frosted windscreen, when suddenly there's a brief flash and something streaks across the clear night sky.

"Shit!" says Emma, grabbing my hand. "A shooting star. Quick, close your eyes and make a wish."

We both do, but somehow I feel that neither of us is going to get what we wish for.

FIVE
THE CRYING BOY

The rattle of the alarm clock heralds Monday morning. I extend one arm into the bedroom's freezing air and silence the clock before withdrawing back into my duck-down womb for just another five minutes.

Half an hour later I'm leaping into the darkness, late for work, realising I haven't ironed a shirt and simultaneously knotting a tie and pulling on my boots as I lock the front door. Ah, what would life be like without these little habitual certainties?

I'm supposed to be in early to call round the emergency services to see what's happened overnight, but naturally Stephen is in ahead of me. Did I mention we work together? I'm fucking his girlfriend, and I sit behind him at work. Is that low? He glances at the clock as I walk in, mentally noting that it's four minutes after seven-thirty, and turns back to the Telegraph. Christ, it's not as if he's my boss or anything, the supercilious twat. He's just the chief reporter. What really nettles is that he probably had great sex with Mags last night. Not that sex with Mags could be anything else, whoever you are. Putting it all out of my mind, I head to the news desk, mumble greetings to the news editor and the deputy, and see what's on the diary. I'm down to meet a delegation of farmers in the office at eleven.

"What's this, George?" I ask the news editor.

He's surrounded by a small phalanx of IT blokes stroking their chins and writing down serial numbers from the backs of the news desk computers.

"For God's sake!" he roars eventually. "Is it not enough that every electrical appliance I own has packed up in the past 12 months and I have had to get people in to see to the TV and the washing machine, and I have had to buy my wife a new personal organiser because it's cheaper than getting it repaired? Can I not have peace from you people at work? Away, away! I've a bloody newspaper to get out!"

He hands me a couple of national tabloids to peruse for local news or stories we might follow up as the IT people melt away, and says: "Oh, the farmers. They phoned over the weekend but Jerry didn't get the chance to speak to them because of that fire at that mill. They reckon they've got some new sightings of the Beast of Shotmoor. Thought it might be up your street."

"The Beast of Shotmoor?"

"Yes, yes, you remember," says George, turning up the radio to catch the morning news. "Few years back the farmers reckoned some big black cat, like a panther or something, was worrying the sheep. Apparently it's back."

I wander slowly over to the reporters' desks, flicking through the tabloids. Stephen Doyle is returning from the coffee machine, a plastic cup of hot brown liquid - I hesitate to call it coffee - for each of us. That just makes me madder. He behaves like a wanker, and then does something that makes you think he's okay, really. It's all part of his plan.

I take the cup, grunting gracelessly, and sit at my

desk, three behind his. He's looking over at me, as though he's expecting conversation, and then I vaguely remember something Mags said about him having to baby-sit some guy up from London. I sigh and realise some kind of social intercourse between us is inevitable until the other reporters come in, and look up from George and Lynn to ask: "So... you had some big job on last night, yeah?"

He launches into his anecdote so quickly I can tell he's been just dying to tell someone. I smile and nod in all the right places... this guy from town, spent eight years in jail... crime he didn't commit... while he was inside, woman who fingered him for the bank robbery starts writing to him... they get a regular pen pal relationship going, etc etc. The guy's just got out of the nick and came home at the weekend for the first time. He's a reformed character, they're going to get married, a good tale. Ought to earn Stephen a few bob flogging it to the nationals. Stephen had to stick with him all night to make sure none of the freelance news agencies got to him before our story's out today. He's still rabbiting on when he says something that turns my blood to ice: "...so there's the four of us, him and the woman and Margaret and myself, and we're in Partington's, you know, the brasserie on the square. All on expenses, naturally, and the duck there is to absolutely die for. Anyway, it turns out that the woman this fellow's marrying now runs a hotel in Brighton and she thinks she recognised Margaret. Asks her if she had a nice time when she came with her husband when they visited in August. Well, we had a right laugh, because Margaret and I haven't even been to Brighton. Complete case of mistaken identity. If I didn't know better, I'd say that my Margaret had a chap on the side."

He brays like a donkey, and I manage to squeak a token laugh through my concrete-set grin. The woman wasn't wrong, she did recognise Mags. Only it wasn't

Stephen she was with, it was me. Christ, what are the odds of that happening? “Well,” I say breezily. “Better get on with the morning calls.”

But instead of calling the police, I dial Mags. She answers after two rings and when I whisper her name she says: “He’s told you then? Bloody hell, I nearly pissed myself in fear. That stupid woman was adamant, hanging on to it like a bloody Rottweiler, until I managed to kick her in the shin under the table. Then she got the bloody message. Christ.”

“I thought we’d be safe in Brighton, of all places.”

“Well, you know what to do next time,” laughs Mags. “Take me to Paris, you cheap bastard. Listen, I’ve got to go to work. I’ll call tonight if I get the chance.”

Then I’m listening to dead air. Yeah, call me if you get the chance, Mags. Then I push it all away and my fingers dance across the telephone keys, dialling the number of the police station. “Good morning, it’s Dave from the Post here. Anything for us?”

“Only admiration,” says the voice on the other end of the line. Christ, I wish I had a pound for every time I’ve heard that one.

The house is a gutted shell, blackened walls reaching up in jagged teeth, forlornly grasping for the roof. Shattered panes of browned glass crunch under the boots of the firemen as they kick apart ruined furniture and turn the hoses on the debris to blast the life out of lurking embers. A pall of black smoke hangs wispily in the white cloud sky, a fittingly funereal silence upon the watching neighbours, broken only by the crack of something breaking as the fire-fighters continue their damping down.

Three dead, husband, wife, four-year-old kid. They’ve already zippered up the charred remains and ambulanced them off to the morgue. I caught a glimpse of what must have been the kid when they were fastening up the body bag; a hand that looked like roast chicken left in the oven too long, blackened in its own juices. If I'd had breakfast, I would probably have lost it there and then.

The leading fireman, a tall man with a smoke-blackened face, strides over to the small throng of reporters, unfastening the straps of his white helmet and pulling it off with a grunt. He runs through the basics of who, where, when, what and why. Why becomes apparent when a fireman staggers out of the house, holding a burned and smoking chip pan. Usual story.

I wander off in the direction of the house, talk to neighbours, get some quotes. As always, they were a quiet couple. Kept themselves to themselves. It's a real tragedy, especially the kiddie. Lovely she was, that little girl. It's as if they've been given a script to recite, that certain responses are required of people in situations like this. So many times they've read in the papers or seen on the TV that people kept themselves to themselves that they now believe it's what they should say as well. By the time the TV cameras get here, someone will undoubtedly have prepared floral tributes to place at the charred front door. A case of life imitating art, or at least the media.

I sniff at the shoulder of my suit. It stinks of bonfire night. I'll have to get it dry-cleaned again. These are the thoughts that pass through my head. I don't think about three people dying agonising deaths. If I did that every time I came on a job like this, I'd probably go mad.

I'm just about to call it a day and ring the office when three firemen emerge from the house gingerly carrying a vaguely familiar-looking painting between them. A blond-haired boy pouts out from the cheap frame, crocodile tears rolling from watery blue eyes down ruddy cheeks. Now where have I seen that before? What is remarkable, however, isn't its familiarity but its condition. The painting is totally untouched by the fire. It must be the only thing in the house that is. The firemen exchange wordless glances and throw it on a pile of debris on the front lawn.

Shrugging, I turn away in search of a quiet corner from where to phone over copy. I almost run straight into a man I hadn't noticed, a tall, dark, shadowy figure wearing a long black greatcoat and carrying, bizarrely, a battered violin case. His silver hair is cropped close and his beady, black shark's eyes twinkle beneath a tombstone brow. His lips writhe together in what I can only think he imagines is a smile. I remember to breathe finally, and nod at him, trying to push past on the pavement, wondering if he's a doomer who's lost his sandwich board.

"The Crying Boy."

I stop and glance at him. "Pardon? Are you talking to me?"

He turns his heavy gaze on me. "The Crying Boy. Did you notice it?" His voice is rich and accent-less, with an odd, unplaceable burr to it.

Something clicks. "You mean the painting?"

"Yes, the painting. The Crying Boy. Completely untouched by the fire."

I stop and look at this guy properly. His big square fingers clasp the handle to the violin case so tightly that they've gone white. Any minute now he's going to unload some religious bollocks on me, I can tell. I nod politely and carry on walking, adding over my shoulder: "Pity the family aren't alive to appreciate it."

"Unfortunately, they won't be the last. God knows, they certainly aren't the first."

Okay, I'm a sucker for the sniff of a good story. I'm hooked. Deadline's approaching rapidly, but I stop in my tracks. I turn and the man with the violin case is still standing as he was on the pavement, gazing towards the scene of the fire, his back to me. "What do you mean?"

He carries on speaking without turning to me.

"Check your archives. Ask those firemen how many times they've attended a blaze at a house where the only item undamaged is a picture identical or similar to that, a mass-produced print of a crying male child."

Abruptly, he seems to decide he's said enough, and begins walking away from me with bold, long strides. He passes the house, the fire engines, the puddles of water, and the neighbours without a glance back at me or at the scene of devastation. I watch until he turns a corner and is gone from view, and then shake my head and bring myself back to the job at hand. Plucking my mobile from my inside pocket, I hit the dial button and ask for copy. Let's see if I can't knock Stephen Fucking Doyle off the front page.

I'm back in the office a full ten minutes before the deadline for the first edition with the pick-up picture of the dead family begged off the wife's sister round the corner. George whisks the pic away to be scanned and I sit smugly at my desk. Stephen glowers at me; they've put his prisoner story on page three. Even though he's still got a colour pic and a nice exclusive by-line, he's such a fucking prima donna that nothing less than the front page will do for him. Wait until he sees what I've got up my sleeve.

I immediately go to work in the library, trawling through computer files and back copies for stories on big house fires. With growing wonderment I discover that what the man with the violin case said is absolutely true: over the past twenty years I discover no fewer than nine house fires where the only thing to survive unscathed was a picture of The Crying Boy. I take copies of all the stories and get back to my desk. Stephen is hovering on the pretence of getting the coffees in again, but I know that he can sense I'm up to something. With great deliberation I shuffle the printouts and turn them upside down on my desk.

"Ah, good job on that fire death story today, Dave,"

he offers, and I know it's practically killing him to say it. He's glancing down at the printouts, wondering what I've got. His favourite trick when you're on a good story is to declare that he's either been working on it secretly himself for weeks, or knows the background to it all, and if he doesn't actually nick the whole bloody story off you, he'll at least get a joint by-line. Not this time, matey.

As soon as Stephen's done lurking, I'm on the phone to the guy in charge of the fire-fighting operation at the house. I exchange a few pleasantries, chat a bit about the fire, then I drop into the conversation that I saw his lads bringing out The Crying Boy. His intake of breath tells me I'm on the right track. His official response is measured and careful: yes, an unusually high number of similar paintings have been found untouched at the scenes of fires across the country; yes, the painting at the house today was fine when everything else in the same room was burned to a crisp. No, there's no scientific evidence to prove that The Crying Boy has anything to do with anything, and it would be in bad taste to speculate. Finally, no, he wouldn't have one in his house, and he doesn't know anyone in the fire service who would.

Then it's searching through the phone book trying to find these previous "victims" of The Crying Boy. I hit jackpot on the third attempt. An old woman who lost everything but her Crying Boy in a fire seven years ago. Yes, she believes it brings bad luck. Yes, she's convinced that family who died today would be alive if they hadn't put that tacky painting on their living room wall. Yes, she'll happily have her photograph taken ripping up a copy of The Crying Boy if we can get one to her.

Half an hour later the news editor shouts across the room to ask if there's any update on the fire for the next edition. I run this by him: "Family killed by curse of Crying Boy?" He loves it. The story turns to a background on page three. Stephen's prisoner story gets knocked back on to five. This is shaping into a very good day.

SIX
THE BEAST OF SHOTMOOR

"Now then, what d'you think of that?"

It's cold on the moors, bloody cold, especially when all you've got on is a suit. The wind whips my tie over my shoulders and I can feel my shoes squelching. The farmer is poking at a furry, bloody, tangled mess with his stick. I feel a bit unusual.

"What is... was it?" I ask weakly. There's a smell like an abattoir. The farmer brings the point of his walking stick up close to his grizzled, wind-beaten face and inspects the red pulp on the end. For one awful moment I imagine he's going to lick it.

"Sheep, tha's what it was. And there's more like it an' all. This is about thirtieth we've had in three week."

There's a dull murmur of agreement from the other three crofters present. They're all looking at me, waiting for me to say something. "Could it be a fox?" I offer.

They laugh without smiling. "Hurr, hurr, hurr," just like that. It gives me the creeps, being up here on the moors with four inbred mutants, all wearing shapeless, soiled trousers and carrying big sticks. How do I know they haven't lured me up here to kill me or eat me or rape me or something? Christ, I don't know what goes through the heads of yokels like these. I glance across the scrubby grasslands of the moor down Beacon Hill towards distant town, nestling comfortably in the valley, the office blocks and smoking chimneys oddly inviting. I finger the bulk of my mobile in the inside pocket of my jacket and try to come up with a reason to phone the office, at the same time desperately trying to shake off the paranoia that's suddenly gripped me.

The farmer, Levi Cartwright, has begun to move, sinking his stick into the spongy heather and hauling himself up-hill like a rural Moses. The others wait until I move to follow him before falling in behind me. I take a last glance at the ravaged sheep before the farmer stops on top of a small rise, overlooking the wilds of Shotmoor, dotted with white. Behind us is civilisation, the town and the urban sprawl beyond. Here in front is nothing, steel-grey skies merging seamlessly with the iron-green of the moor, no sound but the whistling of the wind, miles and miles and miles of emptiness stretching until the next cloudy county.

Only it isn't empty.

The farmer ruminates then through brown teeth spits a smooth stream of tobacco which splashes off a lichen-splattered rock. He is, as he promised, about to tell me the story of the Beast of Shotmoor.

"It's out there," he muses with gravity. "It's back."

It first appeared about seven years ago. The crofters on Shotmoor began to lose an abnormally high number of sheep to something that did more damage than a fox, than a pack of foxes. The thinking at first assumed that a big dog, a Rottweiler or Doberman, had gone wild, tearing into sheep on the moors. Then there was a sighting.

According to Levi, an Australian tourist and his wife were driving across the moor when a deer bounded over the dry-stone wall into the road in front of them. The tourist braked and watched the terrified animal jump across the opposite wall with a single leap. Then another animal followed it into the road. It jumped over the wall from the same direction and landed crouched in the road, frozen in front of the stalled car for some ten seconds. It was about the size of a Great Dane, black as midnight, with white, dripping fangs and green eyes. The creature, indisputably a cat of some kind, then uncoiled and leaped over the wall in pursuit of its prey.

Over that summer there were more and more sightings, and more and more sheep lost their lives, throats ripped out. The farmers took to forming vigilante patrols, criss-crossing the moor with shotguns on the look-out for the beast. A year after the first sighting, one of the posses came across a dark shape hunkered down over a freshly-killed sheep, and it was shot. It turned out to be a domestic Labrador, escaped from its home, sniffing a carcass it had chanced upon. Whether it was the Beast of Shotmoor or not, its death served to satisfy the crofters and the sensation-hungry public, and the sightings stopped.

"But t'weren't the Beast," assures Levi. "No dog could've kilt so many head of sheep in one summer. The killings carried on, oh aye, but nobody were interested by then. Even the crofters put it all down to foxes, like they didn't want t'think about it any more. But it's back with a vengeance this time, thirty sheep in three week. It wants us to know it's back, that it never went away."

It's late afternoon now, and the clouds are black and rain-filled. The darkness seems to fall more rapidly here on the moors, and I don't mind admitting I'm spooked. I scan the greying landscape for a tell-tale black shape slinking between the scrub, but all I can see is grass and sheep. It could be anywhere out there, watching us.

"What do you want to do about it then?" I ask eventually.

Levi and his cronies exchange glances. "We want it caught. We want it kilt. It's our livelihoods at stake and things are bad enough wi'out some Beast chewing its way through our stock. There's four of us, and a couple o'other crofters, been thinking. We've got some money together. We wants to put a price on the Beast's head."

At last, the story. "How much?"

"Five hundred quid. Each. That's three thousand all together, for whoever catches or kills the Beast of Shotmoor."

I look across the darkening moor one last time before we leave. Three grand. That should get half the people in town up here with everything from bows and arrows to Uzis. I wonder if the beast knows. I wonder if it knows that the hunter is about to become the hunted.

Levi and the other crofters give me a lift back to town, sinking into silence the closer we get back to civilisation. They usually stick to their crofts up on Shotmoor and they don't mix with townsfolk unless they have to. Gangs of them loiter around battered and untaxed Land Rovers on market days, occasionally one of their sons will be up on an indecent assault at the Magistrates' Court after taking too many liberties on shore leave, but by and large that's as close as our respective worlds' orbits cross.

Throughout the journey I don't take my eyes off the shotgun that lies across the front passenger seat. The interior of the vehicle stinks of rotting flesh and sheep shit. I catch one of the farmers rubbing the cloth of my suit jacket between a brown, cracked thumb and forefinger and nudging his mate. It was the right thing to do to accompany them up to the moors, to get a feel for the story, but I'll be a lot happier when I'm back in the office in front of my PC, with the phones ringing and the TV mumbling and the coffee machine humming.

My relief as Levi noses the cold, uncomfortable four-wheel drive into a parking bay outside the Post is palpable. I'm glad I'm back on familiar ground. I thank Levi and the other crofters and - sniffing at my suit jacket, convinced I smell of sheep dung - I hare up to the news room with my notebook.

George loves it. We get a picture of Levi posing beside the ripped up carcass and he's going to run it as a page one splash tomorrow, underneath the headline BRING ME THE HEAD OF THE BEAST OF SHOTMOOR.. After trawling through the archives I come up with another three or four good sightings from the first time the Beast was doing the rounds, then I've got a last-minute appointment with the big cat expert at the zoo on the coast road. It's making for a long day, but it'll be worth it to have two splashes in two days and to see the look on that bastard Stephen's face.

The drive out to the zoo is pleasant usually, as it crosses the moors. But this time I'm hunched forward in my seat, knuckles white from gripping the wheel so hard. My heart leaps into my mouth at the sight of rags flapping in a naked tree, the brooding wings of a raven scooting low across the road causes me to stamp on the brakes. It's only when I'm across the moors and on the well-lit coast road that I relax again.

Doctor Teddy Bell at the zoo is, luckily for me, a Beast of Shotmoor buff. He takes me into his cluttered office and after ordering tea pulls a big file marked ABCs out of a cabinet and hands it to me.

“Alien Big Cats,” he explains. “That's what we call them.”

“Them?” I say alarmed. “You mean there's more than one out there?”

Doctor Bell, his bald head shining in the strip

lighting, drops four sugar lumps into his tea and stirs reflectively. “On Shotmoor, probably not. But across the rest of the country there are sightings of literally dozens of Alien Big Cats. Mostly in the Home Counties and Scotland, funnily enough, very few in this part of the country.”

“So you believe in it, then?” I pull out my notebook and pen. I never like to go straight in with the notepad until the interviewee’s at ease, but Doctor Bell isn’t fazed at all. Looks like he loves talking about the Beast.

“I don’t think it’s a question of belief,” he says. “Don’t let the word *alien* put you off, David. We’re not talking about some kind of supernatural beast here. It merely means it is out of place, and if the Beast is out there, and I’m fairly sure it is, it’s more likely to be a puma or even a panther. Pumas often tend to be favourite, and there have even been a couple caught and stuffed in some places. But the fact that the Beast of Shotmoor is usually described as black suggest something a little more exotic.”

“But what is it doing on Shotmoor?”

The doctor shrugs. “Who knows? Perhaps it escaped from here and we didn’t notice.”

I stare at Doctor Bell for long seconds. “Are you trying to tell me something?”

He laughs loudly and takes a long drink of tea. “Of course not, David. All our panthers are present and correct. But if we had lost one, or some other zoo had, it would naturally take to the hills and live off local livestock, especially the placid sheep up on Shotmoor. It’s all natural, there’s nothing paranormal going on.”

I flick through the file and the room grows silent, punctuated by the occasional chattering of monkeys and the chirruping of birds from cages and aviaries outside. It includes fuzzy photographs of beasts that could be anything from domestic cats to lionesses, some of them even supposed to be the Beast of Shotmoor. “You make it all sound rather... disappointing,” I suggest.

Doctor Bell drains his mug and shakes his shiny head. "Oh no, don't get me wrong, David. Just because it's all quite natural doesn't mean it can't be exciting or mysterious. Think of it, a feral big cat roaming the moors near our homes, slaughtering sheep. Even in these enlightened days, we still don't really know what's out there in the dark."

"Do you think it could kill a human?" I ask, awestruck, remembering that drive back to town in what is now full wintry darkness.

"There are no recorded cases. In fact, there are instances of big cats fleeing humans, even children. But that's the thing, David. You never can tell."

Even the monkeys go quiet.

I drive across the moor like a maniac, full-beam headlights sweeping across the black moor every time I take a hair-pin bend at sixty. Christ, but I'm scared. I turn the radio on full, but the reception's crap, so I hunt in the glove compartment for some tunes, eventually settling for some relentless pounding techno that'll keep my mind off big bloody cats stalking me. I wonder how fast panthers can run, keeping the car at a steady seventy as much as possible. Fuck, what if it's a cheetah? I step on the gas a bit, and I might never be as thankful as I am when the lights that signal civilisation rear up ahead of me, and slowly I'm absorbed back into town. I can get the local radio station on the stereo again, and thoughts of snarling cats can be left far behind.

I park up at my flat and notice my lights are blazing. Either I've got burglars, or Mags has managed to sneak away from Stephen. Grabbing my notepad and papers, I'm fumbling for my door key when a huddle of milk bottles scatters like skittles and a pair of lime-green eyes peers unblinkingly from the shadowy foyer. I breathe in sharply and my heart seems fit to burst out of my chest as the scraggly moggy scampers away, its collar bell tinkling hollowly. Jesus. Christ.

Later, after sex, I'm telling Mags about the Beast. She's peeling a tangerine and she giggles as she pushes a slice into my mouth. "Yeah, Stephen mentioned it tonight. He reckons George's gone soft, with all these stories about paintings burning people's houses down and now tigers on the loose on Shotmoor."

"Bastard. Besides, it's probably a panther, not a bloody tiger, and the twat's just pissed off because they're my stories."

I think I might have gone a bit too far. Mags looks hurt. "He's not a bastard or a twat, Dave. Don't let it get too personal, hey?"

I sit up in bed. "Yeah, sorry," I mumble. She's right. Stephen's not that bad. He's all right, in fact, no worse than most. I feel Mags' hand running up my inside leg, and I'm forgiven.

"Anyway, we've still got an hour before I have to go, so come here, tiger," she laughs, low and dirty, and pulls me towards her tangerine-tasting lips.

As I watch her dress fifty minutes later, getting horny again just from the sight of her, we pick up the conversation. "The story you're going to run tomorrow'll probably cause a mass exodus up to the moor, you know," she says.

I sigh, grabbing the remote control and flicking on the portable TV to take my mind off the stockings that Mags is buttoning on to her suspender belt. "Yeah, I'm wondering if I've done the right thing."

Half-dressed, Mags sits on the corner of the bed, contemplating her Wonderbra. "It'll be awful if someone kills it. Or worse, what if they capture it and stick it in a cage, after it's been so free on the moors?"

"I suppose the best we can hope for is that all the activity on the moors over the next few days'll frighten it away, out of the county." I feel really horny still.

"Where are you supposed to be right now?"

Mags gives me a mock-reproving look. "Emergency baby-sitting for my sister, as far as Stephen knows. I said she'd be back by nine."

I flick off the TV with the remote. "She just phoned to say she'll be another hour. Come here."

Mags crawls slowly towards me on the bed. "That panther's not the only bloody beast around here," she whispers, sliding back under the covers, still wearing her stockings.

SEVEN
THE ISLAND OF LOST WOMEN REVISITED

One wing stands awkwardly, like a bent flagpole, black and white feathers limp in the breathless hot air. One of the bird's eyes bulges from its blood-slicked head, its entrails neatly spread out on the Tarmac, as though ready for divination by some pagan shaman. The black road merges at infinity, cutting a swathe through the yellow desert, heat shimmering in the middle distance.

"What's this one called?" asks Emma with unhidden distaste.

I peer at the label beneath the big, lurid photograph and check my programme. "Um... *Magpie, Death Valley, July 14 1996*, apparently."

We move on. *Rabbit, A66 Brough, February 23 1998* stares at us glassy-eyed, its snow-covered corpse split by a neat tyre track and its tongue bulging obscenely. "I feel sick," says Emma. I feel a bit odd myself, and I'm no vegetarian animal-rights campaigner like she is. Still, it's all in the name of work. What other job allows you to spend Tuesday night looking at pictures of squashed animals?

We can't get near *Fucking Dogs, Glastonbury, June 25 1995*, because of the throng of people gathered before it. I catch a glimpse and grimace. A black Labrador and an unidentifiable grey mongrel, still locked together in coitus, both the worse for an encounter with an articulated lorry. Beats throwing a bucket of water over them, I suppose.

"Perhaps it's best not to bother," I suggest, hurriedly steering Emma back towards the free champagne bar. We grab a couple of glasses and I look around for the star of the show. I spot Ferdinand Shelley, tall and brooding, at the centre of a growing crowd of liggers. I need to get the interview over and done with then we can get back to the free champagne for as long as it lasts, then be away to Steam.

I quickly review the biography on the back of the programme: Ferdinand Shelley, born locally thirty-four years ago, studied photography at the local technical college and then at university in London, began controversial career with pictures of celebrity turds. His latest exhibition is entitled Roadkills, and features photographs of animals reduced to fleshy lumps by a variety of vehicles. He's launching Roadkills for one week only in the small gallery in his hometown before it moves on to London, Manchester and New York.

I pluck Shelley from his bouquet of admirers and manage to grab a few quick words with him in front of a photo of a long snake completely flattened by a truck in a Delhi suburb. We go through the motions, talking about the controversial aspect of his work, how he's outraged animal-rights campaigners and local councillors. He counters with how his work is a comment on the twenty-first century road obsession which will stop at nothing, even the taking of life.

"Of course, what I'd *really* like to do," he confides languidly, "is to take pictures of *people* killed in road accidents. Imagine that."

Imagine that. Imagine tomorrow's front page. "Is

that on the record?" I ask cautiously.

Shelley shrugs and winks at me. "If you like. Between you and me, David, I've never shied away from controversy. Write what you like."

The Post photographer turns up fashionably late, downs a quick glass of bubbly, then snaps Shelley in front of the rabbit, before stuffing a vol-au-vent down his neck and dashing off. Me and Emma have a final glass of champagne and head for Steam. The cold air of the clear night brings us up short, making us realise we're quite giddily drunk, and we head off for the park and a short cut to Steam, holding on to each other and laughing.

The park is very quiet, bony, leaf-less trees rearing up into the starry night, pathways picked out in glistening frost. Plumes of hot air tumble from our mouths as we half-walk, half-slide along the slippery paths. Our route takes us past the frozen duck pond and I stop, peering out at the black mass of the island, remembering my last visit on Sunday.

"What's up?" asks Emma.

I say: "I don't know. I was here at the weekend. I think I went over to the island, but I can't remember properly."

"Christ, what were you on?"

"Nothing. I just can't remember."

Then Emma's standing on the creaking ice, holding out her hands to me. "Come on, then, let's go and investigate."

I hold back nervously, warming my hands in the pockets of my jeans. "I don't know, Emma, the ice..."

She stamps the heel of her Doc Marten hard on the ice, which holds convincingly. "Come on," she urges. "It's fine."

Unwillingly I take her hands and she pulls me on to the frozen pond. With each step I remember, remember the night-time visit of seventeen, eighteen years ago, remember the secret of the lost women.

"Emma," I whisper urgently. "It's coming back to me."

"Hush," she says, propelling us on across the ice. After what seems an age we're at the bank of the island, hopping on to the frozen mud. Emma turns to look at me, her white face bright in the starlight. She's quite lovely, her hair falling in strands across her round face, the baggy shirt hiding the firm contours of her body. "Dave, I can feel something about this place."

Emma reckons she's a bit psychic, like most women I seem to meet. Tarot cards and crystals and stuff. "The only thing I can feel is the fucking cold," I say nervously. I want to be away, don't want Emma to know that there's some kind of male conspiracy cloaking this island, and I'm a part of it, albeit peripherally. But she's taking my hand and leading me on, unerringly, to the hut at the centre of the island.

We push through to the clearing, stopping on the edge and peering nervously at the hut, the grave marker, the frosted fireplace. There are still no signs of life. What is it about this place, what makes people forget about it as soon as they've left? It's like it wants to be forgotten, like it's a place of shame. Men came here, respectable men, ordinary working men, visiting a pair of wild teenage girls for sex and then returning, shamefaced, back to civilisation, back to their wives and girlfriends and families. It's as though the denial of the men, their refusal to speak about it, even among themselves, in private, threw up a wall around the place, stopping anyone asking questions or discussing it too much on the other side. There must be a reason why the park keepers never venture out here, or they would have discovered the hut as well. It's like a huge, unspoken secret, bound by an unbreakable code of silence, so strong it actually forces people to forget about the place as soon as they've left.

It's like magic.

Emma is sliding down the slight incline to the

clearing. I hiss at her to come back, then follow her shakily down. I lose sight of her for a minute, panic, then spot her squatting before the crude grave marker. She's breathing heavily when I approach, and she flinches when I put a hand on her shoulder.

"You knew about this, didn't you Dave?" she says accusingly without looking at me.

"Only since Sunday," I say, not asking how *she* knows about it. She puts her bare hands on the frozen ground. "I can feel it here, Dave. It's a place of secrets. It's a place of sexuality. It's like one of those ancient fertility sites of the druids, full of strong energy."

She's frightening me a bit. "Come on, Emma," I say, still whispering despite myself. "It's freezing. Let's go to Steam."

Emma stands and turns to face me. She looks serene in the pure starlight, and puts out a hand to my face, tracing the line of my jaw from my ear to my chin. "The energy's strong here," she says again, taking a deep, shuddering breath through her nose. "Oh, Dave."

Suddenly nothing seems to matter. Ferdinand Shelley and his squashed animals, Steam, the Post, alien big cats, Crying Boys, Mags... something in my chest lurches briefly at the thought of Mags but then I feel Emma's body up close against mine, and the involuntary spasm in my jeans. She plants her lips on mine and I feel her pushing me backwards, steering me to the hut. We push through the curtain and I get a sudden whiff of decaying duck, then it's gone and I'm lost in the scent of Emma's pungent perfume. Her tongue probes my mouth, her champagne spit mingling with mine. She's tugging at my belt and I help her before sliding my hand up her shirt. Her back arches at my cold touch, but then she relaxes as I fumble with the catch of her bra. With my left hand I catch hold of her skirt and inch it up until I can feel the cool flesh of her thigh. By now she's loosened my jeans and there are only a couple of layers of thin cotton separating us.

"Wait," she gasps, stuffing her hand into her coat pocket. She presses a thin foil packet into my hand. "Use this."

We fall down together on the packing crate bed, our heads devoid of any thoughts. As she rolls the condom on for me I lick at her nipples then mount her. Just before I enter her I try to conjure up Mags' face, but I can't. A second later, I can't even remember who Mags is as I lose myself completely in Emma. Oh yes, there's magic here.

We dress in silence. The spell is broken, we're embarrassed. I hold the used condom nervously for a second, then surreptitiously fling it to the back of the hut. Emma pretends not to have seen. She retrieves her knickers from where they had been thrown, hanging on the beak of a rotting duck nailed to the wall, then decides against keeping them. I return the favour and turn a blind eye as she balls them up and shoves them between the packing crate bed and the wall.

"Dave," she says uncertainly. "It's not that I didn't want to..."

I turn and silence her with a finger on her lips, but she shakes me off and continues: "No, I want to say this. You know how I feel about you, I think, and yes, I have wanted to sleep with you, but this wasn't... I don't know. Like I said, there's a lot of energy here."

Strangely, I feel hurt. "You didn't like it," I say quietly.

Emma sighs, like a mother talking to a rather dim little boy. "Of course I did. If it's any consolation to your male ego, I came three times."

I glance at her and can't contain a small smile. "Did you?"

"Yes, but Christ!" Emma slaps her forehead in frustration. "That isn't the point. It wasn't *real,* Dave.

We didn't sleep together because we wanted to, because we have real feelings for each other. We didn't even sleep together for a quick, physical fix. There's some strange shit on this place, Dave, and it isn't all from the ducks. I think we should get off here and not mention this again."

"But I thought it was what you wanted."

"Not like this!" she shouts at me. Then quietly: "Not like this."

Then she's up and out of the hut, and suddenly it stinks of decaying ducks again, just like it did on Sunday. Shivering, I pull on my jacket and follow Emma across the clearing and through the undergrowth. We don't speak again until we're across the ice and back on the slippery paths.

We hit Steam at eleven. We've lost two hours somewhere. I point it out to Emma, but she just looks at me quizzically. "No," I insist. "We left that exhibition at nine, and it's only a ten minute walk through the park. What happened?"

"You're taking the piss, Dave, and I don't like it," says Emma firmly as we push into the warmth of the bar.

I look at her with a pained expression. "No I'm not, Emma. I just don't understand."

She smiles at me, and her eyes seem wet. "No, I don't suppose you do, Dave. I think your watch must be knackered."

I look at the Tag. "What?"

Emma shrugs. "It was after ten-thirty when we left that exhibition. Nothing happened on the way here, we didn't get kidnapped by flying saucers. Your watch is broken."

I shake my wrist and hold my watch to my ear. "Well, it seems okay now. Do you want a drink?"

Emma spies Fi and Kex in their regular booth. "Yeah, I'll have a Red Mist please. I'll be over there."

I chat to Mick and Mark behind the bar, and we talk about my birthday bash in a couple of weeks.

"Invite who you like," says Mick, tinkering with one of the beer pumps with a screwdriver. "Your townie mates, workpals, bring that Mags girl along as well. She's nice, her."

"Yeah," I mutter, suddenly thinking about Mags. Inviting her and Stephen along could be a bit much. Although I don't think Stephen Doyle would be seen dead in a place like this. Ah, it'll work out.

I take the drinks over, and Fi says: "I was just saying to Emma, you two're late. It's last orders. You said you'd be here at nine-ish."

I shrug and look at my Tag again. "Uh, yeah, I can't really work it out."

Emma searches my face as I hand her the Red Mist, as though she's looking for some sign that I'm lying or taking the piss about my watch being knackered.

"What?" I demand, getting vaguely annoyed with all of this.

She downs the drink almost in one and stands up. "Let me out, Dave, I've got to go."

"But we've only just got here! Mark and Mick'll serve for ages, yet."

She pushes past me, nods at Fi and Kex, and heads for the door. She seems upset, and I consider going after her, but I don't know what good it'll do. Probably time of the month.

Instead, I raise the bottle of Red Devil and toast Kex and Fi with my eyebrows. "Women," I say sagely.

Kex nods in agreement, and Fi boots him in the ankle. As he winces and grabs his foot, she picks up her coat and goes after Emma.

"Christ," she mutters on her way out. "Fucking men."

EIGHT
THE HUNT

The news desk secretary is just slapping copies of the final edition on the reporters' desks when the phone buzzes into life. I cradle the receiver between my neck and shoulder as I unfold the paper and note with satisfaction the splash headline: DEAD ANIMAL ARTIST SAYS: PEOPLE NEXT.

"Hello, newsroom?"

There's a dry pause, and then an uncertain voice asks: "Is that Dave? The reporter?"

It's Levi Cartwright, the sheep farmer. Shit. He's probably about to go crackers over that story. I consider pretending I'm someone else for a second, then sigh and decide to face the sheep-shit. "Yep, this is Dave. What's happening, Mr Cartwright?"

It turns out he isn't complaining, not about my story, at any rate. "You want to get yer photographer up here. The moor's gone mad. There's hundreds up here, all looking for t' Beast."

The paper falls to the floor as I grab my jacket and toss the half-full plastic cup of coffee into the bin.

"George," I call to the news editor as I stuff my notepad into my pocket. "It's kicked off on Shotmoor. The hunt's underway."

Levi Cartwright wasn't exaggerating. Just beyond Beacon Hill, at the edges of Shotmoor, the country roads are lined with abandoned vehicles. The grey moorland is dotted with herds of bright, waterproof jackets, moving around aimlessly. I'm with Geraldine, the trainee photographer, and we manage to park as close to the action as possible, then climb over a stile and tramp uphill to where most of the people are. Geraldine wisely keeps a pair of wellies and a waterproof jacket in the boot of her car for such eventualities. After getting shitted up yesterday I'm more prepared and have brought a stout pair of boots with me in a plastic bag, which I quickly change into. I pull the coat tight for protection against the wind.

Leaning on a dry stone wall are Levi and his pals, spitting tobacco and hurr-hurr-hurring at each other. The old crofter tugs his white beard at me in recognition.

"Right old can of worms we've opened here, Dave," he says, nodding at the moor.

He's not far wrong. There must be six hundred people scouring the moors, many of them armed with air rifles, catapults, sticks, nets.

"Christ. How long has it been like this?"

Levi actually glances at the dull ball of the sun in the cotton-wool sky. Surely he's taking the piss. "Since about half one."

I glance at the Tag, but don't trust it since last night, so I confirm that it's now two forty-five with Geraldine, who is busy firing off shots. The readers have had twenty-four hours to get themselves worked up for this and they haven't let us down.

One of Levi's cronies speaks for the first time in our two meetings: "If tha' cat's not fled to't next bloody county after this I'll eat a bloody sheep masel'."

He's right. This bloody circus has as much chance of catching the Beast of Shotmoor as... well, as of something extremely unlikely happening. I groan inwardly as I see a crew from regional TV struggling up the hill towards us. Rosie Lambert, the on-screen reporter, beams at us all as she urges the crew on like pack horses. She holds a rolled up copy of yesterday's Post, the one with the first Beast story on the front. Recognising Levi from the photo she elbows past me and thrusts out a manicured hand.

"Levi, hello," she barks with conspiratorial friendliness. "Rosie Lambert, we're here to do a report for the six-thirty bulletin. Now, have they caught it yet?"

"Only thing this lot are going to catch is 'flu," I mutter. Rosie looks sharply at me, recognising me as one of the press pack but as is usual for her, failing to remember my name. She thinks for a second, then forces a shrill laugh, turning back to Levi.

"Now, we want to do a bit of a funny package, you know, big-monster-on-the-prowl type of thing." She makes a fair balls-up of humming the theme from The Twilight Zone and laughs again.

I raise an eyebrow at Levi and turn to Geraldine, saying: "Come on, let's get into the thick of things."

As we yomp over the mossy moor, Geraldine pulls out a tight joint. "Fancy a smoke?" she offers. I pull out my Zippo and light it for her; she puffs on it until the tip glows orange. Geraldine's all right, she drifts into Steam occasionally, and on appropriate occasions, such as any outdoor job like this, we'll often share a joint. She passes it over as she snaps a couple of kids poking at a dead lamb with pointed sticks, and I inhale deeply, scanning the horizon for the Beast but seeing only people. Away towards town a line of cars is wending its way up Beacon Hill. Three grand plus an unknown Beast is a big draw, even on a Wednesday afternoon. I wonder how many people have pulled a sickie for this?

"Hey, look at this," says Geraldine. Coming up the hill road is a police patrol car, blue lights flashing silently, leading two white police vans. "The big guns have arrived."

Police spill out of the two vans, and officers begin to bring out rolls of blue and white crime scene tape. Geraldine kills the joint and grinds it into the dirt under her heel as we trot down to where the officers are setting up some kind of cordon along the dry-stone wall. I recognise Chief Inspector Babbage from police headquarters and wave at him. He scowls back in return, and when I arrive at where he's standing, glancing at maps of the moors, he snaps: "Now see what you've bloody well done? We'll be taking this up with the Press Complaints Commission, you know."

"What for?"

Babbage sweeps his hands across the moors. "Inciting mass panic, for one thing. Causing an obstruction. Look at all the cars parked on this road. Trespass. A dozen more things I could probably get your rag on."

"With due respect, Chief Inspector, you're being ridiculous. All we've done is report the truth."

"Truth! Truth!. You call spinning yarns about lions and tigers on Shotmoor telling the truth? Christ, it'll be double-decker buses on the moon, next. Complete bollocks, Dave, and you know it."

I pause to watch three police officers armed with rifles climb out of the back of one of the white vans, checking their weapons in the daylight and adjusting their goggles and padding. "Complete bollocks, eh? So why've you got an armed response team here, Chief Inspector?"

I leave Babbage blustering to himself and make a few notes as Geraldine gets some snaps of the armed police. It's gone three and daylight is failing; I wonder how long this will go on. As we walk aimlessly across the moor, between the groups of hunters, I spot a tall, familiar figure: Ferdinand Shelley. I hail him and he nods in recognition, changing direction to meet us.

"Dragged yourself away from the roadkills, then?"

He smiles and holds up his camera. "Thought I'd try to shoot something living, for a change. Just got today's paper before I came up here, by the way. Nice piece... I understand from the gallery that I've already had fourteen telephone calls of complaint."

I leave Geraldine and Ferdinand comparing f-stops and wander off across the moor. I almost literally bump into Pete and Tony, armed with air rifles and a big box of lead pellets.

"Christ, it's Butch and Sundance." Pete slaps me playfully on the back, Tony looks around nervously. "What's wrong with him?" I ask Pete.

Tony decides to answer for himself: "This bastard made me take the day off sick from the petrol station so we could come looking for this fucking big cat you've dreamed up, Dave. I'm terrified I'm going to get caught."

"We bag this cat, you can tell the old fart to fuck off," says Pete, running a hand through his hair.

Tony looks pained. "That old fart's my dad, dickhead, and how far do you think three grand's going to go between the two of us?"

"It's not just that, though, is it?" insists Pete. "Think how much we get from selling our story to the Sun."

A look of mock-upset crosses my face. "Lads, and I thought you'd promise the exclusive to me."

Tony grins and says: "Christ, Dave, the Post can only just afford to pay you, never mind us. I think we'll stick with the Sun."

"Fair enough," I concede.

"Anyway," says Pete, looking at his feet through the sights of the pellet gun. "Fancy a pint tonight?"

I shrug. "Depends what time I finish up here. Where are you going?"

"Cross Keys," says Pete, still not looking up from his gun. "Couple of games of pool, watch the Chelsea match on Sky. We'll be in there from seven, sorting out details for the Amsterdam weekend. You're still on for that, yeah?"

"Try and stop me. I'll probably catch you later, then," I say, and wave them off. It's getting gloomy now, and colder, but that isn't putting people off. I scan the horizon for a tell-tale black shape, but there isn't one. There's more noise on the moor than the town centre on a Saturday afternoon, so that's hardly surprising. I wonder where the thing is, what it is, and what it thinks of everything that's going on.

I jump out of my reverie as a hand gooses me in the ribs. "Hiya, sexy." It's Emma, with Fi, Kex and a couple of others from Steam.

"Hey, folks. Three grand on your mind?"

"No chance," says Kex vehemently. "We're here to stop these bastards shooting that cat. That was a very irresponsible story yesterday, Dave."

I frown, not in the mood to explain myself. "I thought the local hunt saboteur group stuck to saving foxes and hares."

Emma, wearing a *Meat Is Murder* T-shirt under a combat jacket, pouts: "We're against all bloodsports, Dave, including this hunt for a poor panther."

"This poor panther has killed at least thirty sheep in three weeks," I snap. For some reason I've become terribly irritable with Emma. "Who's fighting for their rights?"

"The animal's got to eat, it's only doing what comes natural," argues Emma.

"I'll remember that the next time you get on one because I fancy a Whopper from Burger King," I warn her.

"That's different. You are *supposed* to be an intelligent human being who has enough nutritional alternatives available to him that he no longer needs to eat the flesh of another creature to survive."

I cannot be arsed with this. Emma seems to have picked up a real attitude with me. Christ, it's not as though we're going out.

A potential row is deflated by the dull crack of someone firing a gun away to my left. Everyone looks up like startled meercats then sets off at a run towards the source of the shot. I shout for Geraldine to follow then race up the mossy hill to the throng surrounding a big rough farmer type with a shotgun cocked in the crook of his arm. A Rottweiler lies there with its backside blown away, heaving out one great sigh before dying in a pool of blood and drool. Suddenly there's a cry of "*Rocky! No!*" and the shamefaced farmer holds up his hands in surrender as a young woman sets about him with a rolled umbrella.

"I'm sorry!" he yells. "It were black and it were snuffling about and... and what's it doing up here anyway?"

Babbage huffs up, red-faced, to spoil the fun. He separates the sparring partners and straightens his cap. "*You*, madam," he puffs, pointing at the now-weeping woman, "have behaved irresponsibly in bringing that animal up here when you know full well there's a hunt for a big cat in full swing, and *you*, matey, I bloody well hope you've got a licence for that thing."

"But I thought he might help find the cat," sobs the woman. "Oh, Rocky…"

As Geraldine flashes off a few shots in the gloom, I stick around long enough to get the name of the woman and her dog and then head off to where a group of people is gathering excitedly around a lone tree in the middle of the moor. People are taking photographs and measuring a series of deep gashes in the trunk of the tree. One woman is saying: "Big cats, just like domestic cats, sharpen their claws by scratching bark."

The moor is busier than ever, people coming here straight from work. There must be more than a thousand here now, armed with flashlights and even one or two flaming torches. It's like a Frankenstein movie, with the villagers out to get the poor monster. Suddenly there's a whooshing noise and a strong wind, and a white helicopter swoops low overhead. Rosie Lambert has mysteriously materialised at my side.

"Look at that," she says in disgust. "The BBC. Always has to go one better." Her mood changes, and she goes on brightly: "Anyway, we're after a couple of good yokels to interview. Have you spoke to anyone... ah..."

"Dave."

"Dave, of course. Have you spoken to anyone, Dave, who might be good on camera for us?"

"Christ, Rosie," I snap. "There must be a thousand people here. Can't you just pretend you're a fucking journalist for once and find one yourself?"

She turns puce. I probably shouldn't have said that. But she's pissing me off, and I feel like I've had enough shit today. She regains her composure enough to flip the finger at me as I walk off looking for Geraldine to take a picture of those scratches in the tree before the light fails totally.

I wonder how many people here actually want to find the cat, and how many are driven by a simple thirst for the unknown? I know which camp I fall into. Even though seeking out the truth is supposed to be my job, in this instance I'd rather not know. If someone manages to put a bullet into a black shape flitting from tree to tree, what will it turn out to be? A dog, a cat, something no-one's ever seen before? Do people really want it explaining, or are they happier with the excitement and thrill of know that *something's out there?* The world's becoming smaller and smaller every day. Let's have some mysteries remain unsolved.

I kick about on the moor until seven. It's fully dark and it's fairly obvious that nothing is going to happen. That hasn't stopped the people coming though, with dogs and guns and torches. A third of the town must be up here now. I tell Geraldine I'm heading home. She says she'll stay on for another hour, but then she's a trainee and she's keen. I give her my mobile number and tell her to call me if anything happens. As I walk down the Beacon Hill road I realise we came in her car and I'm stranded up here. I'm just contemplating going back to find Geraldine when a familiar, battered four-wheel drive screeches up at the side of me. It's Levi Cartwright, tugging at his white beard. "Need a lift?"

I settle in beside him and say: "I thought you'd be there until the bitter end."

As he forces the protesting vehicle into gear he shakes his wind-burned head. "Not much point. It's a circus, Dave. They ain't gonna catch the Beast."

I mumble something vaguely apologetic. He shrugs it off. "Ner, it ain't your fault. You've done us a favour, like, getting them people up here. At least it's forced the police to listen, and it might get the Beast frightened off for good, all that commotion."

Town's quiet, as if everyone has deserted the streets and gone wild on themoors. "Where do you want dropping off?" says Levi, pulling up outside one of the banks.

"Here's fine. Where are you headed?"

He nods at the bank and pulls out a cash-card from his shirt breast pocket. "Need cash to pay the bills, Dave. And no doubt we'll have some dry-stone walling to do by the time the townies have finished up there."

Yeah, all right. He doesn't half bang on. It was his idea to do that story after all. We climb out of the Range Rover into the deserted street.

It's a toss up who I see first, the man with the violin case or the big black cat, peering out from between two dustbins in the alley beside the bank. Levi swears softly; it's obvious what he's seen.

My throat goes dry and I try to whisper to Levi but it doesn't matter, he's already reaching gingerly inside the still-open door of the four wheel drive for his shotgun, resting on the back seat.

The cat just stands there. For a crazy moment I wonder if it's stuffed, if it's a prank by Pete and Tony and the lads, but then it moves its head, bringing its lime-green eyes round on to us.

The man with the violin case is standing on the pavement, staring at us and not the cat, wearing the same topcoat and blank expression as when I first saw him outside that house that had burned down. Christ, what if it goes for him? It's as big as a Great Dane, black as night, and when it opens its mouth wide to display its white, wet teeth at us I almost shit myself. Levi is chanting to himself quietly, a brief mantra: "Got the fucker, got the fucker, got the fucker..."

My balls feel funny. The Beast is looking at us, lazily licking its chops after scoffing whatever it's found in those bins. Christ, everyone's up on the moor looking for this bastard and here it is, right in the town centre.

There's an audible click beside me. The cat flickers its ears. Not wanting to move too much in case I startle it, I shift my sweating head sideways, enough to see Levi levelling his shotgun at the Beast, pulling back the safety on the second barrel.

"Got the fucker, got the fucker..." he's whispering to himself. I look at the man with the violin case. He looks at me. Why doesn't he shout, or clap, or *something?* The Beast will disappear into the alley. But he's looking at me, he's looking at me. I can feel Levi's finger tense on the trigger as though his hands are around my throat instead of the shotgun. I try to say something, but my mouth's too dry. Levi's breathing is heavy, like he's having sex.

"Got the fucker, got the fucker..."

"No," I whisper. "Don't, Levi."

He can't hear me. His knuckles are white. He's going to fire.

"No!" I scream. The cat's neck extends, startled. I push the barrel of his gun up and away, it cracks loudly, and the window of a grocery store across the road shatters, the report from the gun echoing down the street.

"You bastard," seethes Levi. I think he's going to turn the other barrel on me. "You bastard," he repeats weakly, throwing his gun into the car and climbing into the driving seat. Distantly, there's the sound of a siren. The police.

"We almost had it," he says without looking at me, gunning the engine.

The man with the violin case has gone. As Levi screams away in the four wheel drive, I know he won't mention this. I know that he partly understands why I did what I did. The alley is empty. The Beast is gone. I don't think it will be back.

NINE
THE TART WITH THE ART

The Cross Keys is full, half the interest on Chelsea getting their arses kicked in Europe, the other half on telling tall tales about the Beast of Shotmoor. The hunt has already passed into local legend and it's still underway up on the moor, although I know there won't be any trophies tonight. Still, I feel an odd swell of pride that something I've done has in equal measures polarised and united the whole town. I'm still shaking, too, from the sight of the Beast right here in the streets. If, in fact, that's what it was. The light wasn't too great, I was hyper from the adrenaline rush of the whole day. Maybe it was just a big dog. But Levi saw it too, and that man with the violin case. Perhaps we were all caught up in some kind of mass hysteria. It happens.

I'm thinking more about the man with the violin case than the Beast as I walk into the warmth of the Cross Keys. Who is he? Just some doomer who's taken a bit of an interest in me? It's the most likely explanation. I forget sometimes that my name's in the paper on a daily basis. People see it, absorb it, and if they see it often enough they're going to remember it. With the number of weirdo stories I've done recently, it was probably only a matter of time until some nutter latched on to me. What's in that damned violin case, though? As I order a bottle of Red Mist at the busy bar, I hope briefly that the guy isn't carrying around a gun or an axe resting snugly where a violin should be. That sort of fan I can do without.

There's the shout of my name from behind me, and I turn to see Tony and Pete, who have managed to secure a small table in the corner. I fight my way through a throng of football fans staring up at the big screen, and settle on to a stool between my mates.

"Waste of fucking time," says Pete immediately, taking a long draft from his lager. Tony's on Red Mist. I swear, this stuff is addictive.

"Nah, good night that was," says Tony. "Like the X-Files or something. Dead exciting."

Pete looks at him over the rim of his pint glass. "You're fucking soft you, you know that? Tramping around up on the moors in this weather. Freezing my nuts off, I was."

"It was your idea," says Tony quietly. "I'm still going to get bollocked for missing work."

"I take it you didn't bag the Beast then, lads?" I grin at them.

"What do you think?" snorts Pete. "And to top it all, look at this shower of shite on the telly." He nods at Chelsea, three-one down. "I've got a bloody tenner on this."

"What have you done with the guns?" I ask, remembering the small arsenal they were armed with up on Shotmoor.

"Back of my car," says Tony, draining his bottle of Red Mist. "They wouldn't let us in the pub with them. It was like The Sweeney: 'No shooters, lads'."

Pete looks at him incredulously. "Jesus, you fucking live in TV land, don't you?"

As they start bickering, I offer to get a round in and leave them to it. They're still at it when I return with two Red Mists and a pint. "Christ, will you both shut the fuck up?" I almost yell. "I don't know why you don't just married and have done with it." From then on the night degenerates into increasingly drunken verbal brawling, and I almost forget about big cats and men with violin cases. Almost.

Come chucking-out time, Tony and Pete are heading off for a taxi. "Want a lift?" asks Tony.

"Nah," I say, jamming my fists into the pockets of my coat. "Think I'll walk. Might pass down Jepson Street on my way home."

"Get out of it, you dirty bastard," laughs Pete, punching me playfully on the shoulder. "There'll be plenty of that in Amsterdam, and a damn sight better fucking looking as well. Anyway, I hear they've got an offer on down Jepson Street at the moment: free clap with every shag."

I leave them laughing their way to the taxi rank as I take the opposite direction. "Jepson Street," I hear Tony laughing. "He fucking kills me, you know."

Funnily enough, Jepson Street is exactly where I am heading, although I wouldn't have told them that if I thought for a single minute they would have believed me. Jepson Street, a once-respectable residential area now given over to street walkers, rooms rented by the hour, porn shops, junkies and crack-addicted children begging for enough change to buy a few rocks. Nice place, and not the sort of area most people would walk home through on purpose. But then, I'm coming to realise I'm not most people.

Jepson Street hits you in the face. You turn a corner off an innocuous looking road, and wham! There it is in all its seedy glory. The police here have a fairly forward-thinking policy towards prostitution and the vice trade: if it's all on Jepson Street they can keep an eye on it, and it isn't spilling over into nice, respectable people's lives. Whatever it is you want, you can find it down Jepson Street, and if you don't want it, you can pretend the place doesn't exist. And everybody's happy.

Having said that, Jepson Street isn't usually a very pretty sight. The first person I encounter is a kid aged about twelve, grimy and snot-nosed with a grubby coat buttoned up to his pale face. He's jumpy and shifting his weight from foot to foot as he pleadingly holds out a pathetic hand to me, not saying a word. Crack kid. Born to a junkie mum, addiction forced upon him in the womb. Probably never seen the inside of a school in his life, and it's only a matter of time before he's old enough to go to jail. I pause, meeting his dead eyes for a moment, then look away, fumbling in my pocket for a couple of quid. There's always a slim chance he might go and spend it on food or a can of Coke, but I know I'm kidding myself. He takes my money without a word, and leans back against the wall, waiting for the next punter. Christ, poor kid. I walk on.

The first of the working girls leans out of a shadowy doorway just a few yards on. She's in her twenties, dressed in boob tube and micro-skirt despite the freezing weather. Not un-pretty, but kind of... *soiled* looking. "Hello, darling," she says in an almost bored-sounding monotone. "What you looking for, then?"

Not her, that's for sure. I mumble something to the negative and walk on. More girls appear and whisper similar proposals, but none of them are what I'm looking for. Further down Jepson Street the operations get a little more classy, and some of the prostitutes have their own flats here, for the more discerning gent who has more time and money than for a quick knee-trembler in a piss-stained alley. This is where I'm going.

About halfway down Jepson Street there's a porn shop, still open at this hour. A hand-painted board on the pavement outside advertises: "Continental mags. Adult toys. Poppers. Models wanted." I side-step it and the crack kid leaning against it with his head down, and go to a thick wooden door at the side of the shop's window grill. There are eight bells there, all with flat numbers, some with names. The one I press has both: flat four. Cheryl. I wait long seconds in the cold night until the intercom buzzes into life: "Yeah?"

"Cheryl, it's Dave. You busy?"

The flat voice that answered suddenly bursts with life. "Dave! Jesus, no, not busy. Having a night off. Come up."

There's a click and I'm let into the dark hallway. I close the door behind me, and start up the stairs, to where I come to really get my head together. To Cheryl. To my secret.

I first met Cheryl about a year ago. I was doing a feature on crack kids, and wandered down Jepson Street to try and interview some. Almost got myself beaten up by a pimp within five minutes of blundering about with stupid questions, until Cheryl intervened. She was doing the doorways at the top end of Jepson Street at the time, and she hauled this guy off me and told him to fuck off. I was surprised when he did just that, but I didn't know Cheryl then. Me getting beaten up would have brought the police down, and that wouldn't have been good for Jepson Street. And if there's one thing that Cheryl wants, it's what's good for Jepson Street. If there was a union for tarts, she would be running it. She'd heard me asking questions, and after the pimp had gone she told me she would find some crack kids for me to interview, providing I promised not to sensationalise the story, and not to do the usual hackneyed, insensitive, clichéd job on Jepson Street. I kept my end of the bargain, and we've been something approaching friends ever since.

I pop down to see Cheryl once a month or so, sometimes more often. And all we do is talk, sometimes she gives me tip-offs for stories. Yeah, I know what you're thinking, but it's true. Cheryl's about the same age as me, but has that wisdom and seeming agelessness beyond her years that most prostitutes seem to have. Once I got to know her, I realised she was really intelligent, planned to go to art college and everything before things went wrong. She got pregnant when she was in her teens and ended up in a council flat, her dreams of college and a career rapidly evaporating as she struggled to make ends meet after being thrown out by her father.

The prostitution began through a boyfriend who quickly became more of an employer than a partner. She's had some rough times; sometimes she talks about them, sometimes she doesn't. But every line in her face tells the story of a beating or a near-rape or an insistent punter who wanted something that wasn't on offer.

I once asked her why she did it, why she carried on. Her dad had died a few years ago and she had been reconciled with her mother, who looked after her son while she was working.

"Because I can't do anything else," she'd said. "You write; I fuck. You have a pen and notebook; I have my body. We all have to earn a living."

During our chats Cheryl will sometimes betray the secret that she keeps deep down inside her in the special place that no punter or pimp can ever get to, no matter how much money they pay her or how hard they hit her. She'll start to talk about life outside prostitution, with her son, Andrew, and her mother. I can almost taste the salt on the breeze and see the roses climbing up the walls of the seaside cottage she imagines for herself when it's all over. Those conversations never last long, though. She'll bring herself up short, dousing the spark in her eyes with a flinty blackness, and look around her room at the bed, the table, the TV, the stereo, all earned on her back. "One day," she'll say, then change the CD or make us a coffee and then tell me that I've got to go, she's got to work.

I knock briskly at Cheryl's door and she opens it immediately, beckoning me in to her room. She's got a nice little place here, a big, clean bed dominating the room, all soft-lighting and classic art prints. It isn't hers, of course; she rents it while she's working from her pimp - not the old boyfriend; he's long gone, replaced since then by three or four pimps who fight it out up like old-time gunslingers to control the cleanest, fittest most presentable girls on Jepson Street. That's as well as handing over most of her earnings as well. Still, it's better than working the streets like she used to. She's got Massive Attack on down low in the background.

"Cosy," I smile, shedding my thick coat. She picks it up from the floor where I dropped it and tuts mock-disapprovingly at me, throwing it over a chair. "Like I said, having a night off.."

I sit on the edge of her bed and pick up the book she was reading before I interrupted her. "Ivanhoe. Very romantic. Can you see yourself in the age of chivalry then, Cheryl?"

She comes sits beside me, sighing. "Knights in shining armour are in very short supply on Jepson Street."

I flick through the book. It's been years since I read it. "So who do you fancy yourself as, then, the glamorous Lady Rowena, or the despised Jewess Rebecca?"

Cheryl ponders for a moment. She has dark hair, very straight, and a pixie-ish nose. Almost pretty. She must make money, especially renting a place like this, which means she can pick and choose her punters and not have to bother with the real low-lifes who come sniffing around Jepson Street.

"Bit of both, really," she finally answers. "I think that's what Scott intended. Ivanhoe is torn between the respectable Rowena and the outcast Rebecca, the virtuous maiden and the forbidden fruit. Different aspects of all women, really."

I cough. "And when was the last time you were described as a virtuous maiden, Cheryl?"

She hits me playfully with a pillow. "Don't get cocky, sunshine," she warns. "I've been taking karate lessons."

We talk easily for an hour or so, chatting about her son, business, new faces on Jepson Street. "We had a bad beating a couple of nights ago," she says.

"Who got done?"

"One of the transsexuals. She gave as good as she got, though. Three pissed wankers came down in a car and just pulled Lola off the street and gave her a right kicking."

That pulls me up. "What did you say? Lola?"

Cheryl shrugs. "Cheesy, I know. Calling herself after the most famous song about trannies ever. But Lola swears that's her mum's name."

Then I'm thinking back to that club, to Pete trying to pull that drag queen, Lola. Can't be co-incidence. That night's when all this weird shit seemed to kick off. I can feel the whiff of a story here, somehow. If I can find my way back to there, I might be able to get another look at those strange, forgotten streets in daylight. And if Cheryl knows Lola, she might know that club.

"Tell me, Cheryl," I say slowly. "Have you ever heard of a place called Arcadia?"

Cheryl says nothing for a bit, lights up a Marlboro, then says after a drag: "I have. But I'm surprised you have."

"I've not only heard of it, I've been there. What's so special about this place?"

Cheryl looks visibly impressed. "You've been to Arcadia? You? Wow. I know Lola kicks around there, but she doesn't talk about it. No-one who goes to Arcadia talks about it. I sort of think that's part of the deal."

"Have you ever been?"

"Shit, no. I don't even know where it is. It's a very exclusive place. So exclusive, in fact, that I'm not sure it's entirely legal. I've only heard a few whispered rumours out on the streets. They say some weird shit goes on there."

I shrug. "It did seem a bit odd, but I didn't see anything too mad. Truth to tell, I was a bit pissed. Can't remember much about it."

Cheryl seems to be looking at me with new eyes. "They say you've got to be a bit... I don't know, *special* to even find Arcadia, let alone get in. I'm very impressed, Mr Reporter. Maybe you're not as straight as you make out."

"*Et in Arcadia Ego*," I mutter to myself, suddenly remembering that stupid password you had to use to get a drink. "I don't even know what that means."

"I do, it's Latin," says Cheryl. "Literally, and in paradise I am, or I have been in paradise. Wait a sec."

She goes to a small shelf and comes back with a hardback book on art. She flicks through for a minute and then passes it to me. Four people in classical dress are assembled around a tomb set in an idyllic landscape, one of them tracing those very words inscribed into the stone.

"Nicolas Poussin," says Cheryl. "French. This is called The Shepherds of Arcadia, but it's also known by the inscription on that tomb, Et In Arcadia Ego. Arcadia was a legendary paradise in Greece, a place without sin or pain. Poussin was trying to get across the message that even in paradise, things are not always perfect. Even in Arcadia, there is death."

I sit and stare at the painting for a long time, feeling exactly like these shepherds of Arcadia. Suddenly, in my perfect, ordered little world, I have come across such a tomb, one that contains mysteries, uncertainties. Slowly, I close the book and hand it back to Cheryl.

She returns it to the shelf, then pauses at her window. She lets out a small sigh and says: "Look at those two."

Two women are standing on the street, dressed in shabby clothes and shouting loudly at men. Cheryl shakes her head. "They're new. Don't know their names. Sisters, twins I think, they only turned up a few days ago. Making a right dog's dinner of it, as well. Don't know where they learned their trade, but they're not good for business. Shouting at the punters, shagging openly in the doorways at this end of the street. They're no spring chickens, either. Must be in their thirties. I had a word with them yesterday, told them to get their act together, but I don't think it sunk in. They seem a bit retarded, actually."

I watch the two girls for a moment longer. There's something familiar about them, although I don't recall ever seeing them before. Cheryl said twins... I suddenly get a glimpse of the park in my mind's eye, almost catch a fleeting memory, but it's gone. I shake the cobwebs away and stand up. "Better get moving, Cheryl."

"Yeah, you're at work tomorrow, poor baby. Thanks for calling round."

She gives me a chaste kiss on the lips and walks me to the door. She busies herself with the lock, pretending not to notice as I surreptitiously slip a couple of notes on to her bookshelf. It might buy the kid something nice. We go through this pantomime every visit, and when the money's down she turns around and opens the door. As I leave, she blows me a kiss and mouths a silent "thanks" at me, before closing the door of her flat behind me.

It's quieter now, being midweek, and most of the girls have called it a night, except for the twins Cheryl pointed out. When I exit the building, they spot me and immediately begin shouting across the road: "Mister! Mister! You wan' come wi' us? We both do you, for money? You wan' come wi' both of us?"

Instead of turning up my collar and fleeing with embarrassment, I stand rooted to the spot, staring at these two girls. They're grimy and thin, almost otherworldly in their appearance. I just can't shake the feeling I've seen them before. I keep getting images of the park in my head, of being a kid on the duck pond, and, most bizarrely and disturbingly, of Emma. But I can't quite make the pieces fit together.

"Mister! Mister!" shout the girls again, and then one of Cheryl's neighbours hauls up a window and yells: "That's enough! You two get off the fucking street now!"

The girls look up at the old whore and bolt for the darkness and safety of a doorway. One of them whispers loudly to me: "Come on, mister! It's okay! We do you here..."

I turn on my heel and hurriedly leave. Jepson Street's getting weirder every day. Just like everywhere else.

TEN
TEARS FOR COLIN

Over breakfast, it dawns on me that I'm drinking far too much. I try to run through some kind of checklist of the past few days. Saturday: far too much alcohol to count. Sunday: a couple of Red Mists in Steam. Monday: a bottle of red wine with Mags. Tuesday: all that champagne with Emma at the Shelley exhibition. Last night: seven Red Mists with Pete and Tony in the Cross Keys. I look at breakfast, a piece of dry toast and a stale bottle of Bud I opened last night just before I collapsed senseless in front of the TV. I think I need to cut back a bit.

It's seven. I don't know how I managed to get up early. More to the point, I don't know how I'm going to get through today. I feel like shit. Still wearing yesterday's clothes, I go to the bedroom and fumble in my dresser drawer, my fingers finding at last a small paper wrap. Speed. I'll feel like fucking Christ knows what by this time tonight, but at least it'll get me through the working day. I lick the wrap clean, grimacing at the bitter taste, which I wash away with a couple of gulps of warm, flat Bud. Not bothering to change, I just have a quick wash, brush my teeth, and straighten my tie. By the time I hit work half an hour later and only five minutes late, I'm as fresh as a daisy. A few cups of coffee to supplement the whizz and I'll be ready for anything.

After writing up my story on the hunt for the Beast of Shotmoor - without the epilogue known only to me, Levi Cartwright and the man with the violin case - I relax for the afternoon. It's a quiet news day and we're going to splash on the hunt, which means four front pages in four days and a big two fingers up the nostrils of Stephen Fucking Doyle. The thought of him and Mags in bed gives me a bad downer for a few minutes, so I call her at work.

"Hi."

"Hi yourself. How's things?"

I shrug and she senses the movement even over the phone. "You know. Bit knackered." I tell her about the hunt, and about the Roadkills opening night. She freezes considerably when I mention Emma's name.

"What is it with you two, are you seeing her, or what?" says Mags with surprising hostility.

"We're just friends," I assure her. At least, I think we're just friends. Emma's been acting a bit weird lately.

"It's none of my business, I suppose," says Mags quietly.

I pause and reflect for a moment. "True, it's none of your business, Mags. But I'm not seeing her. I'm not seeing anyone. I'd tell you if I was, I owe you that much."

"Yes, I know," sighs Mags. "I'm sorry for being like that. It's just... I know you don't owe me anything, really, Dave. There's nothing at all to stop you seeing other girls. Christ, I'm surprised you don't. It's just, sometimes, I wish we were together all the time, that's all."

I'm thinking, well, we could be, Mags, but I don't say anything. I've never asked her to leave Stephen, and I never will. I just wonder where it's all going to end, that's all. Instead I change tack completely. "You won't get in trouble for me ringing you at work, will you?"

"Don't be silly," she says. "You can ring me any time, you know that."

The call to Mags gives me a taste for conversation, so I spend the next couple of hours making personal phone calls to mates up and down the country, taking down fictitious quotes in my notebook so George thinks I'm diligently at work on tomorrow's splash. Ah, give some other bugger a chance. I glance over at Stephen. Let him try to recapture his slipping crown, if he wants. I've done my whack this week.

While I'm chatting, I'm scrolling through World News Link on the Internet, catching up with what's happening in the rest of the world. Wars in breakaway Soviet states, the Balkan crisis spreading to the Greek and Turkish borders, elections, Japanese bombings, a vision of Mother Teresa of Calcutta by a woman in Oregon. The usual. But it's not the big stories I'm after, it's the little ones that fascinate me, the odd little tales that happen to ordinary people in small towns and cities like this one. Here's one, for example: a man in Milton Keynes narrowly escapes death when a block of frozen piss ejected by a passing aircraft misses him by yards. And then in a remote Italian village, there are frogs falling from the skies. Another sighting of Nessie by a boatload of American tourists. In the West Midlands, police find a tramp who has nailed himself to a park bench, through the flesh of his thigh, because he's fed up of falling off in the night. In a small town in Kent, locals are being targeted by an unknown sniper pelting people with cabbages.

I'm on the phone to a friend in London, and I get to thinking about that guy who drove us to Arcadia on Saturday night, the unlicensed cab driver and his theory that strangeness is more acute, more magnified, in the suburbs. "Do you get weird shit where you live, Paul?"

"Well, I got all my expenses paid last week, which is a fairly paranormal experience. What do you mean?"

I toss him some examples, and throw in the personal experiences of just the last week, like that mysterious club, that odd part of town with Lethe Lane and Fugue Street, the Beast of Shotmoor, the Crying Boy. When I remember that something odd also happened in the park at least twice this week, though I can't quite put my finger on exactly what, I stop short. Is it my imagination, or have things suddenly got a lot weirder?

"There's always some odd shit going down in London," muses Paul. "Probably Manchester and Birmingham and Newcastle and Glasgow, too. Stands to reason that the weirder stuff is going to happen out in the suburbs, because that's where most people live."

Perhaps he's right. Perhaps the taxi driver was right. But the suburbs have grown so much in recent years, urban sprawl snaking out and connecting towns and cities with vast residential areas. The suburbs are much bigger than the centres they surround now. All that scope for weird shit. There's too much weird shit. My head's racing with possibilities. It must be the speed. I need to calm down.

I'm grabbing my coat to head to the car park for a sneaky joint when George calls over that there's been a fatal house fire. The address is oddly familiar, and I'm actually on the scene before I realise that it's Colin's road.

It's Colin's house.

Abandoning the car in the middle of the road, I rush past the three fire engines. There are a couple of doomers with sandwich boards taking the opportunity to hassle the rubbernecks. One of the firemen recognises me and grabs my arm. "Fuck *off,"* I snarl, pulling my arm back. "This house belongs to a friend of mine." He looks worried and calls for his boss.

The house… Oh, God. I was only here on Sunday, pushing through Colin's unlocked front door. Which is now gone. There are shards of coloured glass on the front lawn, smouldering scraps of curtain and upholstery in the flower beds. . The roof is practically non-existent, its slates scattered and hanging in the remains of the gutters. The windows are blackened and cracked. I can see straight into the front room through the gaping, open door-way. It's just a charred, gutted mess. Then I notice someone shutting the back doors of an ambulance. It drives away without using its lights or sirens. It's in no rush. I feel sick.

A fireman with a white helmet strides over. I recognise him as one of the assistant divisional officers. Brown, I think. He shakes my arm. "You all right, son?"

I blink and look at him. "Hello. Yes, hi. Ah, is he all right? He isn't, is he?"

Brown looks at the other fireman doubtfully. "You know the occupant?"

"Colin." I search for his surname. "Colin, Colin. Colin Carroll. He's a friend of mine. Known him years."

Brown looks at me suspiciously. "This had better not be some journalistic trick," he warns.

"For fuck's sake," I hiss at him, tears bubbling up. "He's my friend. He's dead, isn't he?"

Brown nods wordlessly. Eventually he says: "It looks like he'd been tinkering with the refrigerator for some reason. There was a window on it. He must have tried to rewire it, and it looks like the fire was caused by an electrical fault. If it's any consolation, he was probably overcome by fumes and died pretty quickly."

"Can I go inside?"

Brown shrugs. "I'll take you. You can't touch anything, the police will want a look. Just routine."

The kitchen is just a black hole. Fire investigation officers are gingerly poking around near the fridge. Something crunches underfoot; a blackened comic book.

I can't stand the stench of burn and death any more so I push out of the kitchen into the hall towards the doorway, getting caught up behind a crew of firemen ruminating about something on one of the charred walls. There's a picture still hanging on the wall, the only thing in the house untouched by the flames.

The Crying Boy.

"Oh, fuck, no," I moan, biting back tears. I roughly push past them into the street, gasping for air. Christ, my heart rate's going ten to the dozen. My hands are shaking. I need to get away from here.

I walk until it's dark, ignoring the insistent bleep of the mobile. I've no idea what time it is, but I suppose everyone in the office has gone home. I wander aimlessly, zigzagging a route back home, forgetting all about the car. What's going on in my life? The last few days just seem to have been mad. I think I might be cracking up.

"No drink or drugs, that's the ticket," I say out loud. "Lay off. Get away for a while."

It dawns on me that I'm going to have to arrange the funeral. I don't even know if Colin had any family. Christ, this is all too much for me. I need to speak to Mags.

Leaning on a lamp-post, pooled in sodium yellow, I take out the mobile and jab her home number. She answers after two rings: "Hello?"

"Mags?" I say in a cracked voice.

There's a long pause, then she says: "Oh, hi, ah, Julie, how're things?"

I take the phone away from my ear and stare at it for a long while. "Mags? It's me, Dave."

"Good, good, glad to hear it," she carries on breezily. With a sinking heart I realise Stephen must be there. "Mags, I need to see you..."

"Of course we must get together Julie," she says, and I sense a tinge of irritability. Her hand goes over the mouthpiece and I hear her muffled voice tell Stephen: "It's Julie. Who I used to work with."

"For fuck's sake, Mags!" I'm shouting now. "Colin's dead! I feel like shit. I just need to see you..."

There's a longer pause. Mags doesn't say anything.

"Please..." I whisper. Big, stinging tears are rolling down my face. A group of kids passes me in the street, laughing at me, but I'm oblivious.

Mags composes herself. "Remind me of your number, Julie, and I'll call you sometime."

"I'm on the mobile," I mumble, then kill the connection with my thumb. I stay slumped on the lamp-post, my head in my hands. Christ, I've got to get a grip. I carry on walking, by accident or design passing the house that Emma shares with three other people. I stand outside for long minutes before shakily banging on the door.

Thankfully, Emma answers. Her smile turns to a frown. "Jesus, Dave, you look like shit. Are you all right?"

I stagger into the house, everything tumbling out. She steers me away from the buzz of conversation in the living room into her bedroom. "It'll be quieter in here," she says. "I'll get you a brew."

Later, after I've drunk the tea, I lie on the bed, Emma enfolding me in her arms, rocking me slightly. "Thanks, Em. I mean that. You've really sorted me out."

She takes my face in her hands and kisses me on the forehead, then on the nose, then on the lips, deep and long. I start to pull away, but she just says: "Shush," and loosens my tie. I really don't want this, but as my hand involuntarily traces the contours of her body, some dim memory surfaces of, making love with

Emma, and I surrender myself, allowing her to slowly undress me and then shedding her own clothes. We rock together quietly and gently, deep inside the covers of her bed.

She's on top of me, holding me down by my arms. "Do you remember?" she gasps. "Dave, do you remember?"

There's something like a half-remembered dream hovering around in my head, but I can't latch on to it.

"Dave, is this real?" Emma asks, breathless. Good God, what am I doing? I'm in bed with Emma. This isn't fair on either of us. But I'm locked into a programme now, and there's no turning back. "Dave," she urges. "*Is this real?*"

"Yes," I gasp. "Oh, yes, Emma, it's real." What is she talking about?

She bends to kiss me. There's a familiar click, and then my mobile leaps into life, muffled by my jacket. We pause, slowing the rhythm, both waiting to see what the other will do.

It's Mags. I know it's Mags. I feel terrible, I want to answer it.

But I don't. Enfolding Emma tightly in my arms, I block out everything except her, and the dull, warm lighting of her bedroom, the Morrissey poster on the wall, the soft music from her stereo, the stench of butter long gone off, the draught coming under the crude wooden door…

Wait, that's not right. I open an eye, focusing on the winking digits of her radio alarm by the bed. There's a dark shape above it, hanging on the wall, which slowly emerges from the gloom to become… what? A duck? A dead duck?

Emma senses my subtle shift and pulls me tighter to her. The bed feels hard and uncomfortable, all of a sudden, and I slide my hands along its packing-crate base. The wind is whistling coldly around us now. I feel as though I'm split down the middle, divided between

Emma's bedroom and a dingy, dark hut that lurks in the deep black lake of half-remembrance, struggling to break the surface, my two selves joined only by the scent of Emma's warm body.

"Do you remember?" she whispers again.

And then I do.

"The island," I say. She holds me to her and nods wordlessly.

The phone continues to ring for a short while, then it's silent. It won't ring again tonight.

Weird shit happens in the suburbs, but sometimes just shit happens.

ELEVEN
ET IN ARCADIA...

"They say you've got to be a bit... I don't know, special *to even find Arcadia, let alone get in. I'm very impressed, Mr Reporter. Maybe you're not as straight as you make out."*

Cheryl's words haunt me. I'm starting to become convinced that my life went straight down the toilet the moment I stepped inside that club. But what do I mean by that, really? Sure, there's the stuff with Mags and Emma, but then that's always been there, and all the weird stuff like the Beast and the Crying Boy, and poor Colin. Of course, you can't really legislate for things like your friend dying in a house fire, but everything else... maybe it was always like that, and I've just been papering over the cracks. But I can't shake the feeling that Arcadia was the catalyst for it all, that if indeed my life was a little insane before and I just never noticed, it was Arcadia that finally opened my eyes.

There's only one thing to do. I've got to go back.

Which, of course, is easier said than done. I decide to

take the day off, and then I realise with a start I don't even know what day it is exactly. I start trying to count the days from the Saturday night when we went to Arcadia, but I can't quite make it all add up. I telephone the office and leave a message with the switchboard that I'm "still sick". Besides, I've got Colin's funeral tomorrow, so no point going in today and then missing another one. I'm sure George will understand.

I try to find Arcadia first in the phone book and the Yellow Pages, but I'm not really surprised when there's no entry. Digging out my A-Z map, I search in vain for Lethe Lane and Fugue Street, but it's like the taxi driver who took us home on Saturday night said, they're just not there. I follow Segg Way with my finger to the end of a page, turn over, and Segg Way has merged into a whole host of other roads, none of them Fugue Street or Lethe Lane. Forgotten, even by the map-makers. I sit in silence in my flat, pondering. Two streets can't just not exist, especially when I've walked on them. And in a litter-blown alley just off Lethe Lane, there's Arcadia. Well, I've talked the talk, and now there's only one thing for it. I'm going to have to walk the walk.

The day is dull and darkening by the time I pull the car up on Segg Way. The road is quiet, fields off to one side and low factory units, all looking shut-up, on the other. No people walking their dogs, no workers coming on for the afternoon shift, no other cars on the road. I consult the map again. If I've got it right, this is just about where Segg Way turns on to the next page of the A-Z, by rights where Lethe Lane should be. I frown and look down Segg Way. It just goes on for what seems like an impossible distance, fields to the right, factory units to the left. The more I stare, the more I frown. The very act of looking down the street is making my head hurt. I can't seem to focus properly, in fact it's almost like... almost like...

It's almost like I'm looking into a vast mirror, the same stretch of fields behind me reflected ahead, the same blocks of shuttered factories repeated again. Only I'm not in the reflection. The more I stare, the more unreal it seems, like a huge stage set, and the more my eyes hurt. I pinch them tight between my fingers, and shake my head. When I open my eyes again, the street looks almost normal. But as I try to stare down Segg Way again, I get the same feeling, almost nausea. I have to look away, rubbing my temples where a dull headache has begun to throb.

Still, I've come so far, not going to let a little exhaustion put me off. I turn the ignition and gun the engine, easing away from the kerb slowly. There's a protest of gnashing gears and the fan belt begins to squeal. What the fuck? I try to ram the car into second gear but it won't go, almost refusing to inch forward despite me stamping hard on the accelerator, causing the engine to whine unhappily. I give up, pulling back to the kerb, and kill the engine. Looks like I'll have to continue on foot.

I stand beside the car for a long time after locking up, trying not to look straight ahead down Segg Way. A fierce wind has whipped up, howling down the road towards me, driving grit into my eyes and creating violent little eddies of litter and leaves. Suddenly I'm aware of another presence, a small dog that's padding up the pavement on the other side of the road, heading in the same direction as me. It's some scraggy little mongrel, the wind flattening the wiry russet hair on its face. I watch it walk slowly up the road until it's level with me, where it stops, sniffing the air and struggling to stand still in the howling wind. The dog tries to nose forward, then gives up and turns around. And then it looks at me like I've never been looked at by a dog, gazing at me levelly, its eyes full of almost human understanding, unflinching. I nearly speak out, unformed questions rising on my lips. What? What? What is it trying to tell me?

Then it gives up, both on me and its chances of getting down Segg Way, and turns tail and bolts back the way it came, disappearing into a side street far down the road. I watch it go for a long time, wondering what it knows, what it was trying to communicate. Was it trying to show me the futility of my actions, trying to tell me that if not even a dog can walk the paths I'm choosing for myself, then what possible hope can I have?

No. No. It's just a dog. Dogs don't try to tell us anything, except when they want to eat, or shit, or take a run in the park. I slump on to the car, suddenly completely exhausted, half ready to crawl back into the driver's seat and sleep right there. But I won't be beaten by this. I fumble in my pocket and my fingers close around a tight paper package. Speed. Pulling it out I shield it from the wind inside my coat and unfurl it, quickly licking the bitter powder in one go, grimacing as it textures my tongue, almost making me gag.

Zipping the coat up to my chin, I close my eyes and push forward into the wind. It howls harder, pushing me back, whipping my breath away, but I don't care, I forge on relentlessly, Cheryl's voice urging me forward. *"They say you've got to be a bit... I don't know,* special *to even find Arcadia, let alone get in. I'm very impressed, Mr Reporter. Maybe you're not as straight as you make out."*

The amphetamine kicks in almost immediately, adding power to my legs as I push on through the wind, eyes still tightly clenched. The powder is cleansing the fog in my brain, rushing through my veins like a tornado, matching the gale gust for gust until I'm not only fighting against the wind but working it, shaping it, folding it behind me and letting it carry me on.

And then it's over. The wind dies abruptly. I open my eyes. I'm still on Segg Way, my car's ten yards or so behind me, but something's different. Where this side of the street seemed unreal before, this time my car and the factory units and the fields which merge off into infinity look as though they're the mere painted backdrop of some false life. I've crossed over, it feels like, made the leap into the unknown. I turn and look down Segg Way, and notice things I hadn't seen from the other side. The road doesn't seem half as long as it did before, I can see it curve round to the left, a wooded area nestling at the end of the fields on the right. There are shops, and streets meandering away from the main road, and the vague hints of movement on the far edge of the limits of my vision.

And then I'm laughing, almost hysterical, but not caring because there's no-one here to see me. I've just had one of those super-lucid speed moments, when something is so obvious that you've been missing it and then it comes and smacks you right in the face. Segg Way. *Segg Way.* I haven't just moved somewhere else physically, I've *segued* there, shifted from one state to the next, almost seamlessly, but just about noticeable. Here, where I stand, and there, where my car sits, are all part of the same tune, but played at different tempos. It's symphonic in its hilarity. Much jollier, I set off at a jaunty pace down towards my destiny.

The speed is kicking in now, coming up much faster than I anticipated. I feel out of step with myself, as though I'm watching one of those TV shows filmed on video which always looks a millisecond slower than real-life. The dusk is landing heavily, and streetlights are buzzing into life, dull orange embers warming slowly to yellow. A car, a blue Triumph Dolomite, cruises slowly past me, the driver looking at me intensely then gunning the engine and driving on. I'm coming up to where Lethe Lane cuts across Fugue

Street, where there are shops, and a pub, and houses. I pass a small corner grocery store, tins and jars displayed in spartan fashion in the window. Behind the counter, an old woman looks impassively at me, meeting my stare. At the doorway a mother and a small child appear, looking at me in the same measured yet disinterested manner. They seem to be waiting for me to pass before they'll step out of the doorway. The child has a small lollipop in his hand. Without smiling he offers it to me and speaks.

I don't know what he's saying. He forms his words as a question, but they make no sense to me. He proffers the lollipop again, repeating his words, which seem to be formed of all the wrong vowels and letters. Not exactly a foreign language, just a... *different* one. He begins to laugh and his mother looks mirthlessly on at me. I shake my head and move away, conscious of the shopkeeper staring through the window at me until I pass by her line of sight.

Suddenly, the street seems full of people, milling aimlessly, a quiet hum of unidentifiable conversation rising all around me. I strain to pick out words, but I can't. Christ, I feel fucked. It's cold but I'm sweating, and I know I must look as pale as a corpse. I think I'm whiting out. I stop and steady myself on a lamp-post. It buzzes harshly, flickers, and goes out, causing shadows to dance and submerge. An old man stands in front of me, waving his walking stick and jabbering animatedly without uttering a single sound. He seems to be pleading with me, gesticulating wildly. Someone else pulls him away, glowering at me and tracing a convoluted symbol in the air in front of my face. There's a sound of tinkling laughter, as though heard at a party from another room.

I push on and the crowds, now thronging the darkening pavements, open to let me through. My head's thumping and my throat's as dry as sandpaper. Need a drink, anything. I'm sure I saw a pub around here last time and I cast about, looking for it, until I spot an illuminated sign creaking softly in the wind across the road. The picture on the sign hurts my eyes, all the angles are wrong, writhing shapes turn in on themselves. I squint and try to read the name of the pub, but the letters won't stay still, swarming over each other like living things. Regardless, I force myself across the road, my tongue feeling thick and dry inside my parched mouth. The door is open and I stagger into the almost Stygian gloom of the vault, my feet sucking on the sticky carpet. There are shapes in here, people huddled around tables. The bar is faintly lit, but darkness seems to be pressing on the periphery of my vision. I lean on the bar, digging for cash in my pocket. A thickset man framed by a dull halo of lights from the optics frowns at me, looking uncomfortably at the other unseen drinkers, as though seeking guidance as to how to deal with me. I slap a handful of change on the dark oak of the bar and beseech him wordlessly, imploringly, for help. Seemingly at some signal from somewhere behind me, the barman reaches under the bar and brings out an open bottle, pouring me a measure into a glass. He doesn't take any of my money, and I slug the liquid down in one go, the harsh, bittersweet taste scalding my throat, but at least offering some measure of relief to the desert on my tongue. The alcohol in the drink hits me a second or two later, causing my head to swim as in a nightmare. I feel surrounded by the other punters, hemmed in, claustrophobic. The bar man proffers the bottle at me again but I shake my head. "Arcadia," I say, the act of enunciating the words alien and painful. "Where is Arcadia?"

Then he's laughing at me, throwing his head back and roaring, but the sound's muted as if we're underwater. The other drinkers join in, slapping each other's shoulders and rubbing tears from their eyes, the dull howl building up until it needles into my head. My ears are sore, and I can feel something wet trickling down my jaw line. I touch my face and draw my fingers back. Blood. My ears are bleeding. I shout at the barman, at all of them, but even my own words fail to make any sense to me now. Turning, I stagger out of the pub, on to Fugue Street.

Which is now deserted.

Except for a single car. A shiny black car of indeterminate marque, the windows tinted, parked up with its engine idling across the street, pooled under the light of a lamp-post. Where did all the people go? The street is deserted, litter blowing unsteadily on the cracked pavement, the shops and houses darkened. I glance at my watch, but I can't compute the patterns of hands and numbers into anything that makes sense. Suddenly I feel very, very afraid. I turn back to the pub, but someone has closed the door behind me, and the building is shrouded in darkness.

I'm not wanted here.

But I won't go until I find what I came for, until I find Arcadia. There was an alley, I remember, long and tight, which opened up on to this very street. I cast around for it, half-spotting ginnels and passages on the edge of my sightline, but when I try to focus on them, they aren't there. The whole street seems to twist and move, re-shaping itself constantly. From the corner of my eye I spot an alley, and then look away, not gazing at it directly. It's still there on the outside of my field of vision, and I edge towards it, not looking full on. When I think I'm but a yard away, I reach out my hand and can't help turning my head to the uninviting, dark passageway. My fingers touch cold bricks, a section of an unbroken and uninterrupted wall. There is no alley.

The car is still there, the unseen occupants watching my strange, uncertain ballet on the darkened and deserted street. I could go up to it, bang on the window, ask them for directions. But I don't want to, I don't want to approach the car at all.

In fact, I want to get out of here.

And that's exactly what I do. Sweating yet cold, I start to walk back the way I came, and it's mere seconds before I'm breaking out into a jog and then a full sprint, my breath jagged and rasping as I run away, back to my car, back to real life. The running and the speed are making my heart hammer, beating in cadence with the slapping of my feet on the cold, cracked, empty pavements. I run and run, seemingly for longer than I walked to get here, until I see a car. My car. I get to it easily, no pressure or resistance like when I tried to get to Fugue Street.

And suddenly everything seems normal once again. I lean on the car, trying to regain my breath. The same fields roll off to one side, the same factory units shuttered and darkened on the other. I can read the signs. SMITH FABRICS. EMPIRE TECHNOLOGIES. The graffiti is refreshingly mundane. FUCK U. Fumbling for my keys, I open the door and sink gratefully into the driver's seat, exhausted. I put my head in my hands and close my eyes for a moment, and seem to sleep.

I awake with a start. Everything is as it was before. My watch, no longer an alien dial of incomprehensible messages, tells me it is nearly seven-thirty. I glance along the gloom of Segg Way. Did all that really happen? Did I even get out of the car, or have I dreamed it all?

I make a mental note to discuss this latest turn of events with Colin.

And then I remember.

TWELVE
THE FUNERAL

I'm the only one here. I even put a notice in the paper, but I'm the only one here. Can it really be that I'm the only friend he had?

Appropriately enough, it's raining; big, black, boiling clouds spew fat cold raindrops on the chapel and surrounding graveyard. Inside, piped organ music plays as the vicar potters around. A cheap coffin stands on the dais. The chapel is lit by electric lights made to look like flickering candles.

Colin had made a will with his parents' solicitors. I shouldn't imagine he left much money, but it did make provision for his funeral. He has specified cremation rather than burial, a sign of someone who has read far too many Edgar Allan Poe stories and EC horror comics than is really good for them.

I didn't think Colin would have thanked me for a full church funeral, so I settle for a mercifully short service in the crematorium, the vicar looking awkward at my sole presence. He shakes my hand at the close of the ceremony and says that if I care to wait a short while I can have the ashes.

Outside, in the rain, I wait for what's left of Colin.

I'm sitting on the wrought iron bench outside the chapel, not caring that the rain is soaking into my trousers, chilling my gooseflesh. It's Tuesday, I think. I'm not sure when I last ate, or slept. All I can recall is doing far too much speed over the last couple of days just to keep me going. I dimly remember George calling me at home, asking what the hell was going on, then apologising profusely when I numbly told him. I haven't been to work since. I suppose I should go tomorrow.

I run the rain off my face, surprised at the stubble on my cheeks. Jesus, I must look like shit. What's wrong with me, why has Colin's death affected me like this?

But it isn't just Colin's death, it's everything. In the past week I feel like my world has been turned upside down. All that with Emma and Mags, all the odd stuff happening like the Beast and the Crying Boy. The strange, nightmarish journey through forgotten streets. I rest my chin on my chest and sigh raggedly. If I had the energy I'd weep.

I sit like that, getting wetter and wetter, for some minutes, until I become aware of distant sounds, deep inside the graveyard. I open my eyes and suddenly everything's gone misty. The chapel is still and quiet, but something is going on away among the headstones. Shadowy figures in the smog.

Bored with waiting for the vicar to bring me Colin's ashes, I decide to see for myself. My legs and arms have gone to sleep, they're as heavy as lead. I feel like an unwieldy robot as I drag myself to my feet and stagger off along the shining wet path. The mist closes in behind me and as I glance back I can hardly see the chapel any more. The noises from ahead are still distant and indistinct, but the figures, seven or eight of them, seem to be closer.

I slow almost to a halt as I realise they're standing around an open grave. So that's why the vicar's taking so long with the ashes. But as I slide closer, it becomes apparent that it isn't the short, bearded vicar who officiated over Colin's service. It's a big, broad-shouldered man with his back to me, short-cropped, grey hair high on a thick neck. He's got a bag in his hand, I notice as the mist clears around the open grave.

No, not a bag. A violin case.

As soon as I clock that I gasp, and the man with the violin case turns his heavy-lidded gaze upon me, the uncomfortable smile playing gently on his thin, bloodless lips. "Come," he intones. "We've been waiting for you."

This is ridiculous, I realise. Even more so when I see who else is standing reverently around the open grave. There's Pete and Tony, Ferdinand Shelley, Emma, George, Mags. "Ah, I get it," I say, smiling with visible relief. "This is all a *dream*."

Emma looks at me annoyed. "Is this real, Dave? *Is this real*?"

Mags starts laughing. "He doesn't know what's real, any more. Do you, Dave? You don't even know who you are yourself. Which mask are you wearing today, Dave?"

Pete and Tony are laughing, too. Tony puts his arm around Mags' shoulders, and reaches down to squeeze her breast, grinning lecherously at me. Pete grabs Emma and kisses her hard on the lips, she gropes his buttocks in return. Christ, this isn't a dream. It's a fucking nightmare.

Shelley whips out his camera and starts clicking off frames, pointing his lens in my face. "I thought you only did dead things," I protest.

"You look in a worse state than anything I've photographed this year," he laughs from behind the camera.

George suddenly pipes up gleefully: "Deadline, David. You're on the deadline. This is it, boy, the deadline. Can you cut it, can you meet the deadline?"

A deep modulated voice cuts into the rising cacophony. "If I might remind you all, we are here for a funeral."

It's the man with the violin case, and I'm grateful when everyone stops yelling and stands still around the yawning mouth of the open grave.

I stare impassively at the coffin beside the grave. Who's it going to be? If this is classic nightmare stuff, then it must be for me. But perhaps not.

Pete, Tony, George and Ferdinand begin to manhandle the coffin and try to slide it into the hole. But it won't go. It's too big for the grave.

"There's too much shit in here," gasps Tony, sweating profusely. "We need to lose some."

"Then do so!" cries the man with the violin case. He throws open the lid of the coffin, reaches in, and tosses something at me. It grows into a snarling, black panther which leaps over my shoulder and bounds away into the cemetery. George dips in and pulls out a copy of The Crying Boy, flinging it frisbee-like into the mist. Then things start to leap out of the coffin of their own accord, crazy, fantastic things. My dream hands clutch my dream head as a flying saucer with flashing lights zooms straight up, a two headed sheep gambols about the gravestones, booming voices and hollow banging noises emerge. The man with the violin case is laughing horribly amid the chaos. "Yes... yes," he urges. "All out. All the mystery, and the terror, and the horror, and the unexplained. They want to bury it all, but it won't work. It won't go away."

The graveside is like the eye of a whirlwind now. A long-necked dinosaur, a bit like what I imagine the

Loch Ness Monster to look like, swims past, turning its yellow-eyed gaze upon me. Bigfoot lopes towards the trees which line the cemetery. More flying saucers buzz about my head. Everyone else has disappeared except the man with the violin case, grotesquely dancing among the stones and swinging his case around with abandon, shouting in rich, rumbling tones: "Ashes to ashes! Dust to dust! Ashes to ashes!"

I clamp my hands over my eyes, trying to block out the madness, but all I can hear is the man with the violin case. "Ashes to ashes! Dust to dust! Ashes to..."

"...ashes?"

I sit up with a start and a small yell at the hand on my shoulder. It's the vicar, leaning over me with a small wooden box in his hand, concern on his face. He smiles apologetically. "Sorry to wake you. I have Mr Carroll's ashes."

It takes me a few seconds to get my bearings. I glance over at the graveyard, to the scene of my nightmare. All quiet, though a little darker than when I first dropped off into my fitful sleep. Numbly, I take the box from the vicar, wondering for the first time what the hell I'm going to do with Colin's ashes. The vicar makes to walk away, then changes his mind. "Would you like a cup of tea? I've nothing pressing this afternoon, and if you'd like to talk..?"

To be honest, I could do with something stronger than tea, but I'm wet and cold and haven't spoken to anyone properly for about three days, so I nod wearily and follow the vicar into the small room at the back of the chapel.

I sit wet and gently steaming in a wooden chair, gratefully sipping the sweet, strong tea. The vicar pours himself a cup from the brightly-coloured, cracked teapot, and sits across from me, wiping the rain from his big round forehead. "Were you and Mr Carroll, ah, close?"

I know what he's thinking. He's thinking that I'm Colin's boyfriend. I can't be bothered to contradict him. "No. Well, fairly close," I say, a little confusedly. "Well, he was just a friend. I saw him quite often."

The vicar looks at me closely. "Are you all right?"

I don't answer his question, but instead counter with one of my own: "Why has everything gone weird?"

He sets his cup down on the table and appears to consider the question carefully. After a long time he says: "Has it? Depending on how you look at it, things have always been weird."

I drain my cup. "Maybe they have. Maybe I've only just noticed. When did you notice?"

He shrugs. "Who's to say I have? Look at recent world history: the Berlin Wall brought down by bare human hands, the collapse of old empires, the rise of Federal Europe, September eleventh and the war on terror, old diseases being cured, new ones being discovered. Two decades ago, most of that would have been considered unthinkable."

"But all that's on a global scale. I've been noticing a lot of... strangeness... here, locally, in our town."

The vicar shrugs again. "Who knows what we see when we finally open our eyes?"

His face blurs and the suddenly familiar, heavy eyes cast their unblinking gaze on me, the violin case sitting on the table between us. My scalp crawls across my head and I leap up, the chair crashing to the floor behind me.

"What's wrong?" says the vicar, himself again, but a second later he's the man with the violin case again, smiling impassively at me. Wordlessly I flee the chapel, running out into the night that's fallen while we've been inside, and I don't stop running until I've pounded up the wet path to the big cemetery gates and burst out on to the road, into the path of a pair of sweeping headlights.

THIRTEEN
MAGS DROPS A BOMBSHELL

For a long moment there is silence and stillness, me standing with my hands slapped on the bonnet of Mags's MG, the headlights shining up into my face, illuminating a halo of rain around my field of vision. I look up to see her shocked and speechless at the wheel of the stalled car.

Ten minutes later, we're on our way to my flat and we still haven't spoken a single word. Mags breaks the silence at last as we sweep into my road. "Jesus. I could have killed you. Jesus."

"Rather you than a stranger." My attempt at levity doesn't raise a smile from Mags. I'd forgotten she was supposed to be coming to the cemetery for Colin's service.

"I'm sorry I was so late. I got held up at the office."

"It's okay. You didn't miss much."

Mags pulls up outside my flat, hauls up the handbrake, but leaves the engine idling. "Was it bad?"

I think back to my weird fever dream, no doubt fuelled by lack of food and sleep and speed exhaustion, and the conversation with the vicar who may or may not have been the man with the violin case. "No worse than you'd expect for a funeral."

Mags thinks I'm being facetious, even though I'm genuinely not, and lets loose a loud sigh. Glancing sidelong at me, she comments: "You look like shit, Dave."

I open the door and pull myself ungraciously out into the rain. Leaning into the MG I say: "Thanks for the lift. Do you want to come in?"

"I think I'd better," she decides, reaching in the back for her handbag. I'm touched by what I imagine is her concern for me, and I wait for her to run with her head down through the lashing rain before unlocking the door to the house.

The flat looks like a rodeo team have been using it for practice. The TV blares a greeting to us as we enter, and all the lights are burning. Mags almost steps in a half-eaten ready meal as she enters, and she eyes me disapprovingly as she picks up an empty Absolut bottle from the coffee table. I aimlessly wander around, picking up discarded clothes and dirty cups, finally saying: "Want a drink or anything?"

Mags is taking off her wet mac. "Why don't we get this place cleaned up first?"

As we get to work, the atmosphere warms considerably, and we no longer seem like the strangers we were when we came through the door. By the time the lounge is back to a liveable state, I'm running some hot water to clean the pots and Mags is forcing clothes into the washing machine. "Not that shirt," I warn. "It's dry clean only."

Mags tosses the top into a plastic bag with the other awkward wash items, and nods at the washing up bowl. "Don't use all the hot water, eh?"

I look down at the foaming sink. "Why not?"

She stands and encircles my waist with her slim arms, kissing me for the first time tonight. Her lips lightly brush the nape of my neck, causing the tiny hairs there to raise like hackles. “We want to save some for the bath,” she breathes.

Wearing my bathrobe, Mags pours a capful of sandalwood bubble bath under the steaming stream of water cascading from the hot tap. “Go on, be reckless,” I urge. “Pour another capful.”

I’m wearing Mags’ Calvin Klein knickers. It’s her idea. Underneath the robe, she’s wearing my Ralph Lauren boxers. She found some strawberries in the fridge that were miraculously still in date, and she leans over to push one in my mouth, the robe falling away to reveal her petite breasts. “You know what I’d like to do?”

I mumble in the negative through the mouthful of strawberry, and she goes on: “I’d like us to go out, to the pub, you wearing my knickers and me wearing yours. No-one would ever know but us.”

“Unless we crash the car,” I counter. “My mum told me always to go out with clean underpants in case I got run over, but I don’t think she meant my girlfriend’s”

Mags sits up straight, and turns her attention to testing the heat of the bath. “I think this is just about right,” she smiles, but I can tell I’ve said something to upset her. Her brow crinkles in that way it does just before she’s about to cry.

“Mags?” I say gently.

“Later,” she smiles through wet eyes. “Let’s get in.”

I recline against Mags, my head on her breasts, while she massages sea kelp shampoo into my scalp, her long legs wrapped around my waist. “Do you remember how we first met?” she asks through a mouthful of the last of the strawberries.

I stroke her thighs, relishing the memory. "It was a hot day, Christ was it hot. The best summer we've had for years. A Sunday, wasn't it?"

She nods. "I was supposed to be going for tea at Stephen's parents' house, but it was so hot and glorious I made up some lie about baby-sitting for my sister and went to the park. I was reading-"

"The Tenant of Wildfell Hall."

"The Tenant of Wildfell Hall. You were playing football with your mates." She pauses to rinse my hair with a cup of bathwater. "I'd noticed you as soon as you started playing."

I twist to look at her. "Why, because I was so crap?"

She giggles and slaps my face gently with the wet flannel. "No, not because you were crap at football. There was something about you. I must have read and re-read the same page for about an hour. I couldn't keep my eyes off you."

It's a nice line. Then she says: "You were crap at football, mind."

We laugh together, easily, naturally. God, I feel as though I've finally come back to life after three or four days in limbo. Just being with Mags has rejuvenated me. That, and the bath, and the sex that's hopefully going to follow. I say hopefully because even though she's rubbing sea kelp into my head and we've been wearing each other's underwear, I find it better not to take anything for granted where Mags is concerned. We're on borrowed time as it is, I can't make any assumptions.

I'm in danger of becoming maudlin again, but Mags is still reminiscing. "I'd finally got down to trying to read again instead of watching you from behind my sunglasses. If I had been watching you, I might have seen that crap kick and the ball coming straight towards me."

"You were down to the strawberry bit on your Fab lolly when the ball knocked it clean out of your hand. You just stood up and said-"

"'Have you got two left feet, you fucking dickhead?'" she finishes for me. "We're out of strawberries. And this bathwater's getting a bit cool."

I deftly manipulate the hot tap with my right foot, letting it run until the satisfying heat spreads through the bathwater, warming us both. I twist round until I'm facing Mags, and she slides further down the bath until I'm practically on top of her. "God, you're gorgeous," she breathes, planting urgent kisses on my soapy face. "Come here."

Later, when we've towelled off, we sit wrapped in blankets in front of the TV, me building a spliff in the flickering light from the screen. It's the end of the news, the funny bit just before the local round-up and weather. "And finally," beams the presenter, "a rather fishy story. Residents of this quiet suburb have found it isn't raining cats and dogs where they live - but mackerel."

I glance up at the pictures of bemused suburbanites carrying buckets of dead fish. A week ago this might have interested me. Now it seems rather commonplace. I finish rolling the joint, light it with the Zippo, and pass it over to Mags after a few deep tokes. "Going back to that first day," I say when I finally exhale. "Why did you go for a drink with me when you were seeing Stephen?"

She takes a long drag on the spliff and lets the smoke drift out of her mouth before answering. "I don't know. I liked you. It just seemed like a bit of fun, then, a drink with a guy I liked."

"A bit of fun then? So it isn't fun now?" I tease.

She hands the joint back. "That's not what I mean. What I mean, Dave, is that it's a lot more serious now. I'd had flings before you while I was with Stephen, but that's all they were. This is weird shit."

We both reflect on it quietly, then Mags goes on: "That's why it makes what I've got to say all that more difficult."

My breathing slows and smoke catches in my throat. "Go on."

She looks me dead in the eyes: "Dave, I'm getting married to Stephen."

I try to look away from her gaze but it holds me, compels me. I don't know what to say. I mean, it's hardly a shock, she's been with him for about ten years. But I'd sort of begun to assume that while we were still seeing each other she wouldn't be able to do it. I've broken my golden rule. I've made assumptions.

"When?" I ask. Easter at the earliest, surely. More likely a June wedding, if I know Stephen Fucking Doyle. I'm right.

I feel wretched. I've been at the bottom, then Mags brought me up again, and now she's dashed me back on the rocks. I just want her to go, but she's babbling on, trying to make excuses and give me explanations.

"So that's it, then," I cut in.

Mags looks visibly shocked. "What? What do you mean? Hey, I know it's heavy, Dave, but it doesn't mean-"

I silence her with a finger on her lips. Her eyes are beginning to fill with tears and I can feel mine prickling as well. "No, Mags. I can't carry on seeing you while you're planning a wedding. Not while you go shopping for your dress and Stephen comes in crowing about his stag night. Sorry."

"No, I'm sorry," she says, crying openly now. "I've really fucked this up. It shouldn't have gone so far between us. I shouldn't have let Stephen talk me into getting married. Shit, I don't know." She buries her face in her hands.

Something occurs to me. "That's the last time we'll sleep together, then," I say thoughtfully.

Mags looks up, a look of near-panic on her face. "No," she says, grabbing me and urgently kissing me through her tears. "No. No."

I don't want to, but I feel my body respond. Her hands seek me out, stroking and pulling at me until despite my better judgement we're lying amid a tangle of blankets on the carpet, thrusting together. Mags is moaning and weeping at the same time, but I feel strangely detached, reaching a quick, unemotional climax and rolling off Mags coolly. While she dresses I take a quick shower, washing her scent off me.

"I have to go," she says, biting her lip. I shrug. "I'll call you," she promises. I just shrug again, reaching for the TV remote control. I can hear her sniffling as she closes the door of the flat behind her. I think briefly to ask her for her key, but decide that's a little too callous. Shit.

It's after midnight, and despite my exhaustion I can't get to sleep. I dress quickly in the dark and decide to go for a walk. On the street, the rain has stopped but everything is covered in a silver sheen, the yellow of street lamps distortedly reflected on the wet Tarmac.

I wander aimlessly, my route taking me past the shell of Colin's house. The windows and doors have been boarded up. The roof isn't there any more. Impulsively, I push open the gate and step into the small garden. Following the line of the house round to the rear garden, I almost trip over a low, white box. It's the fridge, on its side after the firemen dragged it out of the house. The window installed in the door by Colin reflects what little light there is.

I bend down and press my fingers against the cool, wet glass. Did you find out before you died, Colin? Did you solve the mystery of Schrodinger's Fridge? I just accepted the weird shit, went through life like most people do, noticing the odd and the strange occasionally, contemplating it briefly, then carrying on with a more material existence. But Colin thought about the weird shit, questioned it, wanted answers. Perhaps that's where he went wrong. Perhaps we're not supposed to have answers to some questions. If we don't have mysteries, what do we have left? A nice, orderly world where there's a place for everything and everything is in its place? A world where you can fly to the furthest, most remote point, in twenty-four hours? A world with no frontiers, no unmapped territories, no here be dragons?

"Perhaps the world's trying to tell us something," I say to the fridge. "We think we're so bloody sophisticated, think we've conquered the world. Perhaps all this weirdness is just a little reminder: you don't *really* know what's out there in the dark."

The fridge doesn't look in too bad a shape, despite the firemen saying it was the cause of the fire. I bet I could take it away, plug it in, and find out whether that bastard little light stays on or not when you shut the fridge door.

"Nah." I stand stiffly, and leave Colin's gutted house behind me. It's late, but I carry on walking. I don't really know where I'm heading, until I'm there. Emma's house. I stand outside in the rain for a long time, just beyond the orange corona of a humming street light. There's a light burning in Emma's room, upstairs at the front of the house. Why am I here? Because Mags has pissed me off? Because I want to be? I wait for a bit longer, searching for a motive, then eventually step up the garden path and bang loudly on the door. I hear someone running heavily downstairs and then the door swings open. It's Emma. She looks a bit ruffled, and is pulling a bathrobe tight around her.

"Dave?" she asks, surprised. "Christ. What are you doing here?"

I shrug. I feel wretched. I just want someone to hold me. "Can I come in?"

Emma casts a glance back at the dark staircase. "Umm, it's not really, ah..."

I don't get it. "What, is there a problem?"

"Emma, are you coming back, or what?" shouts a new voice, a male voice, from up the stairs. Ah. The problem.

Suddenly, she's angry, narrowing her eyes and hissing through clenched teeth: "What, did you expect to just come round here when you fancy a fuck? It's not like that, Dave, it's not on tap. Did you think I'd just wait for you for ever?"

Wordlessly, I turn on my heel. "Dave," she calls quietly, but I ignore her. Another bridge burned. I walk straight out of there in the rain, not stopping until I come to the inviting light of a piss-stinking telephone box. Inside I hold the receiver gingerly, pondering who I have left to call. I settle on Tony. The phone rings for ages before it's answered and I quickly say: "Tony?"

"No, it's his dad. Who's that, is it Dave?"

"Yeah, Mr Benson. Sorry to call so late. Is Tony in?"

"No lad, they're still in Amsterdam. They were trying to get in touch with you for days. In the end they had to sell your ticket. Are you all right, lad?"

I stare at the receiver. Amsterdam. Shit, I completely forgot. I put the phone down on Tony's dad's tinny voice, then step out into the rain, alone.

FOURTEEN
NO SURRENDER

No, not completely. True, I've lost Mags, and seemingly Emma too, and the lads are in Amsterdam, but I've still got my old bolt-hole, where I can always go no matter how bad things get. Cheryl.

It's raining heavily as I leave the telephone box, but I don't think to head home for the car or take a taxi to Jepson Street. I set off on foot, at first hunching and turning my collar to the downpour, but eventually straightening up and letting the rain wash over me, soaking my hair and running in rivulets down my face. Like tears.

Jepson Street is maybe two-and-a-half, three miles from Emma's road. The route takes me from the student quarter to tight terraced streets, through an anonymous housing estate, skirting the town centre, out by the football ground and then along an interminable road of factories and old mills, where Jepson Street first sprang up to service the late shifts many decades ago. It's almost a proper tourist trail, taking in all the sights and beauty spots of the town. I stifle a giggle as I imagine it being down in one of those guide books, like a walking tour of Rome or Prague, every smashed up bus shelter or vandalised wall duly noted for tourists to gaze at and take photographs of. "Here we are outside the football ground. That's me by that graffiti: PAKIS FUKING DIE."

I walk paths that I've never trodden before. It's amazing what you see when you abandon the car and walk, what you see and what you hear and what you smell when you're out of your insulated little tin can, smothered in air-conditioned warmth and taped music. I should do this more often. TVs flicker behind curtains, there's the yell of arguing voices from behind a semi-open door; the deep rumble of an angry man and the brittle shriek of a woman, followed by a brief pause and then a wail of someone damned. There's the bitter smell of the canning factory, drifting on the wind, penetrating the sheeting rain. There are voices, singing, far away, in another street, an incongruous, drunken rendition of Danny Boy. Horns blare on the bypass beyond the houses, traffic swishing through the rain. Somewhere, there's a telephone ringing and ringing, a plaintive, lonely sound made all the more poignant by my unshakeable knowledge that it isn't going to be answered. I pause and listen to it ringing, until it finally stops with a strangled electric choke. Another desperate soul. Another broken heart.

And here the houses thin out, gardens jostle between the terraces, forcing them into semis, elbowing them out into a better class of neighbourhood. Low walls encircle well-tended gardens, the occasional children's bike or toy drowning in the rain-soaked turf. The lighting behind the blinds is more subdued, the homes wider and squatter, giving more breathing space. Yet still the tubes of television sets wink away in the lounges, painting the faces of mesmerised families blue. Still there are arguments, more muted for the kids' sakes and the neighbours' sakes. Still, a telephone rings, and no-one answers.

I want to answer it. I want to answer all of the ringing telephones, to speak to whoever's on the other end, to tell them that it's okay, I'm like them, I'm lost and lonely and desperate too. I want to be in those houses watching television in silence, the kids in bed, my wife passing me a packet of crisps without being asked, me idly wondering if we'll have sex later. I want to pick up the toys from the gardens and take them into the garage, I want to tinker with the car on Sunday morning, mow the lawn, pass the time of day with the neighbours. I want all that. I want to be normal.

Normal. Normal people do all those things. What they don't do is walk through the streets in the pouring down rain on their way to visit a prostitute. To just talk.

I leave the normal people to their children and their televisions and their neighbours as the estate road I'm following winds in on itself and I forge on, on to the bypass, the mist and drizzle thrown up by the hissing cars drenching me even more. The town centre is just over there, people and lights and pubs and kebab shops. People unbothered by Crying Boys and Beasts of Shotmoor and secret, hidden nightclubs. And men with violin cases. Especially, men with violin cases. Maybe I could go and join them. I stand for a moment, wavering between carrying on towards Jepson Street or diving into the nearest pub, throwing enough Red Mist down me to sink me into oblivion, then trying to get into the knickers of the first woman who'll have me. But they'd know. I feel apart from them, marked as someone different. They'd shy away from me, know I was different. I sigh, and trudge on along the bypass, to the darkened, ugly shape of the football ground.

The floodlights thrust awkwardly into the night, the skeletons of dead giants, heads bowed over the turf. I remember my dad taking me there when I was a tiny kid, before it was an all-seater, when there was just a wooden fence separating the crowd from the pitch. I gripped on to the fence, trying to make sense of the action, and got a splinter in my hand. He pulled it out with his tweezers, but he missed a goal while he was doing it. I could see the flash of anger in his eyes. I would never go with him after that.

Beyond the football ground, anonymous red-brick streets of factories and old mills, now given over to small textiles companies in units. The high walls of the buildings are grimy with soot, covered with layer upon layer of fly-posters for bands and technobilly parties. In three-foot high letters across a wall someone has sprayed the word SURRENDER. Maybe I should. There's something pushing at me this way, tugging at me that. I don't know what it is, but maybe I should just surrender, see where it takes me.

Well this is where it's taken me this time. Jepson Street. The rain eases off slightly as I turn the corner, the same crack kid I saw the last time I was here curled up against the wall. He seems to be sleeping, so I drop a quid coin on the pavement in front of him, put my head down, and head on towards Cheryl's.

I ring the bell three times and there's no answer. Shit. She's probably got a client with her, and it won't do much for her concentration to have me pressing the buzzer all night. Dejectedly I turn, about to go and find a cab and get me the fuck home, when the intercom crackles. There's a pause at the other end, and then a cautious: "Yes?"

"Cheryl? It's Dave. Is it a bad time?"

"Dave? Oh Jesus, oh Christ, you've got to get away from here."

"You got someone with you? Sorry, love-"

"You don't understand, Dave!" Her voice is urgent, panicky even, through the intercom. "Shit, you'd better come up. Just for a minute. Make sure no-one's fucking watching you."

Spooked, I look up and down Jepson Street as the door unlatches, but no-one's taking a blind bit of notice of me. I climb the stairs and rap smartly on Cheryl's door. She only opens it a crack, and she's got the security chain on, but it's enough for me to see her face.

"Fucking hell." I breathe. "Who did that to you?"

She's looking at me through an eye almost closed with bruising and swelling, and her lip is fat and heavy with blood. The knuckles of the hand she holds the door with are black and thick. Looks like she's been given a right going over.

"Dave," she says sadly. "You'd better go. It's not safe for you here."

"Not safe for me? What about you? Who did this? Are they still here? Have you called the police?"

She shakes her head and hisses violently: "Just *go*. The people who did this said... they said they'll get Andrew. They know where my mum lives and everything. I can't risk it."

"Risk what, Cheryl? Look, let me in, we need to sort this out. Why has this happened to you?"

She shakes her head in horror and closes the opening in the door to a crack. "I can't let you in, Dave. It's *you*. They said if I talk to you again, they'll get Andrew. It's *you* they're after."

"Who, for fuck's sake?" I'm getting scared now, really scared, and I know what she's going to say next even as the words start to spill out of her poor, bruised, beautiful mouth.

"I don't know who they are, they wouldn't say. Just told me to stay away from you, and then they did this to me, and threatened Andrew. Then they drove off in a car..."

"A car..?"

"A car. A black car. Now get out of here, Dave. Please."

I start to panic. I ask her what the fuck she's talking about, demanding to know who did this, what it's got to do with me, but she shuts the door. And now I really am on my own.

It's really raining now, lashing down, big thick gobbets splattering on to the pavements. Jepson Street is deserted, and I huddle in the doorway to Cheryl's building, casting about hopelessly for a taxi. There aren't any.

In the distance, there's a glimmer of light in the night sky, followed some moments later by a low rumble of thunder. Great. Somewhere in the world it's fucking warm and light, there's a beach and a shack and I should be there, my hands cradling a sweating bottle of beer. But I'm not. I'm here in this shit-hole, and all I get from this faraway paradise is the memory of their hot day, their cast-off heat flowing high on the Gulf Stream, clashing with the frigid air above my town, and bringing me nothing more than a thunderstorm. The lightning flashes again, a jagged fork that rips open the sky and stays imprinted on my retina in red and green for long seconds later. The thunder cracks again. It's coming closer.

There's a sudden movement across the road. I thought Jepson Street was deserted, but I was wrong. In the doorway opposite are two figures, sheltering from the rain in the shadows. Watching me.

"Mister?" calls a voice. "Mister? You wan' lie with us? For money? It dry here, mister, you come here."

They emerge into the dull streetlight together, suddenly grabbing each other as the lightning flashes almost directly overhead, followed only a second later by an angry boom. They're stunningly dirty, dressed in rags, but not un-pretty. One seems to soothe the other, talking in a low murmur, telling her it's okay, it's only thunder. I want to leave, to get out of Jepson Street, but something's stopping me. Those girls. They look...

familiar, and not just from seeing them when I was last visiting Cheryl. They take my hesitation as encouragement, and step out a little further into the downpour. "Over here, mister. You do both, if you like. For money."

There's something... those girls... me, Tony and Pete on a raft, kids... Jesus, it's like I've got something on the tip of my tongue and I can't say it. And Emma... Emma, too...

Then I can see Emma, angry, hissing at me: *"What, did you expect to just come round here when you fancy a fuck? It's not like that, Dave, it's not on tap. Did you think I'd just wait for you for ever?"*

And then we're moving together, tearing at each other's clothes. Christ, when did that happen? I take an uncertain step out on to the road, and the girls become bolder on the deserted street, both of them holding their arms outstretched to me, as if imploring me to come to them, to put one foot in front of the other and walk to them. "Come on, mister."

And then I'm a kid again, trying to run but Pete's holding me, more in fear than anything else, and then he's saying wonderingly: "Look. It's a girl..."

And I take another step towards them. And I'm with Emma, lost in her scent, in her body, and she's whispering in my ear: "Is this real, Dave? Is this real?"

Oh Jesus. Oh shit. I remember.

The park.

And there's a flash of lightning right above us, the end of the world, a smash of thunder that leaves my eardrums ringing. Suddenly the lights go out. The streetlights pop and fade, all the bulbs dim in the houses and shops on Jepson Street. My eyes are burning and my ears are ringing, and when I can look around me again I'm in total darkness, and the girls have gone, vanished into the night.

But I remember. I remember the park.

Far away, alarms triggered by the storm compete in a dull cacophony. Here on Jepson Street, everything is quiet, as though the lightning strike has just flashed everyone away, made them gone. I'm alone in the silent rain, standing in the middle of the road, just me.

No, not just me. I see him, emerging out of the darkness and the rain and standing on the pavement no more than twenty yards away, the collar of his thick greatcoat turned against the rain, his right hand clutching something, his impassive stare on me and me alone.

It's him.

We stand like that for a long time, a frozen tableau, me in the middle of the pitch-black road, standing in the rain, the water sloughing off me in rivulets, him sheltered by a bus stop, levelling his gaze at me, neither of us caring about the storm raging above us. And all around us the rain, the incessant rain, the rain.

He's standing there just as he was at the scene of the fire, as he was when we saw the Beast of Shotmoor. Just staring at me, as though his very presence is a message, a communication. But I'm not receiving it. The lines are down. I don't understand.

"What do you want from me?" I scream, spittle mingling with the rain slick on my chin. "Why are you doing this to me?"

He steps forward abruptly, only a small stride, just taking him out of the shadows and into the squalling rain, but the movement is enough to cause me to jump. "What do you want from me?" I ask more weakly. "Who's in the black car? Why are they beating up my friends? What's going on?"

As if in answer, he holds out the hand clutching the violin case, letting it dangle in front of him, water darkening the battered leather. I'm mesmerised by it, tantalised by its mysteries. "Do you want me to take it?

Is that it?" I ask, almost begging for him to say something.

He shakes his head and lowers the case to his side. And speaks.

"No. Not yet. What is inside may be for you, one day. But not yet."

"What, then?" I cry again. "Why are you stalking me?"

He lifts his head and says in that terrible, mournful voice: "The game is afoot, but it is not yet clear to you. It may never be clear to you. Do you want to know what is in this violin case?"

No, I want to say. I don't give a shit. But it's not true. I do want to know. "Yes," I say weakly.

"Good," he says. "Keep wondering."

And then he starts to walk, slowly, deliberately, away from me.

I follow him along Jepson Street, shouting after him: "What? Now hold on. I'm not playing whatever fucking game you think this is. Either tell me what's in the case or just fuck off out of my life. But don't piss me about."

He stops walking, and without turning around, just says again: "Keep wondering."

He begins to stride off again but this time I don't follow him. "Go on, then, you mad bastard," I scream. "Go on, take your violin case and get out of my hair. I do not need this, I do not fucking need this!"

This is too much for me now, all this weirdness and bizarre shit. I can't take it any more. Suddenly, I remember that graffiti on the walk here, those huge letters spelling out SURRENDER. That would be easy, to just let go, to just give in to whatever madness is infecting him and let it consume me too. But I'm not going to surrender. I'm not going to go mad. I want to be normal, I want to be putting my kids' toys in the garage on a rainy night, I want Mags to be handing me a packet of crisps while we watch meaningless TV, I want to argue about mundane things in hushed voices so as to not piss off the neighbours.

And that's what I'm going to have. I'm out of here.

FIFTEEN
IT'S LIFE, JIM, BUT NOT AS WE KNOW IT

No-one says a word when I return to work, but then there's no real reason why they should. As far as everyone is concerned, I've just had a few days off sick. They don't know how close I came to losing the plot completely.

But that's changed now. Colin's dead, I seem to have lost Mags and Emma, but that sort of shit happens to millions of people every day. There's nothing weird about it, it's what normal people the world over have to deal with all the time. They seem to manage, so will I. High time I just knuckled down, put this weird shit behind me, and tried to get some sort of handle on my life.

But then there's Cheryl. But I don't like to think about Cheryl and what's happened to her, so I don't. I just block it out of my mind. Like it never happened.

Things at work appear to be refreshingly mundane. I go in on Wednesday, flicking through the national tabloids and swilling down sludge from the coffee machine. My first job of the day is a routine robbery at a local sub-post office. I relish the opportunity to immerse myself in work, listening attentively and sympathetically as the elderly postmaster shows me his bruises and points out where he was tied to a chair while the robbers rifled through the shop. It's not the Beast of Shotmoor, true, but it's what I need right now. Back in the office, George is calling an editorial meeting for the afternoon.

The available reporting staff of thirteen or fourteen lounge around the boardroom, sipping sludge. Stephen Fucking Doyle sits alert at George's right hand like a faithful hound while the news editor outlines the plans for some new project or other.

"It's all very exciting," mutters George wearily. He's been in the business since the days of hot metal and he's been through more "exciting" initiatives dreamed up by men in suits than anyone can imagine. Someone, somewhere, has done a survey at great cost to the company and they've come up with a sheaf of papers telling us what the readers want from the Post. As George begins to go through the latest initiative, I realise with a start it's my birthday on Saturday. We were planning that big bash at Steam, but me and Em didn't exactly part on good terms last night. I suppose I should give her a call later. I'll have to speak to Pete and Tony as well, apologise for fucking up the Amsterdam trip. Shit, I could have really done with the break, as well. I blink back to the here and now and realise George is winding up. I smile and nod, even though I haven't got the faintest idea what he's just said. People are looking pensive and grumpy; whatever this thing is, it looks like it involves a shit-load of new work for us all. I'll get someone to run it past me later.

We all file out of the boardroom and Stephen Fucking Doyle catches me by the sleeve of my jacket. "David," he smarms, handing me an envelope. "I don't know if you've heard..?"

It's a wedding invitation. Oh, shit. "Ah, yeah, I think I heard," I stumble. He looks at me expectantly. "Right, ah, congratulations."

He smiles warmly. "Thanks, David. I assume we can count on your attendance? To the night do, of course."

"Yeah, yeah, I'll see what I can do," I say quickly - *too* quickly. I look down at the invite again. "Um, thanks. Got to dash."

A little later, bored, I'm scrolling through World News Link. In Zurich, a smash-and-grab thief cut his finger off on the jagged glass of a jewellers' window and fled, leaving his finger behind. Police arrested him by matching the severed finger with their fingerprint files. Two fishermen claim to have seen a huge reptile in a lake in North Wales. More footage of the Roswell alien autopsy has been discovered in a garage in Utah. I flick off the screen, telling myself I'm not interested in this weird shit any more.

Come the afternoon I'm off to the central train station to do a piece on a group of Star Trek fans going off to Atlanta for a science fiction convention. We've got them all in costume, climbing onto a knackered old InterCity carriage, for the photo-shoot. It's all a bit of a piss-take on our part, purely so a sub can stick a "to boldly go..." headline on the piece, but they do take it a wee bit seriously.

The chief Trekkie (Trekker, he gently chides me) is giving me a list of Star Trek catchphrases for the piece. He glances at me from under false Vulcan eyebrows, his rubber right ear slipping perilously, and in all seriousness adopts the worst Scottish accent I've ever heard: "'The engines cannae take any more, Cap'n'. That's Scottie."

A thin guy with a protruding Adam's apple, got up to look like a Klingon in full ceremonial battle dress, pipes up in a reedy voice: "It's life, Jim, but not as we know it."

As I look around at the commuters, enjoying the outlandish spectacle that's brightening up rush hour, I mutter: "You can fuck say that again," before smiling brightly and allowing myself to be given a lecture on the workings of the phaser gun.

After a thoroughly and satisfyingly normal day, I hit the flat again. I'm restless, pacing about the living room, eager to throw myself into everyday life again. I call Pete.

"What the fuck's been going on with you?" he says angrily. I shrug and sort of tell him. He relents and invites me out for a beer. "I'm meeting Tony at the Green Man at nine."

That's what I need, a drink with the boys. Vague memories of the other weekend surface, the strange club, Arcadia, and those lonely, forgotten streets, but I push them away. I probably imagined most of that, anyway. I put some thumping hardcore on the stereo and take a shower, spending time ruminating on what to wear.

It's an odd place, the Green Man. Tucked in an alley off the market square, it's usually ignored by the usual townie crew and has its own clientele of old soaks and pit bull-necked hard men. We like to call in for a quiet pint and a few frames of pool occasionally, especially if there's boxing or footy on the TV. The atmosphere can be fairly menacing at times, but there are no billykids pinging off the walls and we're usually tolerated as long as things don't get out of hand, for instance if we make the mistake of putting the jukebox on at the wrong time.

I breeze in out of the cold, wet night to find Pete and Tony sitting in the corner of the dim, smoky snug, nursing almost-empty pint pots. They both scowl at me as I emerge from the smog and Pete points a finger at my chest. "Idiot," is all he needs to say.

Over fresh pints I explain as best I can. Tony snorts derisorily at the mention of Colin, then mutters a sheepish apology when I get to the bit about him dying. They both think Colin was a bit strange, which he was, and thought it odd that I hung around him. The pair of them are sufficiently uncomfortable at the news of his death to forgive me for dropping out of the Amsterdam trip. "So who took my ticket?" I ask.

"That sour-faced git Pickering who Tony works with at the garage," spits Pete. "And what a pain in the arse he was. Moaned non-stop from getting on the plane to getting off it this morning."

Even Tony has to agree. "The fucker even complained about the birds in the windows in the red light district, said some of them were ugly. Like he's a fucking oil painting. Bastard."

The alcohol flows, and I enviously listen to tales of their exploits in Amsterdam. Harry, the landlord of the Green Man, drags himself over wearily to clear the rapidly-mounting pile of empties and taps me on the shoulder with a gloved hand. One of the perils of being a reporter in a small town is that everyone knows, and they all think they've got the scoop of the century for you or want something for nothing.

Harry runs a hand through his greasy hair and says: "'Ere, Dave, might have something for you."

"Leave it out, Harry, protests Pete. "Let the lad have a night off, for Christ's sake."

Harry scratches his chin with the gloved hand, and I notice that he isn't wearing a glove on the other one. "What's this, you turning into Michael Jackson, then?" I quip.

The landlord doesn't crack a grin. "No, but I think I might be turning into something. Look."

Glancing around surreptitiously to make sure none of the regulars are looking our way, Harry tugs off the thick gardening glove.

"Wow," breathes Pete. Tony coughs on his beer. I just stare and say slowly: "I've heard of green fingers, but this is ridiculous."

Upstairs in Harry's living quarters, surrounded by junk and dusty tables and piles of old books, we stare in wonderment at Harry's right hand. From the wrist it's covered in a light, furry green... well, *moss*, for want of a better description. Young green tendrils shoot from in between his fingers, and the fingernails are tough and brown like the bark of a tree. Harry's looking a bit stressed out. Can't say I blame him, he looks in bad shape.

"Have you seen a doctor?" asks Tony.

Harry shakes his head. "I was told not to."

"Told not to?" says Pete incredulously. "Christ, by who?"

Harry glances around the room nervously, then suddenly jumps off his chair and dashes to the window sill. Scooping up three potted plants in his arms he bundles them outside the door into the corridor, then slams it shut, listening intently at the keyhole for a moment before returning to join us. I look at Pete and Tony with raised eyebrows, then Harry goes on: "I know this is going to sound a bit funny but... I think the plants are talking to me."

"Christ, it's Prince Charles," mutters Tony. Harry scowls at him, and I interject: "Shut up, Tony, and anyway, Prince Charles talks to his plants, not the other way round. Go on, Harry."

But it's too late. Harry's tugging the glove back on and standing up. "Should've known better than to try and talk to you pricks. Come on, back downstairs the lot of you, and if you're not buying beer you can all bugger off."

I push Tony and Pete out of the door and turn back to Harry. "Look, I really think you should see a doctor about this, Harry."

"Don't you understand?" he hisses. "*They* won't allow it."

"They?"

He looks down at the three potted plants on the floor of the corridor where I'm standing. "It's this pub, Dave. There've always been... odd things going on. But now they're saying it's time. They need a new one."

"A new what?" I'm totally out of my depth here.

"Oh, get out," sighs Harry bitterly.

One pint later and we're out on the street, Pete and Tony not wanting to stay around Harry much longer. As the rain and wind lash us, and Tony and Pete argue about which pub to go to next, I ponder Harry's words. They're saying it's time. They need a new one. What could he mean? The pub sign is creaking in the wind above us, a faded painting of a green-clad Robin Hood character glancing with shining eyes out of thick foliage. The Green Man.

"Come on," says Pete decisively. "The Cross Keys it is."

My mum and dad live in a quiet part of town, and no matter how many times I visit I always get that shiver down my back, that frisson, that feeling of going home. The alleys and ginnels that were so long and dark when I was a child seem trifling little things now, the fields that were my endless battlegrounds and lunar landscapes are filled with houses and business units, the secrets of streets and lanes forgotten, buried deep inside. But just occasionally, when I pass a small boy haring along the wall of an abandoned garage, oblivious to everything except the story that's playing in his head, I remember the adventures of childhood in these concrete car parks and swathes of greenery that were the boundaries of my world so long ago.

My dad struggles out of his favourite chair, still suffering with his bad back, when I walk into the lounge. His hair, always so dark and curly, is flecked with more grey than black now. He's in his mid-fifties, and suddenly it hits me; Christ, they're getting old now. Then his face cracks into that gap-toothed grin and he's just my dad again, eternally older than me, but I bet he'd still take me fishing and carry me on his shoulders if I asked.

Mum potters about in the kitchen, announcing that tea will be ready in half-an-hour. We chat about inconsequential things, work and friends, and mum asks me the usual questions about when I'm going to get a girlfriend and settle down. I've sort of half told them about Mags, but said that things were difficult and left it at that. They'd go ape-shit if they thought I was seeing someone who was about to marry someone else.

Tea is pleasant and we crack open the bottle of red wine I've brought, talking about people who still live here and people who've moved away. Then the conversation takes an almost inevitable turn: "Your dad saw a flying saucer, you know."

"Oh yeah?" I say, nestling into what used to be my favourite spot on the couch, my cheeks rosy from the glow of the coal-effect gas fire. "And this was after a few shots of that blended whisky he brought back from Scotland at Easter, was it?"

"It was not!" says my mum. "Tell him, Bob."

As dad launches into his anecdote about the flashing lights over the cornfields while he was walking the dog two nights ago, I sink into a foul mood. Everywhere I go it's the same: weird shit. Even here, my last refuge, my old home. Just what is going on?

I half-heartedly join in mum's gentle ridicule of dad's flying saucer story until he takes the huff and loses himself in the digital TV channels. I sit there for a while longer, watching the fire with a feeling of longing for the old, childhood days, and I'm almost ready to ask if I can stay the night in my old bed when I decisively stand and say my goodbyes. As I walk out of the front door, I try not to notice my dad scanning the clear night sky for bright lights.

The night is cold and clear, my breath forking out of my mouth in jagged white plumes. I decide to walk the two miles home, hands jammed deep inside my coat pockets, head warmed by red wine and Irish coffee. It's one of those nights when you could believe in magic. The sky is clear and still, stars winking knowingly up in the distant black, street lamps buzzing gently, casting orange pools on to the pavement.

There's no-one about at all. In the distance I hear a dog bark tinnily, and there's the constant whisper of traffic away on the bypass, but here on the streets I'm alone. Curtains in the terraced houses are pulled firmly shut, TV screens flashing behind every pair, people drawing into their hives, shutting out the darkness and the night. Occasionally a window glows dull purple, betraying surreptitious use of a sun-bed.

Down an alley a bin-lid rattles and I almost jump out of my skin. I'm spooked, but it's a good sort of spooked. The hairs on the nape of my neck stand to attention, but it's more from a feeling of being among the unknown rather than a fear of something substantial.

I stop dead, beside the cold, glass rectangle of a telephone box, thoughts tumbling inside my head. Here, amid the silent streets of my childhood, beneath the winking stars and the Cyclopean street lights, with frost-sheened pavements beneath my booted feet and silent breath leaking from my lips, all this begins to make sense to me. Just for a moment, I'm on the brink of grasping something fundamental to the recent cycle of events. It's like a huge epiphany, it's swelling inside me.

And then the telephone rings.

And it's gone.

I stare dumbly at the muted ringing from inside the telephone box. Damn. Damn damn damn. I search desperately inside myself, trying to drag back whatever I had stumbled across, but it's submerged itself back into the murky depths of my subconscious. And the telephone's still ringing.

Sighing, I pull open the creaking door and step into the piss-smelling phone box. Time to do my good deed for the day and inform someone that they've got the wrong number. I lift the receiver and say hello.

"Dave? Hi, it's Emma."

I think it's fair to say I'm surprised, but only for a moment. Trekkies, my dad seeing flying saucers, the Green Man, and now this. It's life, Jim, but not as we know it. But we're going to have to get used to it, I reckon.

"Hi, Emma," I say resignedly, wondering if I should ask just how she knew I was passing this phone box a mile-and-a-half from my home at ten minutes after midnight.

Perhaps I'd just better not bother.

SIXTEEN
THE BIRTHDAY PARTY

We're living in the future and nobody noticed.

Where are the jetpacks and holidays on the moon, the pills that give you a full roast dinner, the cures for old age and the common cold?

They're here, and we didn't even realise. On the television news this morning I saw pictures of Russians and Americans in a space station, smiling and shaking hands and going on spacewalks to fix aerials on their shuttles. When did this happen? When did we get space stations orbiting the Earth, why didn't we notice? Why weren't there fanfares and people dancing in the street, hugging each other and crying and saying it's here, the future's here?

It's here, all right, but we just slipped into it like it was a comfortable, old jacket. Maybe we have filters on our brains that only allow us to take in just what we need to operate on a daily basis. Everything else is just background fuzz that goes on all around unnoticed. Traffic jams, overdrafts, central heating, EastEnders; that's what we sit up and take notice of. If we had to think about wars and lasers and people in space all the time, if the barriers came down and we looked around, blinking, at the world we've created, then... bang. That would be it. Information overload.

We'd go mad.

Oh, the future's well and truly here, but it's slid sneakily into our collective subconscious. In some Pacific Rim nation they've transplanted a pig's heart and lungs into a cystic fibrosis sufferer. There's a mouse that can breathe liquid in America. A guy I used to work with learned to speak Greek from the Internet. I can buy an on-board computer for my car which can tell me the quickest and easiest way to get to Manchester, avoiding road works and delays And I read this morning that the last long-horned, short-haired mountain goat in the world died when a tree fell on it in a remote area of South-West France. The news makes me inescapably sad. Goodbye, then, *Capa pyrenaica pyrenaica*. I hardly knew you.

It's midnight and I'm arseholed on alcohol and pills, dizzily tripping through the *son et lumière* experience of my birthday party.

Mick and Mark have graciously agreed to open Steam after hours for a private bash, and all my friends are here. Everyone threw in a few quid to hire a really swish lighting system, and Delta is blasting out an amphetamine-fuelled line-up of frenetic, trancey, bass-heavy tunes to turn your brain to hot butter. Not everyone's cup of tea, I'll admit, but hey, it's my birthday, and I'll fry if I want to.

I stagger over to the DJ booth where Delta is studiously lining up the next track. I watch him spinning the black record for a moment, filled with an inexplicable sadness for the days of my lost youth when buying an album meant buying an album, walking out of a trendy record shop with a huge twelve-inch by eighteen-inch plastic carrier bag emblazoned with the logo of the place to be seen in. You'd get it home, carefully slide the vinyl from its static-clingy paper inner sleeve, holding it gingerly, nay reverently by the edges, then flip it in the light to spot any scratches on the sensitive grooves. Then you'd sit there on the floor, knees drawn up, wearing huge headphones because there was only one record player in the house and mum and dad and the neighbours didn't want to hear *that racket,* the sleeve propped up on your knees, reading the sleeve notes and lyrics and dedications. When most of the big chains stopped stocking vinyl a few years ago, I always resented walking out of the shop with a tiny, little bag containing a CD small enough to shove into my jacket pocket.

Delta snaps me out of my reverie with a hand clapped on my shoulder. I'm standing near the vibrating amps, the bass line gripping my internal organs and shuddering them to bits. He mouths: "Happy birthday" then leans over and bawls in my ear: "Any dedications for the birthday boy?"

I ask for a track called Millennium Fevre by Desolation Angel, and Delta winks and pulls it expertly out of the DJ box without having to flick through for it. As the current record segues effortlessly into the next I give him a salute and head back into the smoke.

Twenty six. Old man. Emma's words, spoken God knows how long ago. Christ, twenty six. People my age are married, have children, mortgages, dogs, in-laws. I'm pulling in less than twenty thousand, I'm renting a one-bedroom flat, I don't even have a proper girlfriend. Then I look around me, at the people who are here to celebrate my birthday, and I realise that in my circles, my lifestyle is the rule rather than the exception. Mags and Stephen Fucking Doyle are at the bar, him sucking on a Bud and wishing he was just about anywhere else in the world, Mags looking wistfully around at the dancing and at me, half-wanting to play part of the soon-to-be-married couple, the other half of her wanting to let go and just enjoy herself.

I go over to talk to them. I'm pissed, but not horribly so, the pills keeping me bubbling up, the alcohol taking the edge off the buzz, resulting in a pleasant, talkative, I'm-here-and-I-can-conquer-the-world feeling. Stephen Fucking Doyle forces what he imagines to be a pleasant smile. Mags squirms.

"Thanks for coming," I boom, the exuberant host. "And congratulations, Mags," I add warmly. "Stephen's spoke of nothing else but the wedding." She looks at me with hurt almost dripping from her shining brown eyes. Doyle starts talking about work but then Delta winds up the track that's playing and shouts into the mic:

"Don't stop moving, Steam! This one's for Dave. Happy birthday, mate!"

There's a whoop as Delta drops the opening chimes of Millennium Fevre and I grab Mags' arm. "Sorry, Stephen," I interrupt. "This is my birthday tune. You don't mind if I drag the blushing bride-to-be away for a dance, do you?"

I don't wait for him to answer and leave him tugging uncomfortably at his tie in the wet heat of Steam as I haul Mags onto the bouncing dance floor. "Oh God, Dave," she moans. "This is horrible. I'm sorry, I'm sorry."

"Mags," I say kindly. "Shut up and dance."

The church bell intro of Millennium Fevre explodes into a thumping bass and fluted whistle that grabs your intestines and twists them, jerking your feet into frenetic movement and sending wave after wave of sonic rush lapping at your pineal gland. Almost everyone is crushing into the tiny dance space, arms in the air, whistling and cheering and stomping. I look over to Delta and give him the thumbs up and he waves back, basking in the glow of pleasure from a hundred people dancing below him. I'm as happy as a pig in shit.

I still feel sad about the goat, though.

Tony shit-faced in the corner, puke staining the front of his Valentino shirt. Mags gone long ago, I think. Saw her rowing with Stephen Fucking Doyle and him walking out, face set solid granite. She shrugs and out behind him, shaking head. Is someone having a fight somewhere? I hope not.

I think I am, or at least was, or maybe will be, kissing Emma. Is this before Mags left, or after? Does it really matter? Faces looming out of the red mist, trance pounding my head into my head oh my God I think I'm losing it.

"Try it, Dave, it's good shit." That from Kex – when?. Small pill. Just a small pill. What is it?

"What is it?"

"Good shit. Get you there. Go on, it's your birthday."

Good shit there, birthday. Good birthday, get you. Good shit. Shit.

Shit.

I shouldn't take drugs, I think.

I think.

I…

think…

too…

much…

What time is it?

Emma holds me tight on the dance floor. Too tight. "Who cares?" Millennium Fevre is playing again. Or maybe it's still the first time. Good shit.

I think I might be having a bad time.

"Are you having a good time?" It's Ferdinand Shelley. What is he doing here?

"What are you doing here?" He looks hurt. I'm sweating. He's joking. I saw him yesterday, invited him. He takes my picture, steals my soul. Whoa, get a grip, getting a grip. Breathe, for fuck's sake, *breathe*. That's it, getting a grip. I wheel away from Shelley and grab Kex by the lapels of his army shirt. "Christ, what the fuck was that?"

"Good shit," he grins. I'm on a plateau. Need to anchor to reality, now, stop myself from losing the plot completely.

"I think... I'm straightening out," I breathe, remember to breathe.

Kex laughs. Don't laugh. His face comes close. "That's only the start of it! Isn't it fucking great?"

Another? Don't mind if I do!

How many times is Delta going to play Millennium Fevre? I break free from Emma and stumble over to the DJ booth, and ask him just that. He comes close to listen. "Dave, this is the first time I've played it. Do you want it again?"

Another? Don't mind if I do!

"Dave? Hi, it's Emma."

"Hi Emma," I say resignedly, wondering if I should ask just how she knew I was passing this phone box a mile-and-a-half from my flat at ten minutes after midnight. Perhaps I shouldn't bother.

"Look, I'm sorry about before," she begins.

"Who is he?" I ask, trying to keep the accusatory tone from my voice. "Sorry, you don't have to answer that."

"He's... he's no-one, Dave. He was just someone. Forget it, it was just... I was so pissed off at you. I don't know what's going on between us. Look, I'm sorry, and just forget it. I was calling about your birthday. I've spoken to Mick and Mark and they're still on for this Saturday if you are. But we need to start inviting people. Most of the Steam crowd will be up for it, but what about people you work with, and your mates Tony and Pete, and..."

Yes, I'm sure I want it.

Emma leads me by the hand through the back of Steam into the cool, dark storeroom stacked high with walls of Bud and Red Devil. "Just chill out," she whispers. "It's heavy stuff. How many have you had?"

Two, I think, on top of whatever I had before, and all that alcohol. Not good.

"Just chill, just chill..."

She wipes the sweat from my forehead, and then places her cool lips on mine. I return the pressure and she moulds her body against mine, loosening my shirt, tugging at my belt, drawing back and looking at me quizzically.

Yes, I'm sure I want it.

Then she's on her knees in front of me and my jeans are crumpled around my ankles. I feel her warm wetness on me and there's a rush up my spine but it isn't Emma it's something else and suddenly what's so funny?

Emma disengages and asks me just that.

"It's just, I thought..." But I'm laughing too much.

What?

"What?"

"I thought you were a veget-"

Then it's just me and the crates and the red sting of her slap on my cheek. And I can't stop laughing.

It's four o'clock and suddenly I'm dipping, emerging from the clouds like a holiday jet and suddenly grasping the geography all around me. Four o'clock! What happened to the past four hours? The party is showing no signs of abating, but I'm taking a breather in one of the booths, my arm hanging loosely around Emma, who's apparently forgiven me for something or other I said earlier, Kex pissing himself at one of his own jokes, Fi in a huge sulk at him. In an hour she'll be outside swapping spit with my mate Pete, and there'll be a fight between him and Kex. How do I know that? Maybe it's already happened. Maybe it never will.

Delta can't stop, dropping tune after tune into the sweating, boiling pot, forcing the party on to new altitudes. Streets away, dogs must be howling. I feel like doing so myself.

"How are you feeling?" whispers Emma.

"Better. Great."

She smiles sheepishly. "Do you want to, uh, try again?"

I've never been a huge fan of sex in cars. Still, at twenty six you take it where you can, I suppose. It's bloody cold and our gasping breath has fogged up the glass, and the gear stick is digging into my thigh. With all the shit I've had, it's a miracle that I've been able to get it up at all. And then something odd happens. I start to enjoy it. Not that I was hating it, but it gets... different. It starts to mean something, inside. Christ, I must be growing up.

Or maybe it's just the drugs.

Emma passes the joint over and lets the smoke leak from her lips. I take a long drag and then cough violently but involuntarily when she says: "Does this mean we're going out, then?"

Fortunately, she takes it in good humour. "Hey, don't have a fit. I didn't mean it." But I can tell she's a bit hurt.

"No, no," I insist when I recover. "Swallowed a spark."

The question hangs unanswered between us, like a third person squeezed between the vinyl seats. I look at Emma, at her crushed velvet dress, her centre-parted hippy-chick hair, the flush of lovemaking lingering on her pale cheeks, and it doesn't seem that unattractive a proposition. Up until recently, I had never really thought about Emma in that way. She's always just been a good mate, but I suppose that's a good enough pedigree for a relationship, a firmer foundation than one built on a last chance saloon grope at a nightclub chucking-out time.

"So," I say slowly, measuredly. "What are you doing tomorrow night, then?"

We return to Steam hand in hand to find things tailing off. Delta is still spinning the discs, but at a markedly muted volume. Mark looks glum, leaning on the bar and nods to one of the girls helping out to sling us a couple of Red Mists.

"Hi. Party winding up, then?"

"Not through choice. The Old Bill've been round, asked us to turn it down or we'll lose the equipment. As most of it's Delta's we've not a lot of choice."

I peer blearily at my watch. Five thirty. Fairly respectable, I suppose. I squeeze Emma's hand and she makes a wrinkled-up smiley face at me. All in all, not a bad birthday. "Shall we call it a night, then?" I say, and right on cue a yawn builds up which I stifle awkwardly.

I say my goodbyes and head for the door. It looks like Emma's leaving with me and we lean into each other, like cats. Part of me feels self-conscious about it all, like a stranger looking in and thinking it's all faintly ridiculous. As we're leaving Mick hollers me over and thrusts a bulk brown envelope into my hand. On it is the message "Happy Birthday David" in a familiar yet unplaceable spidery hand. I cock an inquisitive eyebrow at Mick but he shrugs. "Some guy dropped it off while you were out. Said thanks for turning up. Don't know what he was on, but he smelled like he'd been standing a bit too close to a bonfire."

I'm looking non-plussed at the envelope in my hand but Emma's pulling me towards the door. "Come on, Dave," she whispers. "Let's get back to mine." I look at the envelope again, and then at Emma.

No contest, really.

SEVENTEEN
TALKING WITH THE DEAD

It's that indistinct time of year, when the seasons shift palpably and become an almost physical territory. Ray Bradbury called it the October Country, far away from high summer, not quite deepest winter, the autumnal border between. The hinterland.

The cemetery is deserted, unsurprisingly given the hour. Eight in the morning on a Sunday. I went back to Emma's but couldn't sleep. After a couple of hours of mad thoughts and teeth grinding, I left her dozing fitfully and went for an aimless walk.

Which brought me here.

Spotless, white clouds scud across a sky of such deep blue that if you stare at it hard enough, you fancy you can see the blackness of space beyond. Earthbound, I walk the gravel paths like a restless ghost, trying to ignore the lights and blots scattering on the periphery of my vision. I fucking hate coming down. I'm sweating and shaking and my heart is pounding, the whole feeling laced with that certain numbness, a peculiar self-loathing that I can only liken to a teenager hating himself for masturbating into a handful of man-sized tissues.

There's a song in my head, Millennium Fevre, branded into my synapses. The wind is up, bending the bald trees, whipping my hair on to my forehead. A closed-circuit television camera mounted on the crematorium wall charts my progress impassively. Christ, CCTV in the churchyard? When did that happen?

I have a sudden, lucid impression of the deepest certainty that this will the last sane thought I ever have. How can I possibly know that? Unless I'm already mad. Shit, I fucking *hate* coming down. My feet have carried me to the recesses of the graveyard, where the old plots tangle together, soldiers and sailors killed in far-off lands, tinkers and tailors dead of ancient diseases we thought we had driven away but which are creeping back into our not-so-immune world.

A pink leaflet blows across my path, surfing the merest gust of wind, a paper tumbleweed. Sighing I snatch it up, resigning myself to the fact that even co-incidences seem to happen for a reason these days. Bizarrely, it's the slickly desk-top-produced manifesto of a group calling itself FRITE - Fight for the Right to Interment in The Earth. Cute. According to the leaflet, within sixteen years the country will have run out of space to bury the dead. Local authorities are not making plans for any more cemeteries and according to this lot the Government is drawing up plans for compulsory cremation. "Don't let them burn your bones!" scream the yellows and reds of the leaflet, hurting my eyes. FRITE members assert their right to return to the clay from whence they came. Sounds a good idea to me. I never fancied being burned to ashes, and Edgar Allen Poe nightmares aside, being buried seems somehow... right. I remember an early acid trip up in the Lake District, sinking my hand deep into the springy moss to the cool earth beneath, my fingers becoming tendrilous roots, reaching down into the loam, my carbon molecules mingling with those of the dry soil. I had an intense feeling of *oneness* with the earth. Of course, that's acid for you. Makes you behave like a fucking hippy.

What really appeals to me is sky burial, as practised by the Tibetans. Take a body high into the Himalayas and leave it there for the eagles to tear and rip and carry away, a little bit of you winging away in a hundred different directions, your unravelling essence spanning out on a majestic, feathery network. I blink, realising I'm staring into the blue yonder, and pull myself back into my body. I glance at the FRITE flyer and stuff it into my pocket. I'm sure I can get a story out of that tomorrow.

I've no idea what time it is; I left my watch at Emma's. I suppose I should be getting back to hers, although I still feel weird. But it's Sunday and people will be wanting to come and lay their flowers and polish the headstones, and tell their husbands and fathers and sons all the latest news. It's a waste of time. The dead don't listen.

"Happy birthday, Dave."

But sometimes they do talk.

I close my eyes, letting the honeyed voice ooze over me like treacle. Consciously or not, I had let my feet drag themselves along the gravel to here. To her grave. I don't need to look at it to see the simple, black, marble headstone, the spray of week-old orchids, the chiselled, gold-leafed "Helen", and its quiet, understated "A beloved daughter, granddaughter, sister, and niece. Cruelly taken from us all." There are two dates, so close together as to make you weep. Twenty-two years between being wrenched screaming from the womb into this world to being taken from it. When she said my name for the last time, it sounded as though she was talking underwater – it was the blood filling her lungs - and I laughed, because I didn't know what else to do, and I was too scared to cry.

"Helen," is all I say. I don't run screaming, even when I can bring myself to open my eyes some moments later and I see her for the first time; except it's just like the last time. I see that she is still wearing the Katherine Hamnett dress I bought her the previous Christmas, except now I can also see the mess the steering column made of her stomach. Her ginger hair is matted with blackened jelly, her make-up, or possibly blood, runs from her eyes like inky tears; her right arm hangs useless and impossibly bent by her side.

She's beautiful.

She stands with her good hand on the cool marble of her own headstone, tracing the words. "Daughter. Granddaughter. Sister. Niece." She turns her terrible gaze on me. "What, no 'Fiancee'?"

"Your mum's decision. I suppose she sort of blamed me for everything."

Helen looks at her good hand. "What happened to my engagement ring? I always wondered that."

I shrug awkwardly, shifting my weight from foot to foot, like I always used to do when Helen was giving me shit for no reason. "At the pub after your, uh, your funeral, your mum, she, well, she threw it at me. Said some things. She was upset, she'd had a bit to drink. Understandable, really."

She smiles, but it's horrible. There are some teeth missing and blood trickles from the corner of her mouth. "It wasn't your fault, Dave. It was his. What happened to him, by the way?"

"Guilty of causing death by dangerous driving," I say quietly. "Three years. He's out now. I saw him, actually, about a month ago, in town. He didn't even know who I was. I wanted to grab him pummel him into the ground, beat him to a pulp."

"Did you?" she says, in that really annoying way that always used to wind me up, phrasing it like a simple innocent question but loading it with barely-veiled accusations.

"No," I say, even more quietly, trying not to get angry with her. She's dead, for Christ's sake. "No. Of course not. I stood there in the street while he walked past, completely oblivious. He was going to the bus station. Still banned, presumably."

She is still running her left hand over the marble, as if she is marvelling at the coolness of the stone. "Do you come here often?" she asks, without any trace of irony. I don't point out the unintentional quip.

"No. Sorry. Not my, ah..."

"Not your scene? No, not mine, either. I just didn't have any choice."

I suppress a sigh. I don't remember her being quite so tart when she was alive. I suppose that's what being dead does to you. "Helen," I begin. Then it hits me like a wave crashing on a beach, a boxing glove of emotion straight to the gut. "Christ, Helen," I almost sob. "I'm sorry. I'm so sorry."

"Hey," she says tenderly, putting her good hand on my shoulder, drawing me to her. I don't resist, burying my face in her earthy shoulder, taking her useless right arm and wrapping it around my waist and holding it there awkwardly, tears being ripped out of my lungs in great jagged sobs.

We stand there, holding each other like that, for some time. But it's no use. Her long-dead body can't absorb enough heat from me to turn back the clock, to take us back to a time when she wasn't cold and clammy and streaked with grave-dirt. She's cold, just as she was the night she died, sitting across from me in the unforgiving vinyl passenger seat of the car, the tundra of an argument stretching between us as I grasped the steering wheel, pissed and scowling. I can't even remember what the row was about. We'd been at a party, someone's house, intending to crash there. Early on we'd started to bicker, probably because I was so drunk or high, until it made the night unbearable and I stormed out in the way I used to do so well. She'd followed me out, still sniping, then shouting as she realised I was climbing into my car.

"Don't you fucking dare even think about driving in that state!" are the only words I can remember from that point. Then we're moving, me driving, hunched over the wheel with that super-lucidity you get when you realise you're driving pissed, tunnel vision on the car in front, over-concentrating. Then I'm relenting and pulling over, and she's shuffling over into the driver's seat as I'm getting out of the car, grudgingly, and about to walk around to the passenger door when the other car comes out of nowhere, fog lights blinding me as it veers across the road and rams with a sickening crunch into the front of my Fiesta, and I'm staring straight into Helen's face when it happens. When she dies.

I've wrenched open the door of my car, and I'm not giving a flying fuck about the other guy, like why should I, and Helen's such a fucking mess, and I didn't know the steering column did that to your gut. This was before airbags were mandatory, of course. And she's trying to say something, but she's making a horrible bubbling sound And the only thing she says is: "...love you..." And I'm laughing, because otherwise I'll cry, laughing until someone puts a hand on my shoulder and tells me to shut the fuck up, and then I do start to cry.

And I do love you, Helen, even though you've been dead for five years. And I probably think that watching you die and listening to you tell me you loved me in that terrible Stingray undersea monster voice is probably the reason I feel like I'm losing my mind.

"Dave, how often do you think about me?" she asks patiently. I stop my wailing abruptly.

"What?"

"How often do you think about me?" She pulls away from me, still holding me at arm's length while her right arm flaps uselessly at her side. "Every day? Every week? Every month? Never?"

It's been five years, I'm about to plead in mitigation, but that won't matter to Helen because she's been dead the whole time. She doesn't even know what day it is. No, scratch that. Of course she does. That's why she's here. "Did you have a good birthday?" she asks, her previous question still hanging in the air between us.

"Yeah, we went to Steam," I enthuse, before realising that she doesn't even know where or what Steam is, that Helen was before this life.

"Did you think about me last night?" she asks.

I turn away from her for the first time, watching a V of southerling geese high in the sky, then answer truthfully: "No. No, I didn't. Thing is, Helen, I probably haven't thought about you properly for about two months, since it was your birthday. But you're still there somewhere, there's a thin strata of you always there, and when I want to think about you I can. But at least it's my choice now, Helen, rather than thinking about you every single fucking day of my life and wishing I hadn't got out of that driving seat, and waking up screaming in the middle of the night."

That last bit's a lie. I never once woke up screaming in the middle of the night. I did wake up crying a few times, and once I pissed myself. When I turn back I half-expect her to be gone, but she's still there, idly plucking a spider off the hem of her dress. That blood or mascara flowing down her cheeks really looks like tears now. "Are you seeing anyone?" she asks in a small voice.

I laugh out loud. Where the fuck do I begin? Well, there's Mags, who I've been sleeping with for some time now, but she's getting married soon, and there's Emma, but the only meaningful time I've had with her was when I had a head full of drugs. "Yeah. You'd like them."

She thinks I'm taking the piss and doesn't push it further. There's another silence and I turn away again, scanning the blue sky for birds, the cemetery for people. Real people. You'd have thought that after five years we would have more to say to each other. Finally, Helen breaks the stillness. "It isn't my fault, you know. It would be easy to blame it all on me, but it goes back further than that. My death might be the trigger, the thing that kicked it all off, but it was in you long before that."

"What was?" I ask without looking at her. "What isn't your fault?"

"The weirdness, Dave. The madness."

"What are you saying, Helen? Am I mad? Is that it?" I turn, but this time she really is gone. I drop down on my knees beside her black marble headstone, pounding on its cold smoothness with my fist, my question unanswered. The dead. They sometimes speak, but they rarely listen.

The living, on the other hand, listen too much, more often than not to what is not intended for them.

There's a cough behind me, not the sort of throat-clearing cough, but one that announces a presence, usually an unwelcome one. I turn to see a tall man in a grey suit, carrying a black leather briefcase. Whoever he is, he certainly isn't going to want to see me here at eight-thirty in the morning, talking to a gravestone. How wrong I am.

"Hi!" he barks loudly, proffering a business card. I take it from him. Rod Baker, of Dignity Inc., apparently.

"Hi," I say weakly. Shit, I feel bad.

Rod squats beside me and places a leather-gloved hand on my shoulder. He looks at me as though he's practising for his sainthood exam. "Friend, do you ever think about dying?"

I start to look around for help. Rod stands up and surveys the cemetery with me. "Fine place, isn't it?" he says in a well-modulated mid-Atlantic voice. "Mighty fine. Can't imagine anywhere else I'd want to have my earthly vessel laid to rest once I'd shuffled off this mortal coil, can you?"

Without waiting for me to answer Rod re-arranges the various components of his face again, this time surfacing with a poignant, almost tearful expression. "But nothing's guaranteed, sir. Not in this day and age. Not even the ground under your feet. Do you know how quickly the cemeteries are filling up?"

I sigh. "I believe people are dying to get in."

"Heh. Quite. But seriously, sir, conservative estimates suggest we may well run out of burial space within seven years. To this end, Dignity Inc. has acquired a sizeable number of plots which we are putting on the market now. Reservations can be made for yourself or on behalf of a friend or relative. It's the perfect Christmas present!"

Rod delves into his briefcase and pulls out a garish brochure. "I appreciate you're young, sir, but you probably already have a private pension scheme. We at Dignity Inc. are just asking you to think one step further down the road. All the information is in this pack, which includes a CD-Rom. Hope to hear from you soon, friend." Then he's off, striding through the gravestones towards a knot of early-morning visitors. I look at the brochure. Happy fucking birthday.

I think I've spent too much time in this cemetery. I need to get the hell out. I'm finally crashing, I feel like I could sleep all day. Question is, do I go back to Emma's, or mine? I should go back to her's, but what I really want is to be on my own. It's been a fucking weird come-down.

I'm halfway to the gates when I pass a shiny new marker, the one that the last of Colin's money paid for, the one that marks the spot where I clumsily and awkwardly scattered his ashes. I pause uncertainly, something bugging me, something half-remembered from last night. Something Mick said as I was leaving with Emma: "Some guy dropped it off while you were out. Said thanks for turning up. Smelled like he'd been standing too close to a bonfire."

Then I'm running up the gravel paths, out of the gates, and towards Emma's.

She stirs as I burst into her room, blinking and squinting at me as I turn on the light. "Dave? Are you okay?"

I kneel beside the bed. "Sweetheart, did we bring a... a package, or envelope, or something in with us last night? From Steam?"

She rubs her eyes. Christ, she looks cute when she's just woken up. "I can't... Dave, can this wait until I've had a fag?"

"Please, Emma, it's important."

She sinks back into her downy pillows and mumbles: "Kitchen, I think."

I find it on top of the toaster. A big manila envelope, Happy Birthday David scrawled on the front. Colin's writing. *Smelled like he'd been too close to a bonfire.* I don't want to think about it. Surely it was just his mate or someone, it can't have been... I don't want to think about it. I rip open the envelope and take out a thick, hardback notebook.

Colin's diary.

EIGHTEEN
COLIN'S DIARY

...I think I might have solved that confounded refrigerator question. A window! A window in the door! Common sense tells me that when I shut the door of my refrigerator, it activates a switch which turns off the light, and when the door opens it releases the pressure on the switch and the relay activates the light. No-one, however, has ever successfully accused me of having an over-abundance of common sense. It has become almost an obsession with me... I must solve the conundrum.

Feel lethargic today. In fact, I'm writing this from my bed, and it's gone three. I would get up, but Jerry Springer starts in half an hour. Women who pretend to be their sisters in order to pick up Uruguayan male prostitutes, or something equally improbable. Sounds like jolly good fun, whatever it is. Then I suppose I should fix myself something to eat. I certainly didn't have lunch or breakfast today, and I don't remember if I had supper last night. There was that tin of Spam, but

I'm sure that was when I was watching Captain Pugwash...

...Marianne came round this evening and we fucked like bunnies. She was surprised to see me still in bed at seven-thirty, but I didn't see any point in getting up before Coronation Street. She had apparently told Arthur it was her bridge club's annual general meeting. Expect he thinks it is quite normal for her to come home from bridge with a face the colour of a fire engine and bits of dried jissom in her hair. Could only manage it three times, though, and I think she may have been a tad pissed off. Must remember to eat more, build up my strength, or I could be in danger of letting the marvellous, mighty Marianne slip through my beard...

...e-mail from the Alpha Geek today. Asked me what I knew about Rudolf II. Apparently he's trying to draw parallels between Rudolfine-era Prague at the end of the Sixteenth Century and our own end time world. Rudolf was a melancholy dreamer, a collector of dwarves and fantastic simulacra, holing himself up in his fabulous castle and filling his court with mystics, astrologers, alchemists and, invariably, charlatans, all the while letting his kingdom carry merrily on without him. Hmm, maybe the Alpha Geek has a point. We are all of us Rudolfs, abandoning the tedium of real life for the unknown and mysterious.

Until real life catches up with us...

...Bumper post today. A month's worth of Marvel and DC comics, a red electricity reminder, my fuck mags, and I may already have won £250,000. No point opening that one, I think the Alpha Geek has won everyone's share of Reader's Digest prizes with his patent "system". Or so they say.

Someone's sent me a picture as well, a big cheap painting of a boy with huge tears rolling down his cheeks. It was addressed to 'The Occupier'. Not mine, I'm sure, but still, it will probably look all right in the hall, over that damp patch...

...Must get out to a handyman's store today and buy some new hacksaw blades so that I can start work on the fridge door. They didn't have any at Safeway, but I did manage to get some food. Rustled up a fantastic steak au poivre, which I washed down with a slightly chilled Puglian red. People think they should drink red wine warm because on the label it advises room temperature. Absolute bollocks. The people who put that on it originally lived in freezing cold French gîtes, so to reach that room temperature means sticking it in the fridge for an hour. I hate people who are so bloody literal. Anyway, fed and watered I now wend my merry way up the wooden hill to Bedfordshire, where I plan to wank myself into a stupor...

...Contemplated shaving off my beard, but Marianne likes it too much. Went for a walk down by the canal today and saw a horse sweating profusely. That is supposed to be a major portent of something huge to come. Strange times we live in. On the way back there was a big black car outside the house. I don't know what make it was, never did know anything about cars. Comes with never learning to drive. Thought at first they might be from the electricity board, but they drove off when I got to the gate...

...e-mailed the Alpha Geek with some stuff I picked up in the library about Rudolf II. My PC's slower than usual. Saw that black car again when I came out of the library. Men in black? No, that's ridiculous. I've never seen a UFO or anything like that. Never really wanted to or expected to. Can't imagine anyone would travel

light years across the trackless wastes of outer space just to flash their headlights at me while I'm half-cut.

Bought the hacksaw blades and started work on the fridge. This is going to be trickier than I imagined. I think I might have to take the fridge door off. Plus, I'll have to get some glass. I wonder where one buys glass..?

...Young David came around today, always a welcome visitor. I think that, because I live alone, he half fancies that I want to fuck him. It's nothing he's said, but young men always feel nervous around middle-aged bachelors. I'll have to introduce him to Marianne, put his mind at rest, although scratch that. She'll probably want to frig his brains out. Finally started work on that damned fridge. Managed to unscrew the door off, although I'll probably have to throw all the food away, David said. Had to punch a hole right through the middle with a nail and then saw out from there. Still, it'll all be worth it.

David has noticed increased weirdness over recent days that corresponds with the approach of our end times. His adventures down the streets of forgetfulness are interesting. Think I'll consult the Alpha Geek on that one.

Saw the black car near the park again today...

...I'm getting rather perturbed now. Awoke early, before eight, and when I opened the curtains that bloody car was there, parked in the street. The windows are darkened and I can't tell who's in there, but it must be four or five times that I've seen it now. Could it be the Inland Revenue? The police? No-one knows about the crop of marijuana in the attic, apart from Marianne, and I don't think she would shop me. Unless Arthur has found out! Christ!

But that's not all. My mail came today, some more comics, a bank statement, the Fortean Times, tickets for the Mozart recital next month, the usual religious garbage that seems to come unrequested every day now. Every single item had been opened and rather clumsily resealed. Everything, even the junk mail from the Scientologists...

...Took the unprecedented step of telephoning the Alpha Geek. He wasn't happy, said he'd only given me that number for emergencies. Sorry, but I'm starting to consider this an emergency. He was interested, but dismissive, as I'd expected. Asked if I'd ever seen a UFO, for fuck's sake. Told me to get the registration number and call the police. I hadn't thought of that...

...It's been three days now. Three days since I saw the car. Christ, I was nervous when I was seeing it every day, now I'm worse since it stopped coming around. I've had no mail, no e-mail, no calls. It's like I've ceased to exist. Still, Marianne's coming around tonight. That should ease my tension, if nothing else...

...I don't believe it. Marianne isn't coming around any more. Wouldn't even let me touch her. She only called in for a minute, said Arthur was becoming suspicious. That's bullshit. I've sent her home with whip marks on her buttocks before now and he's never noticed anything. She looked scared. Looked like she'd been got at...

...My telephone isn't working. I tried to call David at work today, but it kept redirecting me to some insurance office somewhere. I tried every telephone number I know, even Marianne's but the calls kept getting put through to factories, office blocks, people I didn't know. That means the e-mail's gone as well. I'm cut off...

...I think someone's trying to kill me. Heard the sound of smashing glass in the middle of the night and when I came down the little window in the kitchen had been broken. There was a milk bottle full of petrol, for fuck's sake, lying on the floor near the fridge, but the rag fuse had landed in a pool of water on the lino from something that had melted in the fridge, and luckily it had fizzled out. I need to finish that fucking fridge door quickly. Before it's too late...

...I'm running out of food, but I'm too scared to go out. Saw the car again this morning, and in a weird, perverse kind of way it was such a relief, to know I'm not losing my mind, to know that I really am being watched. Remember what the Alpha Geek said and waited for a full two hours until it drove away so I could get its registration number. The car didn't have any plates...

...God, I'm so scared. It's three in the morning and I haven't slept a wink for about two days. Christ! What was that! Sounded like another window

NINETEEN
MAGS DROPS ANOTHER BOMBSHELL

And that's how it ends. "Sounded like another window". No full stop, no comma, nothing. Just left hanging there. The rest of the story is easy to imagine. Whoever had been stalking Colin came back to finish the job properly. Another Molotov cocktail through the window, the kitchen goes up in flames, Colin tries to beat back the fire and loses the battle. His tinkering with the fridge makes it all so neat and tidy, and easy to blame on an electrical fault.

But why? Colin was no threat to anyone. Who on Earth could have been following him, watching him? Who would kill him? And that black car he kept mentioning... Cheryl was beaten up by some men in a black car. I suppose that's an occupational hazard for a prostitute, but something about this doesn't feel right.

I'm sitting on Emma's bed, scoring through lines with a yellow highlighter pen, until she stirs fitfully and opens one mascara-orbited eye to regard me sleepily.

"Dave? What time is it?"

"Eleven-ish."

Emma crawls out of bed and leans across the tangle of sheets to turn on the TV just in time for an old Survivors re-run. She's still wearing the silky drawers that gave me a bit of a thrill early doors and I run a hand over her smoothness as she snuggles up to me. "What you got there?"

She's not ready for all this yet. "Something a friend left me. Nothing important, really. Go back to sleep."

Emma nods assent, burrowing her hands into my crotch. "Mmm. Sleepy. You were great last night."

I kiss her awkwardly on top of her head and mutter something equally complimentary. I was pretty strung out last night, needless to say. I need to get my head round this Emma situation when I've straightened out fully. However, I think she has other ideas. Her fingers are tugging at the buttons on my jeans and she's looking up at me the way she was doing in her car earlierI put Colin's diary to one side. I suppose it can wait. As Emma slides her hand into my waistband, I wonder if I even want this. I don't think I can even help myself any more. I slide down to her level, my lips meeting hers just as my mobile phone jumps into life.

We make a good show of ignoring the insistent bleep, muffled by my jacket pocket, but eventually she sighs and rolls away. "It might be important," she shrugs, turning her attention to the TV.

I fumble around until I get the phone and check the display. It's Mags.

"Hi," I say guardedly.

"Dave, I need to see you." She sounds urgent, in no mood for pleasantries. Well, fuck her.

"I'm sort of busy..." I begin.

"*Please*," she urges. "Benny's. At two." Then she hangs up.

Emma raises an eyebrow at me. "Work," I lie flatly. "Something's come up."

"That's a shame," Emma grins. "Something else was coming up then... What time have you got to go?"

"A couple of hours, yet."

"Good," she says firmly, burrowing under the covers and picking up exactly where she left off.

I haven't had a proper relationship since Helen died, and somehow I don't think I ever will. I was barely twenty-one when that crash happened,, and no-one really knew how I was supposed to deal with it. Was I meant to just throw myself into life again, or lead some kind of monkish existence until a "decent" amount of time had passed? I tried to play it the respectable way. For three months I moped around in our flat, never going out other than to work, where everyone treated me with kid gloves and wouldn't let me do any stories remotely connected with death or car accidents. I sat there in the midst of Helen's clothes, her ornaments, her pictures on the wall, slowly fading away, not knowing whether I should cut loose and forget her or wallow in her memory. Then Pete and Tony literally dragged me out on Saturday night and got me mortal drunk. I woke in a strange bed with three used condoms on the floor and a beautiful brunette asleep by my side, sneaked out of the house, went home and cleared the flat from top to bottom of Helen's possessions. I sent her clothes and jewellery back to her mum, dropped everything else off at Oxfam, spent a night looking at old photos and getting pissed on gin, then the next morning began to live my life again. I never remembered that girl's name or where she lived, and never saw her again, but I'll be eternally grateful to her for fucking some life back into me and making me realise it was Helen who had died, not me.

There have been other women since, mainly casual flings. Girls say I'm difficult to get close to, that I treat relationships like butterflies, knowing that no matter how good and beautiful they are, they're never going to last. That changed with Mags, she was the first girl I had ever really loved since Helen, but if I am honest, I have probably used the fact that she was engaged, and to a colleague at that, to build up this huge wall that I could hide behind, a safety valve that would mean I never had to commit or take it too seriously.

But now there's Emma. Young, free, single Emma. What am I going to do now?

The grey clouds have thickened and darkened, and are now boiling with rain, spitting fat gobs down on me as I leave Emma's and head towards the town centre. I still have an hour before we're due to meet, so I take my time, still trying to shake off the effects of my over-indulgence last night. I know I'm going to be fucked by tomorrow morning, and hope there isn't much on the diary with my name beside it. A nice morning in court where I can sleep off the weekend would be ideal.

The rain's lashing down hard now, but I'm finding it quite refreshing, letting it wash away the grotty feeling I always have after a heavy night. I'll look like a drowned rat by the time I get to Benny's, and I'll probably end up with a stinking cold, but right now it feels wonderful.

Emma lives in the bohemian part of town, tall townhouses converted into multiple occupancy homes in narrow, sometimes still-cobbled streets. Almost every set of curtains is closed; almost every other window has a scrawny cat blinking lazily at the rain. It's so dark with the clouds that some of the streetlights are on, glowing a deep ember red and buzzing angrily in the downpour. I glance in one window and see a thin, long-haired student, bonier than his cat, rolling a fat joint amid the debris of a Saturday night Chinese. Across the street a beautiful blonde girl in a baby doll nightie gives me a suspicious stare as she collects two-day old milk from the doorstep. I realise I'm smiling like an idiot.

A tune rises unbidden in my gullet, starting as a hum as my feet fall into rhythmic cadence. Da-da-*da*-da-da da-da-*da*-da-da. I can't wipe the fucking grin off my face, and suddenly I'm skipping down the street, the tune finding my voice. "Da-da-*da*-da-da da-da-*da*-da-da." It's louder than I intend and a couple of the curtains twitch, but for some reason I can't stop myself, I'm gathering speed. And when I see a huge puddle that's gathered at the kerbside on a quartet of cracked flags, I can see what I'm going to do even before the thought has crossed my mind. I set off at a run and a woman walking her plastic-jacketed terrier huddles into the doorway of a house as I hurtle past, breaking into song. "I'm *sin*ging in the rain, just *sin*ging in the rain!" I land with both feet in the puddle, muddy rainwater soaking my jeans. I leap out again, grinning fiercely at the terrified old biddy, raising my face to the rain clouds and bellowing: "What a *glor*ious feeeeeeeeling, I'm hap-hap-happy again!" The girl in the baby doll nightie is still at the doorway, now with her friends, pointing and laughing. More people are at their windows, some smiling, most frowning. I bark an unattractive guffaw at them all, then begin to uncontrollably weep, my tears mingling with the polluted rain that batters my cheeks.

What the fuck is going on?

I sit at a table in the bowels of Benny's, gently steaming. I'm still a little early, so I leaf through the News of the World and the Observer that I picked up at WH Smiths on my way over. The waiters glanced at each other as I pushed through the door, leaving a pool of muddy water where I stood as I waited to be seated. Eventually they took me to a booth right at the back of the cafe, and one offered me a towel for my hair. I declined, but now I'm reconsidering as rain drips from my soaked hair and muddies the newsprint on the tabloid.

ALIENS STOLE MY BABY! scream the headlines. DOOMSDAY CULT SHUTS FORTRESS DOORS. NO COMET! MILITARY KEEPS MUM OVER MYSTERY METEORS! Whatever happened to vicars and rape and All-Bran? Heh. There's a story here about a normal, usually-sane businessman who is refusing to fill in his appointments diary, he's so uncertain about the future. I wonder how many others there are like him? Every other page has muddy pictures of aliens or UFOs, or adverts from faith healers and rune casters. Maybe the guy's right. Maybe it isn't worth the risk, planning too far ahead. There are so many crackpot theories about the end of the world that one of them must be right. It's the law of averages. Perhaps I should go and sign up with this doomsday cult in the paper, plead with them to let me into their massive mansion in the Scottish Highlands and just wait there with the doors locked and the windows barricaded until it's all over one way or the other.

"Dave."

Mags is standing there, her short hair gelled back severely, no make-up, although she doesn't really need it. She's gently shaking the rain from her folded umbrella and sheds the sopping raincoat before sliding into the booth across from me. "Christ, you look like shit."

Embarrassed, I push the rain-slick hair off my face and trying to unplaster the shirt from my chest. Mags hands me a fistful of napkins and I wipe the water from my face. Once she would have done that for me.

"So..." I begin measuredly, grasping for something proper to say. "Um, how're the wedding plans going?"

Mags looks at me with pleading in her eyes. "Dave, don't. I didn't ask you here to talk about my wedding."

Ah well, cut the crap, then. "So why did you drag me here on a pissing-down Sunday afternoon?"

Mags looks up and nods for one of the bow-tied waiters to approach. "Let's order first." She scans through the menu. "These pizzas. Any chance of prunes on one?"

Mags lets her cutlery clatter to the empty plate before she will answer my questions. My tagliatelli verdi lies untouched in front of me, the Red Mist unsipped. "*Pregnant*?"

She holds up a hand to stop me going further and when she has finished wiping her mouth with a napkin says in a tremulous voice: "Please don't follow that with 'but how?', Dave, because I'll fucking scream."

I finally pick up my fork and begin pushing the pasta around the dish. The piped Beethoven sweeps grandly and when it quiets some I say: "Um, congratulations. Stephen must be delighted."

Mags lets out a kind of low groan and buries her face in her hands. "Oh God, Dave. Do I have to spell this out for you in words of one syllable or less? Stephen doesn't know, and if he did he'd be less than delighted. Trust me when I say that this isn't his baby. It's yours."

Half an hour later my food is still untouched but I have three empty bottles of Red Mist in front of me. Mags has moved around to my side of the booth and I've been hugging her gently, rocking her as she cries into my wet shoulder. "How long?"

"Not long. Just eight weeks now. I only found out three days ago. I wanted to tell you last night but I didn't want to ruin your party. I've been going out of my mind wondering what I'm going to do."

"What *we're* going to do," I correct her, then feel wretched and embarrassed for sounding like someone off a shit TV drama.

She looks up at me through red eyes. "This doesn't change anything. I'm still marrying Stephen. Look, I'm sorry. I shouldn't have come here. I just thought you should know."

As she starts to gather her belongings I look on helplessly, not knowing how I should feel and instead feeling nothing. Mags stands awkwardly and struggles into her raincoat. "Look, I'll call you in a few days. My hormones are all over the place and I'm not thinking straight." She dips into her purse and drops a tenner on to the table then turns on her heel and stalks towards the door without another word.

I give Mags enough time to clear the street then stand up and settle up at the till. I emerge blinking into the daylight from the cafe, the street busy with Sunday shoppers and doomers with sandwich boards handing out leaflets about a dozen different ends of the world. The rain has slackened somewhat, and as I step out on to the street I don't notice the car idling at the traffic lights at first. When the lights change it drives past me at a leisurely pace, sending a finger of familiarity shivering down my spine.

It's a big black car, a big black car with mirrored windows. And no plates.

TWENTY
IN SEARCH OF THE ALPHA GEEK

So, where do you want to go today?

I'm searching for the Alpha Geek in a place that doesn't exist, an electric city that never sleeps, trawling the glowing highways, the humming alleys, the neon streets and, as is more often the case, the cul-de-sacs and dead ends. He must be on here somewhere. Colin managed to contact him and correspond with him, after all.

Most journalists I know are either dismissive or suspicious, or a bit of both, about the Internet, which is odd considering it's the ultimate communication tool. Every desktop in the office is hooked up to the net, but most people just piss about on it at best. A recent report carried out by the boffins in the newspaper's IT department cited a delightful piece of work called Smutworld as the most-visited website, followed by a site featuring old eighties video games like Space Invaders and Asteroids. World News Link, updated every thirty seconds, came in a poor third.

The words 'Alpha Geek' typed into the net search engine produce no matches, although I would have been surprised if it had been so easy. It's after nine and I've been chasing my arse up and down the world wide web for four hours now. Granted, it is easy to get sidetracked, and I spent slightly longer than necessary visiting various unofficial Diana Rigg homepages, but it's still like looking for a very small needle in a very big haystack. I don't even know if the Alpha Geek has his own website. Colin used to communicate with him by e-mail, but he must have made the initial contact somehow. Through some of the more esoteric websites on conspiracy theories and obscure knowledge I manage to get to a few discussion groups, but no-one has made any mention of the Alpha Geek. Perhaps he's all in Colin's imagination.

I'm currently hooked up to some discussion group devoted to old episodes of the X-Files. Someone calling himself (or herself, I suppose, but I doubt it) Fox is holding forth on documented cases of men in black visitations. Wondering if men in black is the same as men in black cars, I bookmark the discussion group page in case it proves useful and go back to the main menu, tapping in "men in black" and hitting search. The search engine comes up with more than a hundred entries.

I call up the first couple and my blood runs cold.

Back in my flat I'm running through the couple of dozen pages of printouts on the men in black phenomenon. I thought it was just a crap film, but apparently the concept's been around for years, practically as long as documented UFO sightings. Mysterious men in black suits, turning up unannounced to silence flying saucer witnesses. I glance through the window but there's no sign of the black car I saw earlier. Come on, got to get a grip here. Why should someone be following me? Then again, why would someone want to terrorise Colin or Cheryl? Cheryl perhaps mixed with more dodgy characters… aggressive punters, pimps pushing to take her on. But she's a tough bird. I've never seen her look as scared as she did when she was standing at her door with her fat lip and swollen eye. Colin was a harmless bloke, eccentric, yes, but not the sort of person you'd want to kill. I was rather hoping that I wasn't the sort of person anyone would want to kill, either.

The mobile rings and pulls me out of my increasingly paranoiac reverie. It's Tony, only just recovered from my birthday party and wanting a hair of the dog. "Green Man at nine?" he suggests.

We stand in the orange pool of a street lamp, Tony, Pete and me, gazing nonplussed at the darkened frontage of the Green Man. The sign creaks slowly in the wind; the big front door is locked and lifeless. "This is uncanny," says Pete. "I've never known Harry not to open up. It's hard enough getting him to shut the pub."

"You don't think he's been busted, do you?" asks Tony, handing over the dog-end of a joint we've been sharing. "You know, had his licence taken off him for serving after hours?"

I inhale the last of it then grind the roach underfoot. "Nah. Half the police use this place for an after-hours drink. No-one's going to bust Harry."

We contemplate the pub for a moment longer, then Pete shrugs and suggests the Cross Keys. As we're turning to cross the market square there's a clatter of bolts and the front door creaks open an inch or two, and then enough to let a suited middle-aged man carrying a briefcase out of the pub. As he begins to lock up behind him Tony shouts: "Mate, what's the score?"

The guy regards us suspiciously for a moment, standing huddled together under the streetlight, and probably thinks he's about to get mugged. I adopt a lighter tone and explain: "We're regulars here. Why's the place closed? Is Harry all right?"

Pocketing the keys to the pub the man relaxes and scratches his head. "Wish I knew. He seems to have disappeared. I'm from the brewery. We had a few calls yesterday saying the pub hadn't been open since Thursday."

"Harry's done a runner?" says Pete wonderingly. I don't believe it either; that pub was his life.

The brewery man shrugs again. "Not in the usual sense. The till was left full of money and all his personal belongings are still inside. There are even a few dirty glasses on the bar. It's like the Marie Celeste in there, like he closed up on Thursday night and then disappeared into thin air."

The brewery man walks towards his car, then stops and turns to us. "Funny thing, though. The private quarters upstairs are literally overgrown with plants. All sorts of stuff, a massive tangled mess. Had to fight my way into his bedroom. Seems he was a bit green-fingered on the quiet, our Harry."

As the guy drives away Tony looks at Pete and me, astonished. "Did you hear that?"

Pete starts walking in the direction of the Cross Keys. "Look, Harry's just gone on his holidays. It's not the fucking X-Files or anything."

"No," insists Tony, jogging to catch up with Pete. "Green fingered. You remember the last time we saw Harry, right? All that stuff on his hand? I've been reading up on it. The Green Man, see, he's like nature, but a man, like the protector of the trees and fields and shit-"

Pete stops and angrily turns on Tony. "What? What are you saying? That Harry's turned into the fucking Swamp Thing? What a load of cock. It's time you graduated to grown-up books, Tony. Try spending more time on page three than the comics, eh?"

As the pair of them bicker their way to the warmth of the next pub, I stay still, quietly watching the impassive, upstairs window of the Green Man. There's a slight twitch of net curtain, and I swear I can see a flash of movement. Something catches my eye for a brief second, and it's like a painting I once saw in a gallery in Prague, by a Sixteenth Century artist called Arcimboldo. It was a portrait of a man but the artist had used fruits and vegetables to depict the details of the face, cherries for his eyes, a pear for his nose, apples for his cheeks. That's exactly what it looks like, up there in the front room of the Green Man, but then it's gone, leaving me rubbing my eyes in the electric glare of the streetlight.

Pete and Tony are still arguing about Harry's disappearance as we get our drinks and find a quiet alcove in the Cross Keys, no mean feat as it's technobilly night and the pub is full of sweating teenagers furiously chewing and drinking water as they take a brief break from the music and dancing upstairs. Pete takes a long draught of his pint and nods at our Red Mists. "You still drinking that shite? I thought it would have gone out of fashion by now."

Tony starts to extol the virtues of the guarana and alcohol mix but that just triggers another row. It's really getting on my nerves, now, and I glance through the window into the darkened street.

There's a black car parked under a streetlight, its windows reflecting the dull glow. "Shit," I breathe slowly, reaching out my hand to get Pete or Tony's attention and instead knocking my bottle of Red Mist into Pete's lap. He leaps up cursing, the red liquid staining the crotch of his cream Levi's as though someone's chopped his knob off.

"Dave, you cock!" he shouts, angry and embarrassed as some of the kids start laughing. I protest and look back through the window, but the black car's gone and a flash sport's car's parked up in its spot.

"But it was outside," I insist. "The black car..."

Pete just shakes his head. "Look, I'll see you two tomorrow. I'm going home. I'm not sitting here with my jeans piss wet through while these little wankers laugh at me all night." He heads for the door, pushing some billykid wearing a lurid purple cowboy hat out of the way. Wisely, no-one challenges him on the way to the door.

Me and Tony sit in silence for a bit. "Uh, do you want another?"

Tony checks his watch and shrugs. "Nah, it's almost last orders, innit? Might as well sod off." There's another pause, then Tony frowns and looks at me. "Dave, ah, are you okay? You've been acting... weird, recently."

I look back from the window where I've been scanning the street. "What? Weird? Nah, just... you know. Had a few things on my mind. You know." Thing is, he probably doesn't. Where do I start? He wouldn't understand. No-one would.

Tony drains his Red Mist. "You still on for five-a-side tomorrow night?"

"Yeah, why not. I need the exercise." Pete and Tony drag me into their Tuesday five-a-side sessions when they can't get anyone else. It'll keep my mind off things, if nothing else.

"Right, see you tomorrow, then." And he leaves me in the pub, the thudding bass of the technobilly upstairs and a group of furiously masticating billykids looming over my shoulder, ready to grab the table when I leave.

The rain has stopped and the streets have that slick sheen, lights reflected and distorted in the wet Tarmac, cars swooshing by. I decide to walk back to the flat. I could take a taxi but it's quite a mild night and besides,

I don't really fancy climbing into the back of a black car tonight. Out of the town centre the streets are quiet, most houses darkened, only a few betraying life of a sort through the flickering of TV screens behind tightly shut curtains. I walk aimlessly, letting my boots carry me through the streets, forcing myself not to look behind for a dark car crawling along noiselessly beside me. Once or twice I can't help myself and spin around, but there's never any car.

This can't go on. I'm infected with something, a fear of the dark. It's got to go, got to be confronted. This is Colin's fault, his stupid fucking diary planted the seed in my head and now it's growing and growing and it might consume me, like it did him. He's got to help me.

I continue along the route I had subconsciously started to follow and within half an hour I'm standing outside the shell of Colin's house. The windows and doors have been boarded up and the jagged teeth of what's left of the roof rear upwards into the dark sky. I pause at the gate, pondering my next move, when I hear a sound; a woman crying. It's coming from behind Colin's house.

I quietly slip into the front garden and make my way around the debris of the fire, the mattress, the fridge with the window, to the path that leads to his wild, overgrown rear garden. Noiselessly I sneak to the corner of the house and peer round.

There's a big woman with flame-red hair, dressed in a mac and squatting by his doorstep, where she's placed a single red rose. She's intent on her grief and doesn't see me until I step out from the path, when she starts. I remember the area I'm in and realise she probably thinks I'm here to rob her or worse. "Please!" I say loudly. "It's all right. You must be Marianne."

The coffee is rich, freshly ground, expensive. I swamp mine with milk and sugar, Marianne takes hers black. I look around her kitchen as she prepares it, the Aga, the stone floors, the pine walls decorated with rustic art. Nice. She must be worth a few quid. Can't think what she saw in Colin.

"Was it you who put the funeral notice in the paper?" she says as she lays down a plate of biscuits on the pine table. "I wanted desperately to come but Arthur had some colleagues over for dinner and I just couldn't make it. I felt terrible."

I shrug. "Don't worry. You didn't miss anything." Marianne is a handsome-looking woman, early fifties I'd say, big and ruddy and, if Colin's diary is anything to go by, rather athletic for her age and build. When she was convinced I wasn't going to rob or rape her she suggested a coffee back at hers. Arthur, apparently, is away on business. Left her with the car as well, which beat walking back to their detached home on the outskirts of town.

"How did you know about me?" she asks as she sips her coffee. "Did Colin talk about me much?"

"Not exactly. He gave me his diary when he, uh, before he died." I realise as Marianne's already burnished complexion reddens even more what I've said, and try to cover myself. "Um, I didn't read all of it, you know, the bits about you..."

She smiles kindly. "It's okay, David. Don't dig yourself a bigger hole."

I munch on a biscuit and try to steer the conversation on to more stable ground. "How did you know Colin, then?"

She nods her head in the direction of what must be Arthur's study and says: "Via the Internet. We both belonged to the same discussion group and got chatting, then realised we both lived in the same town, which is a miracle because the people in that group come from all over the world. We arranged to meet and then things just progressed from there."

Marianne leans forward conspiratorially: "After the first time I couldn't keep away. Hung like a stallion. But you'll know all about that, I suppose."

Then it's my turn to blush furiously. "What? No, I think you've got it all wrong..."

Marianne slaps me heartily on the shoulder. "Come on, man, don't be shy. Colin's memory must be worth more than that. I knew his tastes didn't just lie with big breasts and an accommodating bush, don't worry."

"No, honestly!" I almost shout. "It wasn't anything like that. I mean, I didn't even know he was, I mean, he did, oh shit, I'm not doing this very well. What I mean is, me and Colin didn't have a sexual relationship."

There's an even more embarrassed silence. Christ, I can't believe this woman thought I was Colin's catamite. After a while she says: "So, how did you know him, then?"

I drain my coffee and as Marianne refills both our cups from the cafetiere I tell her how I bumped into Colin in the local reference library while I was researching our town's witch trials of the Eighteenth Century. He proved to be a store of knowledge on all kinds of obscure and esoteric subjects, and he slowly graduated from regular contact to friend over the course of a couple of years.

"Obviously, he had hidden depths," I finish.

"A big man, in oh, so many ways," agrees Marianne sadly. "I shall miss him immensely. Arthur, whom I love greatly, please don't get me wrong, just doesn't seem to... measure up."

There's another awkward silence. Marianne is giving me more information about Colin than is really necessary. "Funny, you met on the Internet," I say thoughtfully. "I've spent most of the evening on the 'net, trying to find another of Colin's contacts. Don't suppose you've ever heard of the Alpha Geek?"

The Internet discussion group where Colin and

Marianne "met" is called the Knights of Avalon. "It's all a bit New Age, isn't it?" I complain, as Marianne powers up the PC in Arthur's plush study. I spin on a brown leather chair as she gently chides: "These days people are looking for new things, David. We are in the Age of Aquarius, you know. In many ways people are demanding changes, but it is just a cycle, returning us perhaps to older ways. It isn't all crystals and runes, you know. Most of us are quite normal people."

As Marianne signs onto the discussion group site I ask: "It's pretty late, are you sure there will be people about?"

She laughs gently, a small sound for such a robust woman. "David, the people who take part are from all over the world. It's always daytime for someone."

"It's always night-time for someone, as well," I say quietly and gloomily.

Marianne signs on to the website and someone greets her almost instantly: HOWDY, AGRIMONY.

I give her a quizzical look. "Agrimony?"

She shrugs. "My netname. Some people don't like revealing their true identities over the Internet. I use the name Agrimony, a flower that some herbalists prescribe for those who hide their worries behind a brave face." She smiles sadly at me.

We spend a good couple of hours on the net, our search leading us to other discussion groups. Almost everyone has heard of the Alpha Geek, but no-one seems to have met him or spoken to him directly, even by e-mail. He appears to be some kind of expert on all things weird and strange, a kind of apocalypse commando. Several of Marianne's contacts promise to post notices on various bulletin boards he might visit saying we're looking for him.

It's late and I've got work tomorrow. Marianne offers me a lift home in her husband's Beamer, the engine idling as she drops me at the flat. I hastily scribble my address and phone numbers for her in case Agrimony's pals come up with anything concrete.

As I'm about to leave the car Marianne says: "David, thank you for a stimulating evening. After Colin's death I thought I had lost something special. It seems to live on in you, that love of mystery and that quest for the unknown. Don't let anyone knock that out of you."

Something occurs to me and I sit back into the passenger seat. "Marianne, in Colin's diary he said that you told him you couldn't see him again. He thought that you'd been 'got at'. What did he mean?"

She pauses, then switches off the engine. After a long silence, she says: "A couple of days before Colin died Arthur came home from his office visibly shaken. Came straight in and poured himself a big whisky. Then he told me he knew all about Colin, about what a filthy bitch I'd been, and warned me that if I didn't stop seeing him, something bad would happen."

"How had he found out?"

"Apparently he'd been visited at work by two men, completely unsolicited. They showed him photographs of me going into Colin's house and told him, in graphic detail, what had been going on."

"Who were they? Private detectives?"

Marianne shrugs helplessly. "If they were, Arthur hadn't hired them. They were just two men who turned up at his office, turned our world upside down, and then disappeared out of our lives. Just drove away in a big, black car."

I don't believe it. Colin, Cheryl, and now Marianne too.

Who's next?

TWENTY-ONE
THE WORD IS OUT

I still can't believe they just gave me this computer. I went into a shop on the high street, filled in a few forms, promised to pay seven hundred quid in a year's time, and three days later they delivered six boxes full of brand spanking new computer kit to the flat. I can't see that I'll have that kind of money this time next year, but then again I can't see it's going to matter. The future is just a dull crackle of interference to me, like a TV set that isn't tuned in properly. The way I'm feeling right now, I don't even know if I'll be alive in twelve months' time.

I think I've got all the leads plugged into the right bits, but I'm not sure. I never was any good at this boffin stuff. But I had to get my own set-up here at home, it was just becoming too obvious at work that I was sitting there surfing the net and firing off e-mails every five minutes. I'm sure they must have some kind of monitoring service for this kind of thing, but I haven't been directly approached yet. Better to do it here, in the privacy of my own home.

I power up the computer and wait while it flicks through the set-up process. A basic Internet package comes with the deal, and once I've loaded up the software I dive straight into registration and within an hour I'm online, logging on at the Knights of Avalon bulletin board.

Through the Knights of Avalon I've met some pretty interesting people. Well, I say "met" when of course I mean conversed with them over the web, and always using obscure code-names. It would be easy to dismiss me as paranoid right now, but when I think of what happened to Colin and the number of times I've seen that black car since then... I just don't like to think about it. With almost a reflex action, I tug back the curtain to the window beside me and give the street a cursory check. It's clear.

I'm still searching for the mysterious Alpha Geek Colin mentioned in his diary. It's amazing the number of people who have heard of him, but no-one's ever been in contact with him directly. I'm beginning to think he's just some kind of urban myth, some legendary Internet Robin Hood who doesn't actually exist. Colin claimed to have spoken to him by telephone, but who knows what his state of mind was at the end? With a start I realise I'm starting to go the same way.

No. I don't really know what this is yet, but I know I'm involved in something. I can sense it. Whatever it is, it got Colin, but it isn't going to get me. The weirdness, the black car, Arcadia, the man with the violin case... it's all connected, somehow. I just wish I knew how, and why it involves me. And it looks like the only person who can help me is the Alpha Geek.

A new bulletin board I've discovered the last couple of days is proving a little more fruitful than the Knights of Avalon, which seems to be populated by various gentle New Agers who don't really move in the kind of circles I need to get into if I'm really going to make contact with the Alpha Geek. This new one's called The Terminus, and is full of people who describe themselves as "Discordian Pranksters", whatever the fuck that means. They seem to want some sort of revolution, but the kind where no-one gets shot. Sounds like a good idea. I just hope that the people they're rebelling against feel the same way about shooting people. When I think of Colin, I wonder whether a gun wouldn't be a handy thing to have under my pillow.

I sign on to The Terminus using my codename Arcadia and check the topic I posted which was a general question asking if anyone had heard of the Alpha Geek. I'm stunned at the response. More than fifty replies have been posted, almost all of them positive. I check them all thoroughly, but I'm disappointed to find no-one on The Terminus has any more hard evidence on the existence of the Alpha Geek than on the Knights of Avalon. One reply, however, catches my eye. From someone calling themselves Eris, it says cryptically: "Beware Echelon."

Great. Just what I need. More mysteries. I yawn and check the clock, and I'm surprised to see it's almost three in the morning. Shit. I've been on this thing since I got in from work and I haven't had a bite to eat or even a cup of tea. Christ, I'm going to be knackered in the morning. I decide to have just one last trawl through the Knights of Avalon before I log off.

It had to happen sooner or later. I'm at work hiding behind my computer, shovelling coffee down my neck to try to kick-start my body after just three hours sleep. I have the phone crooked in between my neck and shoulder, although I'm just listening to dead air and pretending to take notes from an imaginary interview while flicking through The Terminus when George's secretary slaps a Post-It note on my monitor telling me he wants to see me pronto. Making a loud show of finishing my pretend conversation, I slope into his office and say: "Hi, what's up?"

He motions me to shut the door behind me and tells me to sit down. He looks knackered, but then I suppose I'm one to talk. On his desk in front of him he has a sheaf of papers. "Dave, I won't beat around the bush because we're both busy; or rather we should be," he says wearily. He slides the papers across his desk at me. "Mind telling me what the fuck these are all about?"

I glance down at them. They're printouts of all my recent e-mails in and out of the office. Shit. I pause for a minute, and say: "Just a story I'm working on, George."

He pulls the top sheet back and begins to read: "'Looking for the Alpha Geek. Believe you can help me. Any information, especially contact details, would be gratefully appreciated.' Who the fuck is the Alpha Geek, Dave?"

Good question, George. Good fucking question. I lean forward, trying to be animated, and say: "It's going to be a big one, this, George. A cracker..."

He holds up a hand to silence me and pinches the bridge of his nose. "I don't want this sort of shit, Dave. I know you've had a good run recently, what with the Beast of Shotmoor and the Crying Boy, but you've got to get back to Earth, lad. We're not the National Enquirer, are we? Go and get me some council corruption, some police brutality, some fucking cat stuck up a fucking tree if that's all there is, but leave this weird shit alone, eh? Now go on, fuck off, get some work done."

I nod and stand up. I'm about to leave when George says: "Between you, me and the gatepost, Dave, things aren't great at the Post at the moment. I'm being leaned on to cut costs here, and you know what that generally means." He waves the sheaf of papers at me. "Don't give anyone an excuse, lad, because they don't need much of one these days. You're a good reporter, Dave, just remember what I said. Leave the weird shit alone."

I nod again, and say in a small voice. "I'll try, George." I will try. But it's more a question of whether the weird shit will leave me alone.

Stephen Fucking Doyle is smirking as I come out of George's office. Like he fucking knows anything. As I pass his desk I brush his cup of coffee and knock it into his lap. He leaps up like a scalded cat and glares at me, but I shrug and say sorry. The other reporters are snickering behind their screens, and I feel better already. Doyle gives me a menacing look as he hops off to the toilets to bathe his burning balls. But fuck him. Fuck them all. I get back to my desk and grab my coat off the back of the chair, stuffing my notepad into the pocket. "I'm going out," I tell the newsdesk secretary. "If George asks, tell him there's a cat stuck up a tree."

I decide to take the afternoon off and head for the flat. George won't have to worry too much about the e-mails at work now I've got my own set-up at home. I feel knackered, and know I should eat something, but that shit they call coffee at work has taken any edge off my appetite. Hunting around the flat, I turn up half a wrap of speed hidden under a plant pot and snaffle it down, grimacing at the bitter taste. Quicker than beans on toast, and twice as much energy. Head already beginning to buzz, I power up the PC and connect immediately to the Internet.

My head is pounding by midnight. My body is exhausted, but I know I'm not going to sleep for a long time, and it isn't just the amphetamine. Eris from The Terminus has e-mailed me reams of stuff about Echelon, and it's put the wind up me. I don't know how much of this is true or just paranoid fantasy, but according to the stuff he - or she - has sent me, Echelon is a joint British and American surveillance programme that employs all the spies left over from the Cold War. Instead of monitoring the Russians they are now largely employed in industrial espionage, and have this huge network of listening posts that can intercept all telecommunications, including e-mails. Apparently the listening posts run off computer programmes which recognise key words in transmissions and log them for further investigation. For example, one article reckons that Echelon has been used to scupper European business deals among certain companies by passing on restricted information to American corporations, giving them an unfair advantage when bidding for contracts. Fairly underhand, but nothing more sinister than you'd expect. But Eris also claims that one of the key phrases the Echelon computers are programmed to recognise is "Alpha Geek". I go running for where I'd stashed Colin's diary under my mattress and start to flick through it, quickly finding the passage I'm looking for, scored through in highlighter ink.

"...Took the unprecedented step of telephoning the Alpha Geek. He wasn't happy, said he'd only given me that number for emergencies. Sorry, but I'm starting to consider this an emergency."

I'm not fucking surprised the Alpha Geek wasn't happy when Colin telephoned him, if his name is on the Echelon most wanted list. It explains why he's so hard to track down as well. And then I think of that sheaf of papers on George's desk, reams and reams of e-mails from me asking questions about the Alpha Geek. If that hasn't started alarm bells ringing in some underground bunker somewhere, I don't know what will. Jesus.

Got to calm down here, get a grip. Echelon is run by the Government... Christ, why would the Government want to kill a harmless old fruitcake like Colin? Nervously, I glance through the window at the darkened street, but there's no car there. Thank God. My heart's beating to fuck. I need to calm down.

Jumpily, I head into the bedroom and retrieve my stash, and start to shakily build myself a joint. As I twist the tip I become aware of the muted ringing of my mobile phone, hidden away in my jacket pocket thrown on the couch. I ignore it and spark up the spliff, inhaling deeply and feeling the anxiety ebb away somewhat. The phone stops ringing.

By the time I've finished the joint I feel calmer but not really any better. I return to the PC and read the Echelon stuff again. This just doesn't make any sense. Spies? After me? I feel like I should tell someone, but who? The police? My MP? Write a letter to The Guardian? Might as well walk into the nearest bug-hatch and book myself a nice padded cell for the next five years. I've become the kind of person I always used to dread getting a phone call from at work, the wild, tremulous conspiracy nuts who feel the need to ring up their local newspapers and bare their souls to a bored reporter. We used to dread the call from the switchboard telling us in coded terms that there was a nutter in reception who wanted to talk to a journalist. Christ, the hours I've spent patiently listening to outrageous stories from people convinced they were being watched or followed or spied on by secret agents. And here I am now. One of them. If only I'd listened a bit closer, I might know what to do now.

The mobile phone rings again from the living room. Sighing, I decide to answer it. It's Emma.

"Dave? Are you okay? I've not seen you for days..."

"Yeah, Em, just a bit busy, work and stuff. You okay?"

She pauses, the phone crackling in her silence. "Fine, yeah. Do you want to see me?"

And then I have visions of Emma sitting in a darkened room, surrounded by men in black suits, urging her on, murmuring encouragement, scribbling down suggestions of things to say and places to meet. I push them away, this is ridiculous. But is it, though?

"Emma," I say slowly, "Alpha Geek."

I pause, listening for a tell-tale click or squeak that might indicated some bored surveillance equipment monitor in a remote listening station coming alive at the sound of a key word. Emma says: "What? What did you say?"

"Alpha Geek, Emma. Alpha Geek."

Then I'm shouting, holding the phone in front of my mouth, my head pounding, shrieking: "Alpha Geek! Alpha Geek! ALPHA FUCKING GEEK!"

And then it all goes mercifully black.

I come to and I'm moving. My face is pressed up against leather, there's a gentle rocking motion and the intermittent sweep of yellow light across my face. My head is banging and I feel like I'm going to throw up, but I know where I am. I'm in a car.

I'm in a car.

There's a dull murmur of whispered conversation. I pretend to still be unconscious and try to pick up the words, but my head's buzzing too much. Is this it, then? Did I push them too far? They've come for me, haven't they? They're coming to take me away, bum-bum. They're coming to take me away. Ha-ha, hee-hee, ho-ho ho-ho, they're coming to take me away. I stifle a sob. Or is it laughter?

I feel a hand on my sweating forehead, a cool, small hand, not the hand of a spy or a man in a black car. A soothing voice melts away my madness: "Dave? Are you okay, sweetheart? It's me."

Emma. I open my eyes and turn my head. Emma's beside me, leaning over, her face flushed with concern. I'm in the back seat of a car with her, in the front are Mark and Mick from Steam. I'm in their BMW. I force a smile. "I thought they were coming for me."

Emma exchanges a quick glance with Mark, who's leaning over from the passenger seat. "Hey, it's okay, mate," he says softly. "You've just been overdoing it, that's all. We're going to take you to Steam to chill out for a bit, yeah?"

"How did you find me?" I ask dumbly.

"I'd been trying you on your phone but it was permanently engaged. I got you on your mobile but you were, well, I don't know what you were shouting, Dave, but you sounded a bit... any way, I called Mark and Mick and they came to pick you up."

"How did you get in?"

"You gave me this the last time I stayed over, remember?" Emma holds up a key. Mags' old key. She says: "Now I know why I haven't been able to phone your flat for days. You've been connected to the Internet. Constantly. Fuck knows what it's going to cost you."

I slump back into the seat, letting Emma stroke my brow. Yeah. Fuck knows what this is going to cost me.

Later, we're in the chill-out room at Steam, Mick bringing in a tray of strong, hot, sweet tea. I sip mine gratefully as we lounge around on bean bags, Mark arranging some soothing ambient music on the decks.

"I think you should take tomorrow off work," suggests Emma.

I sigh. "I can't, I've had too much time off recently, and things aren't great at the Post at the moment, apparently. Not that I've noticed. I've been a bit too wrapped up in myself."

Emma looks concerned. "You need to do something, sweetheart. What exactly is going on?"

I shrug and can feel my eyes welling with tears. Fuck. "I don't know," I say in a small voice.

She puts down her cup and kneels in front of me, staring straight into my eyes. "Dave," she says levelly. "You need to get some help."

I smile weakly at her. "Don't suppose you know where I can find the Alpha Geek, do you?"

TWENTY-TWO
ALL IN THE MIND

"So, what do you think is the significance of the black car?"

The question sits there between us, the woman sitting back in her leather chair, fingers steepled, staring out of the window at the busy streets below. The eleventh storey office is insulated from the outside world by thick glass which lets no sound in.

I'm not sure whether the question is meant to be answered or if it's rhetorical. I'm not sure that coming here was a good idea at all.

This was Emma's idea. She's been coming to this woman on and off for a number of months now. Apparently it's quite fashionable, in fact, it's considered something of a failing these days if you *don't* have an analyst.

I suppose it was my own fault. After that episode at my flat I stayed the night at Steam in one of Mick and Mark's spare rooms with Emma, and on her advice phoned in sick the next morning. George wasn't too impressed, but sounded too busy to push it. I promised Emma I would sort myself out, and for the last couple of days I have made a show of doing just that; going back to work, meeting up with Tony and Pete, popping over to see my Mum and Dad. Then at the weekend, I went to Emma's to relax after football, and when I was freshly showered, sharing a joint and a Red Mist, pink from lovemaking,. Emma flicked through Colin's diary. I could see the puzzlement growing on her face.

"Dave, what is this? Why have you written this?"

I snatched the pages from her a little more harshly than I intended. "I haven't written it, Em. It's Colin's. He left it for me."

Gently, she took the diary back. "David," she insisted quietly. "It's *your* writing."

"No, it's *Colin's.* We just have similar handwriting, that's all. Why on Earth would I write someone else's diary, Em?"

She let it go and hugged me, stroking my forehead. "Are you feeling all right, Dave? I just mean, recently, you've been..."

"What?" I snapped. "Weird? Go on, say it, that's what Tony said the other day. Weird."

"You were seen dancing in the street, Dave!" she shouted back. "*Singing in the fucking Rain*, for God's sake. The whole street was talking about it."

I went to hug her again, and she yielded, allowing me to bury my head in the fluffy towelling of her bathrobe. "You don't know, Em," I breathed. "No-one knows what I've been through, recently."

"Tell me," she pleaded quietly.

There was a long silence, Josef Suk's *A Fairytale* tinkling gently in the background. Finally I turned away. "I can't. I can't. Not yet."

Emma grabbed my head and made me look at her. "You've got to talk about this, Dave. If you won't tell me, I know someone you can talk to. Please, Dave. If not for me, do it for yourself."

"I'm not sure I understand the question. What do you mean, signify? It doesn't signify anything. It's just there, following me."

She considers this for a moment, taking off her glasses and rubbing them with a piece of cotton. She's in her forties, hair scraped back into a bun, the wall behind her dotted with framed certificates. She reaches for a packet of cigarettes and lights one, not asking me if I mind or offering me one. "Okay, David," she murmurs in her low, hypnotic voice. "Let's step back a little. Why do you think it's following you?"

"I don't know, really. Maybe they think I know something. I'm not really sure."

"And who are they?"

I sigh, slightly exasperated. "I don't know. Whoever's driving the car. Look, if I knew all the answers, I wouldn't have come to you, would I?"

"Do you think I'm going to be able to give you all the answers, David?"

Christ, her voice is so irritating. I take a deep breath. "Look, this may have been a mistake, coming here. Why don't we just call it off?"

She shrugs. "You're paying for an hour, David. Might as well get your money's worth. Now, tell me about the man with the violin case. When did you first see him?"

I sit back and try to relax. "Um, when I went to cover that house fire, the one where they had the Crying Boy painting."

"When was the next time you saw him?"

"I think it was when everyone was hunting the Beast of Shotmoor. He was down in the town, when me and the farmer saw the cat in the alley."

"So your farmer friend saw him too?"

"I don't know. I suppose so. But I think he was more wrapped up in the cat." What's she getting at? Is she trying to make out I've invented it all?

"Apart from the farmer, do you know anyone else who's seen the man?"

"Well, people must have seen him, but no-one who was with me."

She takes off her glasses again and cleans them thoughtfully. "David, what do you think is in the violin case?"

"I don't know. A violin?"

She nods, as though humouring me, then takes a look at her notes. "You also mention two girls, twins. You have seen them... three times now? But never at the same time as the black car or the man with the violin case?"

"Not at the same time, no," I smile humourlessly. "I like to keep my phantoms spread out throughout the day."

She makes a note of the word "phantoms" on the yellow legal pad in front of her. Jesus, this is money for old rope. How hard can it be to listen to people like me, repeat everything they say, and write it down? I'm in the wrong line of work. She pauses, and lights another cigarette. I watch the swirls of white smoke drifting chaotically through the shafts of cold sunlight, and she looks at her pad again then levels her gaze at me.

"Okay. Back to the car. Has anyone else ever seen the black car?"

"Well, Colin saw it. And Marianne's husband was visited by two men in a black car. And Cheryl... Cheryl was beaten up, for God's sake. They told her to stay away from me."

She pauses for a long moment again, reminding me of a teacher who used to give you the chance to change your mind when you'd given a wrong answer in class. "Is there any evidence that the car used by the men who visited Marianne's husband is the same one you've been seeing?"

I shake my head. "Well, no, not evidence, as such..."

"And Colin's diary... well, we can come back to that later. Now, do you think there may be a relationship between the black car and the man with the violin case?"

I look out of the window at the cars rushing below, at the people getting on with their lives, unbothered by black cars and men with violin cases, unconcerned by beasts on the moors and lost women. She gets up to pour us both another coffee, sips hers measuredly, all the while never taking her almond eyes off me. "David, would you like me to tell you what I think?"

Well, she might as well have her say for the money I'm paying her. "Yeah, why not?"

She sits back again, her elbows on the leather chair arms, twisting a wedding ring on her finger, gathering her thoughts before she speaks.

"David, I believe that neither the man with the violin case nor the black car exist as you perceive them. The same goes for the mysterious twin sisters."

I almost rise from my seat. "What? Are you saying I'm nuts? I'm not listening to this for another minute. I thought you were going to help me."

She holds a conciliatory hand in the air and I slowly sit down again. "I didn't say you were, as you term it, nuts. You may well have seen a man carrying a violin case, it is more than probable you have seen a black car, maybe even the same one, more than once. Twin sisters are not uncommon, either.

"I believe these things have become icons for you, David. You are becoming agitated, anxious, fearful, even, of the unknown. You have woken up and realised the world is not the ordered, sensible place you once thought it was. There is still a lot of unexplained phenomena, David, there are things out there that we only barely understand.

"I think the man with the violin case represents the unknown for you, his violin case an analogy for the mysteries and cyphers the world suddenly seems full of."

"And the black car?"

"The black car represents the next stage. Having accepted that we cannot explain everything, that there are mysteries wrapped in enigmas and boxed in puzzles, you are now realising what that entails. The future is here, David, we cannot stop it or put it off. Some people lock themselves away, hoping it will go away, others may even end their lives than face the uncertainty. That's what the black car represents for you, David, fear and uncertainty. Once you have accepted that the world is a very weird place, you are now terrified of the world, and what it has to hide.

"The twin sisters represent your lost innocence now that you have woken up, as you see it, to the world as it really is. That is why you feel compelled to follow them, to recapture how you felt before your world became a very different place."

She looks at her watch and pushes her coffee cup away. "Now, I'm afraid your time is up."

So it's as simple as that. I'm mad. Barking. Three sandwiches short of a picnic. Stark, staring hat stand. I'm sorry, but that doesn't go a tenth of the way to explaining everything that's been happening to me. Well, thanks, but no thanks. If I had wanted to be told that I'm crackers I would have just gone down the pub with my mates. As I leave the doctor's office some other poor bugger stands up in the waiting room and the receptionist signals for him to go in. Christ, but he looks a case. Dishevelled, ill-fitting suit, staring eyes, tangled curly hair, constantly fidgeting and jumping like his nerves are on a knife edge. I walk past him and he nods to me, almost a signal of recognition, although I've never seen the poor sap before in my life. But maybe it's not me he recognises, maybe it's something in me. Maybe it takes one to know one. Christ.

I take the lift down from the eleventh floor. All that baring your soul can really take it out of you. I'm alone until I get to the third floor when the doors slide noiselessly open.

And there stands Mags.

She looks at me like she's just had an electric shock. We stare at each other wordlessly for so long that the doors start to close until we both hit the button again. When I find my voice I say, as naturally as possible: "Mags! What are you doing here?"

A second before she answers her eyes flicker towards the smoked glass doors behind her. "Oh, just here on business." But it's too late. I've already followed her gaze to the discreet sign on the office door: National Pregnancy Advisory Bureau.

Oh, Mags, no.

We sit in a small coffee shop, this time near the window, because this time I look a bit more respectable and this far out of town there's no chance of Stephen Fucking Doyle walking past and spotting us.

"So what did you expect me to do, Dave? Have the baby? Turn up at my wedding with some squalling infant in tow?" Mags shakes her head and looks down at her coffee, her reflection distorted in the ripples.

"I don't know, Mags. I just thought, you know, you'd talk to me about it first." I feel sort of helpless, like I'm on unsure ground, out of my depth. "Um, you haven't had the, uh, operation, yet..?"

"Two weeks. Shit, Dave, I've had no choice in this. You're out of the equation, now. Besides, I believe you're practically shacked up with that student girl."

News travels fast in the information age. "But that's nothing to do with us, Mags. You know that if you left Stephen tomorrow..."

Then she's crying, an unattractive, snotty, hacking kind of crying. People are looking at us. "I just don't know how the fuck it happened. I knew we should have been more careful. God, I've been so bloody irresponsible. I never thought this would happen… it never felt *real* enough.".

"Never felt *real*?" I say. "Mags, it never felt *real*?"

"Poor Stephen," she says. "Christ, this would kill him."

"Poor Stephen? What about me, Mags? It's my baby too!"

She wipes her nose on her sleeve. "A mess down my leg, a few chromosomes, Dave, that's what you contributed. If there was any way for you to bear this child you would be fucking welcome to it. It's my body, my life, and I'm not ready for this shit. It would ruin everything."

I want to hold her, take her in my arms, be in my flat with soft music and snuggled up under my duvet. But I suppose that's how all this started. She knows I would drop everything for her, but she's made her choice. I should just get up, walk away, never see her again, but I'm just not that hard. Instead I put my hand on hers and she looks up, her red eyes betraying nights of insomnia. "Dave, I feel like I'm losing my mind."

I manage the first smile I've had for days. It feels weird. I sigh. "Join the club, Mags. Join the club."

I turn down Mags' offer of a lift and take the train home. We both need to be on our own. I didn't bother driving to the doctor's because I figured it was highly likely I would walk straight out of there and get hammered in the nearest bar. Besides, I quite like train journeys. This one's only forty-five minutes or so, but I like the sense of being carried along, peeking into people's back gardens and seeing brief flashes of other lives, farmers in fields, kids playing football, commuters locked in traffic.

I feel strangely calm, almost numb. Emma will be waiting for me at my flat, and I'm not sure if I care or not. Mags went off to shop to make her feel better.

Christ. I was almost a father. But it's just words, I can't make them make me feel anything. Perhaps the doctor's right, after all.

The carriage rocks gently, almost sending me to sleep. Then it slows and stops, patiently waiting for signal changes ahead. We're in the countryside just before we hit the town, fields rolling off to my left. To the right, across the carriage from me, there's a derelict station, a platform and station house and waiting room, all cracked and falling apart and overgrown with weeds. Obviously one of Dr Beeching's casualties, a rural station serving a handful of farming types, its loss mourned by no-one. Beyond the station there are a few fields then the grey slate roofs of one of the outermost corners of town, the more concentrated conurbations beyond them. The station looks odd, on one of the region's main lines, with trains and life thundering past every few minutes, yet completely ignored, hiding in plain sight.

Then the train lurches and we're off again, the station lost behind a copse of naked trees.

Emma is waiting with a cup of tea. She's a sweetheart really. I collapse onto the couch and gratefully accept the steaming mug from her.

"So... how was it?" she ventures.

I take a few sips of the hot sweet tea then stand, walking to the big window and watching out over the town's rooftops. Mags is gone now, she's jumped ship and signed up for a vessel bound for calmer waters. Emma's here, a willing conscript. She deserves more and I'm going to try to give it to her.

The day has been bright and the light has lasted longer than usual, but now it's failing, the sky overhead a deep blue. Out on the street there's my car, and behind it, as I more than half expected, is parked a big, black car with anonymous windows.

I turn to Emma and give her the big smile she's desperate to see. "Fine. I'm feeling much better now."

TWENTY-THREE SKIDDOO

But I'm not. I know I'm not. But I'm going to try. I've been trying to keep off the Internet, or at least off the Knights of Avalon and Terminus bulletin boards. Found some interesting stuff on that Arcadia picture that Cheryl showed me, and I printed out a quote from the artist Nicolas Poussin, which I've stuck to the top of the monitor at home: "*My nature leads me to seek out and cherish things that are well-ordered, shunning confusion which is contrary to me as dark shadows are to the light of day.*"

Bollocks, of course, but it serves as a warning to me that I'm trying to do things properly and normally now, like a photograph of a model wearing a size ten dress stuck to an overweight woman's fridge door as a reminder to diet. It's all a matter of perspective. Just like the analyst said, these things that have affected my life have become icons for me. Everything has a rational explanation if you want to believe it. The man with the violin case is just another doomer plying his shite, who just happened to pick on me because of the weird stuff I've had in the paper recently. The black car... well, how many fucking black cars are there on the streets? Arcadia is an experience I've built up from nothing, fuelled by too much drink and drugs. The twin sisters, well, there are a lot of lost souls on Jepson Street.

It's a nice try. But it's like trying to convince myself that the sky's green and the grass is blue, I'm afraid. And surely enough, I find myself grazing back to The Terminus while surfing the net at home. Eris, the mysterious Eris who has been so helpful, has posted a reply to a message from someone else, dismissing the previous poster's theories tartly and ending with the phrase: "Twenty-three skiddoo!"

That's something I've seen a lot on the net, especially on The Terminus. Allowing myself a brief deviation from the path of normality I'm desperately trying to stick to, I post a quick query message about twenty-three skiddoo.

Eris comes back almost immediately, implying he or she is either in my time zone, or keeps fucking odd hours at the other side of the Atlantic. The message is short and to the point: "*Arcadia: The origins of the phrase 'twenty-three skiddoo' are murky, but the term was popular in the 1920s, although there is evidence it was in use prior to the First World War. It generally means something like 'get lost' or 'be off with you' and was common Roaring Twenties slang. Various theories as to origin: Skiddoo was undoubtedly a variation on the word 'skedaddle' while there are differing stories about the twenty-three bit. 23 was Morse Code for 'away with you', but there's also a funny story about young men standing on the corner of Twenty-Third Street and Broadway in New York, in the hope that the notoriously strong winds at this corner would lift up women's skirts as they passed. Cops used to shoo them away with the admonition: 'Twenty-three skiddoo!'. For more Discordian aspects of the phrase, you could do well to read some Robert Anton Wilson."*

Skiddoo. Heh. For some reason, I like that word. Suddenly hungry, and remembering Emma's instructions to look after myself a bit better, I shut down the PC and head off to the kitchen to see what's lurking in the fridge.

Later, I'm sitting with Emma in the Fortune bar in town, both of us sipping Red Mist. Christ, it seems like ages since I had a normal night out. The chatting is easy and nicely meaningless, the alcohol's slipping down nicely. She's feeling my thigh under the table with the promise of more exploration to come later at her flat. I've even managed to stop myself scanning the street for black cars for a good hour now, and I'm concentrating on Emma's face as she animatedly relays some tale or other about what someone did in Steam the other night. I'm not really concentrating, but it's pleasant just to sit and watch her mouth working and her eyes shining, and hear the noises without really listening to them. On an impulse I lean over and kiss her. She looks a little taken aback, but smiles coyly, and squeezes my thigh harder under the table. She moves in closer to me and nuzzles my ear, whispering: "I'm glad you got yourself sorted out, Dave. I was really worried about you for a bit there."

"Me too," I say, taking another swig of Red Mist and draining my bottle. "You ready for another one yet?"

She shakes her bottle and nods. "Yeah, I'll just go and powder my nose while you're at the bar."

I order two more Red Mists from the girl at the polished-chrome bar and as she's getting them my gaze lands on the newspaper the guy at the side of me is flicking through. There's a big headline: VICAR SEES UFO OVER CHURCH. I close my eyes, willing it to go away. "Skiddoo," I whisper under my breath. "Twenty-three skiddoo." And sure enough, when I open them again, he's reading a different story, a refreshingly normal article about a footballer and a model. I smile as the girl hands over the bottles and takes my money. I've got a magic word for when the weirdness comes now, and it works. Skiddoo. Makes it all go away.

Emma joins me at the table and smiles lovingly at me. Maybe this is what I need. No complications with Mags, no hassle, just a simple, normal relationship - the kind I haven't had since Helen died. An image of her in the graveyard - surely my lowest point in all of this shit - bubbles up, but I whisper: "Skiddoo" and it's gone, and I'm just looking at Emma's smiling face again.

She cocks an eyebrow at me. "What did you just say then?"

I smile at her. "I said, I love you." And you know what? I think I do.

Two days later I'm with Tony and Pete, flushed and hot from playing football and the showers, heading into town for a couple of drinks with our sports bags thrown over our shoulders. It's just like old times, before the... before everything.

We fetch up in the Cross Keys, and I order Red Mist for me and Tony and a pint of Stella for Pete. We greedily sink our drinks, finishing them with big *aaaah!*s and beaming smiles. We chat about inconsequential things, the possibility of a trip to Budapest early next year, the football, EastEnders. Tony and Pete want to meet Emma again, there's talk of them coming down to Steam at the weekend.

Tony stands up to get the next round. "Ia R'lyeh! Cthulhu fhtagn! Ia! Ia?" he asks.

I stare at him wordlessly. Pete nudges me and says: "N'gai, n'gha'ghaa, shoggog, y'hah, Nyarla-to, Nyarla-totep, Yog-Sothoth, n-yah, n-yah."

Oh Jesus. What's happening? I close my eyes tight and whisper rapidly: "*Skiddoo. Skiddoo. Twenty-three skiddoo.*"

Tony shakes me on the shoulder and I open my eyes to look at him. "You all right, Dave? I asked you if you wanted another Red Mist..?"

I nod helplessly at him. He and Pete exchange glances, then Pete says decisively: "No he fucking well doesn't. That shite is rotting his brain. Get him a pint of Stella."

Tony nods and heads off for the bar, and Pete says: "What's got into you, mate?"

I shake my head, recovering rapidly. "Few late nights, you know how it is."

He nods and taps the side of his nose. "That Emma girl, eh? Say no more. In fact, bollocks to that, tell me everything. Bet she goes like a train, that one, eh?"

By the time I've seen them, they've seen me and it's too late to do anything about it other than balls it out. I've just stepped out of Clobber where I've been buying a new shirt for Steam tonight, and they're walking straight towards me. Mags pretends not to have seen me, but Stephen Fucking Doyle is braying like a donkey and shouting: "David! David!" Fucking great.

Mags is staring at her feet as if it's the first time she's noticed her shoes and she's finding them incredibly interesting. Doyle is prattling on at me but I'm not listening, I'm not taking a word of it in. He pauses and looks at me, and I realise he's asked a question, he's waiting for a response. I hazard a guess: "Um, yeah?"

"Perfect!" roars Doyle. "We'll probably fly over to Dublin on the Friday morning and come back on Sunday, so make sure you get the day booked off at work quickly. We'll have an absolutely monster time!"

Oh Jesus, I think he just invited me to his stag do. I smile wanly and risk a glance at Mags. She's still staring at her feet, arm linked protectively with Stephen's. I'm about to say something to her, something inane and puerile, when I'm roughly jostled and a smelly, old doomer stands there, a woman dressed in a ragged coat and wellies cut off at the ankle to make shoes. Her Aldi carrier bag full of "Are you ready for the Rapture?" pamphlets hangs loosely by her side. I'm about to fumble in my pocket to get some change to get rid of her, but she doesn't look like she's selling. She's looking at Mags, waving her hand in front of Mags' face, who's shrinking back, nose crinkled in disgust.

"Having a babby, darling, having a babby?" shrieks the old bat. Mags' eyes lock with mine for a second, before Stephen crossly pushes the old woman away.

"Not today, thanks," he says loudly.

The woman looks first at Stephen and then at me, saying sadly: "But she's having a babby, she's having a babby, she is."

"Go away," says Doyle firmly. Mags' eyes are wet and shining, and she's still looking at me.

I whisper under my breath: "Skiddoo, skiddoo. Twenty-three skiddoo."

The woman looks at me all sly and cunning. "I heard that, feller, I heard that. I know what you're doing, know where you're coming from, so I do. You've said it now, and I'll be off. Can't do more or less, can I? I'll be off."

And off she goes, delving deep into her carrier bag and pulling out a handful of pamphlets, shrieking at the top of her voice: "Are you ready for the Rapture, luvvies? Think about the little ones."

"Mad old bat," says Stephen as she is swallowed up by the shopping crowds. He punches Mags playfully on the shoulder, and she recoils as though burned. "Mad old bat. Having a baby. As if, eh, pet?"

After an awkward pause I say: "Well, better let you two get on, eh?"

"That's right, and it looks like you've got a big night ahead," says Doyle, indicating my bag from Clobber. "Single guy like you, bet you have the pick of 'em, hey Dave?" he leers, winking at me and nudging Mags. She looks like she's about to burst into tears. "My days for sowing wild oats are over now, but I wouldn't have it any other way." He aims a kiss at Mags' cheek but she moves abruptly and he ends up with a mouthful of hair. He winks at me again and says in a stage whisper: "Still, always the stag night, eh, Dave?"

And then they move off, thank Christ.

The episode with Mags really threw me off balance, but by the time I've had a couple of lagers in Steam I've loosened up some. At Emma's suggestion I'm laying off the drugs tonight, and at Pete's insistence I'm drinking Stella instead of Red Mist. For once, I'm quite happy to go along with other people. I know they only have my best interests at heart, and it really is sweet that people seem to care that much. We're squeezed into a booth, me, Tony, Pete, Emma, Fi, Kex, and a couple of Emma's friends whose names I've already forgotten and who the lads are desperately trying to impress. This generally takes the form of Tony nervously talking about football and obscure indie bands and Pete preening his feathers like a peacock and telling outrageous lies. The girls seem pliable and a bit touchy-feely, but that's because I know they've dropped a couple of Es and would be just as friendly to Hitler and Mussolini. I've a vague memory of some unpleasantness between Kex and Pete at my birthday party, but maybe I imagined it all because everyone seems in jovial spirits now.

Several pints and a bit of dancing later, Pete and Tony are huddled in the corner wondering why they've been blown out by the girls when they were getting on so famously, and Fi and Kex are dancing wildly to some jaw-dropping, acid techno that Delta's furiously punting out from the DJ box. Emma tugs my arm and whispers: "You look so fucking hot tonight. Want to go back to mine?"

I'm agreeable enough, especially as she's massaging my balls through my jeans underneath the table. We stand and decide to slink off without saying our goodbyes, and by the time we get through the door we're kissing furiously and tugging at each other's clothes.

It's a cold night but it's dry, and we decide to walk to Emma's. The street outside Steam is deserted, and we're crossing the road, engrossed in each other, when light fills my closed eyes and there's the roar of an engine.

The car's almost upon us, it's full beam dazzling the pair of us, but the next few seconds stretch to infinity. The street's dark, but I can see clearly that the car is a big black one, with darkened windows. Emma's opening her mouth to scream in crazy slow-motion, and I'm standing there frozen, like the proverbial rabbit in the headlights. Finally my parched mouth begins to work and I squeeze out a single word.

"*Skiddoo.*"

The car keeps coming and I can feel Emma squeezing my arm, her scream finally escaping from her lungs.

"*Skiddoo.*"

And still the car's coming, and the light's blinding me, and now I'm joining Emma's wail and screaming at the car: "Skiddoo! Skiddoo! Twenty-three skiddoo!"

But it's not working, the car's still coming, so I grab Emma and roughly drag her back the way we came, tumbling to the side of the road with her landing heavily on top of me, the fall knocking the wind out of her lungs and silencing her scream, and the car guns its engine and moves on, disappearing down the still-deserted street.

Emma's on her feet, shaking her fist after the disappearing car and shrieking: "You fucking asshole! You almost fucking killed us! Fucking asshole!"

By now two or three of the Steam regulars have run out, followed by our friends. "What the fuck's going on?" says Pete.

Emma answers: "Fucking asshole came from nowhere and nearly ran us down. Jesus!"

"Must have been pissed," says Kex.

"Did you get his number?" asks Tony.

"No, it happened too quickly," answers Emma shakily, shock setting in now she's calming down. "Jesus."

Everyone turns to me where I still half-lie on the road. "You all right, mate?" says Pete, concerned.

No. No I'm not. That was them, it was obviously them. And they wanted to show me, tell me that no matter how all right I think I am, I'm not. They didn't skiddoo, it doesn't work on them. They wanted me to know.

That was a warning.

TWENTY-FOUR
THE ALPHA GEEK, I PRESUME

There can be no doubt now. It's war. Me against them. They know who I am, where I live, everything about me. They have me at an advantage. I need help. And, as though my prayers are answered, help comes.

I've been surfing the net again in search of answers. I even went back on the Knights of Avalon and Terminus bulletin boards, but no-one has been able to help. Still, I have faith. It's just that time is running out. That's what the psychiatrist said, isn't it? *Your time's up.* Maybe it was a warning.

Weekend is approaching and I'm fending off calls from Emma, the guys, my parents, all keen for my time. I can't afford to waste a single moment. Colin sat there and did nothing, and they got him. How many others have suffered the same fate?

I have invested in some good security for the flat, bolts and padlocks for the doors, window locks. I'm considering bars for the windows as well, but that will take time and money, neither of which are in plentiful supply.

I've been spending my evenings by the big window, no TV, no music. The news is full of madness, everyone going down the same road as me. I sit and watch the street, sometimes seeing the black car, sometimes not. I wonder when they'll make their next move?

The harsh buzz of the doorbell makes me jump almost a foot in the air. Probably Emma, or Pete and Tony. Mags, even. I ignore the next two buzzes. Hopefully they'll go away. Within five minutes there's a sharp rap at the door of my flat. One of the other tenants must have let them in the main door. I sigh and answer it.

He's short, maybe five-two, but his presence fills the hallway. He wears one of those little waistcoats with loads of pockets that fishermen have, the pockets stuffed with all kinds of boxes and tubes and odd devices. His short legs are clothed in urban camouflage combat trousers, tucked into tightly-laced, shiny, black boots. Under the waistcoat is an X-Files T-shirt with the slogan Trust No-one. He wears a pair of Ray-Ban Wayfarers balanced on his little button nose and a Star Trek baseball cap hides neatly cropped silver hair. In a tremulous, mid-Atlantic accent that gives nothing away, he announces: "I believe you have been looking for me."

I open the door wider and allow him to step into my flat. "The Alpha Geek, I presume."

The Alpha Geek wanders into the lounge, eyes darting about under the Ray-Bans. "Yes, that is one of my names, young man. It will suffice for now. And I call you..." - he consults a notebook which he whips with a flourish from one of his pockets - "...David, that is correct?"

He doesn't wait for an answer, slipping a small but tightly-packed rucksack from his shoulder and perching on the edge of the couch. "Tea, milk, two sugars, Earl Grey if possible, let it brew for four-and-a-half minutes" he says, reaching for the remote control and flicking through the digital channels until he gets to CNN. As I retire to the kitchen he calls after me: “No word from the Middle East, David. I’m not sure whether that is good or bad. Either nothing is happening, which is a mixed blessing, or it is and they are not telling us.”

I pop my head around the kitchen door. “The Middle East? Christ, what’s happening now?”

He sighs and takes off his baseball cap. “I just told you, David. Maybe nothing, maybe something, but we need to keep an eye on it all the same. Nostradamus, the New Testament, the Concerned Christians, a dozen prophets and soothsayers, all point to the Middle East as playing host to cataclysmic events in the End Times. Only a fool fails to closely monitor politics in the desert states.”

I return with tea for us both, handing a steaming mug to the Alpha Geek. “I presume you got one of the messages I left for you? Was it from Marianne, or maybe Eris?”

He holds up a fat hand and splutters: “Stop! Do not involve others more than is necessary. Agrimony is one of our best operatives, although she doesn’t really know it yet. It would be folly to endanger her.”

“Our best operatives? Who are you? And how can Mari-sorry, Agrimony, work for you and not know it?”

The Alpha Geek slurps noisily at his tea and turns to face me on the couch. “We have no membership cards, no roll call, no headquarters or fnords, but our numbers are legion. There are many like us, who know who they are and why they are such as Eris, many more like Agrimony, who know who they are but not why they are, and many millions more who know neither who nor why they are, and may never even know when they are.”

This idiot is talking in riddles. “What did you say just then?” I ask curiously. “What have fjords got to do with anything?”

The Alpha Geek stares at me impassively from behind his shades for a long moment. "I spoke not of fjords," he says measuredly. "Did you by chance hear a *fnord* in what I said?"

More riddles. He goes on: "I did not say fnord, but if you heard it, that could be a powerful omen. You are on the way to knowing who you are, when you are, why you are. Congratulations, and my condolences."

The Alpha Geek drains his tea. "Now," he says, settling back into the couch as though a long night looms ahead. "It is time for your education to begin. Forget everything you have been told up to now. Have you seen a doctor?"

The sudden turn of the conversation throws me. How much does this old guy know about me? "Uh, as it happens, yes. I saw an analyst."

"I thought so. It is very often the first refuge of the newly-awakened. What was their verdict?"

"Paranoid, mad, in not so many words."

The Alpha Geek barks a strange, hacking laugh. "Like hairdressers, all psychiatrists are in the employ of the Government. Which government is another question, but certainly some government. Tell me, David, did this quack consider these conditions bad things to have?"

I shrug. "I'm not sure. She certainly didn't say it was good news."

The Alpha Geek stands and draws himself up to his full height. Coughing to clear this throat, he quotes: "'Watch, therefore, for ye know neither the day nor the hour wherein the son of man cometh'. Or anyone else cometh for that matter. Matthew 25:13." He comes close to me and hisses: "*Keep watching the skies!*"

I suppose I should be getting worried right about now, that I should throw this guy out on his ear. But the funny thing is, the Alpha Geek is the one person who has spoken the most sense to me since all this started.

"Can we have more tea, David? It's going to be a long night."

Two freshly-brewed mugs of tea sit between us along with a packet of chocolate digestive biscuits. The Alpha Geek has slipped off his waistcoat and tossed it over his baseball cap, but he keeps his Ray-Bans firmly in place. "UV rays," he explains conspiratorially. "Maybe they can, you know, attach stuff to them." He taps the side of his nose and winks at me. I nod wordlessly.

Finishing his digestive, the Alpha Geek asks me: "Do you know when the world will end, David?"

I shake my head. "No. Do you?"

He laughs mockingly. "Come now, do I look like a man who can foresee the future? Many things are possible in these strange times, but not all things are. Keep it in perspective."

"What, like big cats on the moors and paintings which kill people are okay, but seeing the future isn't?" I say angrily. "So where do I draw the distinction?"

The Alpha Geek shrugs. "A good rule of thumb is to believe only what you've seen yourself, David. As for everything else..." he points to his T-shirt with his thumb. Trust No-one.

"Okay," I sigh. "No-one knows when the world will end. So why bring it up?"

He leans into me. "Because many people think they know, David. More and more people every day predict doom, disaster, apocalypse. Do you know how many doomsdays await us? Let me tell you a few. Meteors will strike the Earth on December 21 2012, obliterating all life. Sometime before 2018 an asteroid will collide with our planet. Some Sufi sects place the apocalypse in 2076, the year 1500 in the Muslim calendar. Greenpeace predicts massive starvation due to population growth before the year 2038. A comet will crash into earth in the year 2012, according to some translations of the first five books in the Bible, the

Pentateuch. We live in the End Times, David, the world is holding its breath, waiting for something to happen. We're all wound up like elastic bands. We're eating ourselves, rehashing music and fashion and remaking old films and rewriting old novels. We're on the brink of something."

My tea has gone cold so I go to make more. As I potter round the kitchen the Alpha Geek continues: "Europe is in uproar. Should we have a single state, a single economy, should we not? Technology is moving far faster than our notions of right and wrong. People are in space. People are starving. The Balkan states are in turmoil." He pauses, reflectively. "I went to Yugoslavia for my holidays, once."

I return with the tea and we watch CNN for a while, Charles Manson celebrating his parole win. Apparently he's going to open a restaurant on Rodeo Drive.

"Is it any wonder more and more people are feeling as you do?" he says. "We live in the communication age. Something can occur to me and I can transmit the thought almost as soon as I've had it to someone in Japan or Australia via the Internet or e-mail or ISDN. There's no way to contain the fever in these conditions. You don't get what you've got from dirty toilet seats; you catch it from clear thinking."

"Does it always affect people badly?"

"Not at all. Typical symptoms do include anxiety, panic, outright fear, sometimes just mild apprehension. Others see the End Times as the dawn of a new age for our planet, an attaining of spiritual enlightenment, even the return of Christ."

"Ah, the Age of Aquarius," I say, keen to contribute.

The Alpha Geek nods. "It is true we are now living in the Age of Aquarius, but we've only made the first step on the road to spiritual enlightenment, in my view. And there are those who would seek to hold us back from making the next one."

Oh? I lean forward and encourage the Alpha Geek to go on, but he just looks a bit agitated. "The Anti-Aquarians," he whispers by way of explanation. But he will be drawn no further. Instead he reaches into his backpack and pulls out a clipboard with a printed form attached. He produces a fountain pen with a flourish. "Now, just a few questions to assess your End Times rating."

"What? I already told you. I've already been seen to by a shrink. Mad as a hatter, apparently."

The Alpha Geek laughs in his tremulous way. "She may be all right for piddling little ailments like schizophrenia and paranoid delusions, but a victim of the End Times like yourself needs a second opinion, my boy. Now, question one. Do you keep a personal diary or planner?"

"I suppose so. At work, yeah."

"Question two. Have you continued to fill it in since you began to notice all this strangeness around you?"

"Um, well I was going to Paris next Spring with Mags, but I suppose that's cancelled. Other than that, I'm not really the type to plan ahead."

He looks pleased with that one and scribbles away on the form. "What?" I say, vaguely irritated. "Is that bad or good? What does that mean?"

"Can we wait until after the questionnaire? If I start explaining things now it might prejudice later answers. Now, question three. Do you hoard food? Tinned goods, dried foods, long-life milk, that sort of thing?"

I laugh. "You'll be lucky to find anything within its sell-by date in my fridge. What, you mean like stocking up for a nuclear war?"

He silently notes my answer. "Question four. Have you modified your chimney and/or roof in any way?"

"Modified my chimney? Is Father Christmas due to make an appearance next?"

"No," says the Alpha Geek in his shaky, high-pitched voice. "No. For example, have you altered your chimney so that should the rapture of the Day of Judgement come, your soul can freely and easily rise to the heavens, that sort of thing."

This is getting silly, now. "Look, I don't think this is helping much," I say as sympathetically as I can. He nods ruefully. "One more? Do you get neck-ache from constantly watching the skies?" I shake my head quietly.

He throws the clipboard to one side. "You're right, this is useless. Look, maybe you better just tell me everything you told that shrink. Start at the beginning."

It's after midnight when I finish my story, and I'm exhausted. The Alpha Geek looks stunned. "I don't believe it," he breathes. "You're actually being stalked by the Anti-Aquarians." It's the second time he's used that term and I ask him to explain. That same, strange, hunted look comes over him again. "Can you put some music on, please?" he requests. I shrug and switch on the system, a Charlatans CD bursting into life. "No, something louder, something that will drown our voices," he insists. I shrug and switch it for an old album by The Prodigy. If anyone really is listening in, as the Alpha Geek seems to suspect, this should sort them out good and proper.

"Now," I say, raising my voice to be heard. "Tell me about the Anti-Aquarians."

"No-one knows who they work for," he shouts back. "The Government, someone else's government, an independent organisation, some extra-terrestrial entity. We don't even know what they want. What little information there is suggests they visit people who make discoveries or sightings of the unknown, UFOs, lake monsters, ghosts, that sort of thing. The people they visit either don't talk about it again, or just... disappear."

"But why?" I say, thinking of Colin and his stupid fridge. "What does it matter to them?"

"One theory is that they have been for some reason charged with making our transition through the End Times as smooth as possible. All this getting caught up with mysticism and mysteries isn't doing us any good, in many people's opinions. If we are thinking about the Loch Ness Monster, we aren't giving the single economy our full attention. If we are watching the skies for flying saucers, we aren't guarding our borders against flesh and blood enemies. You can't tax runes and crystals."

"You're saying the people who killed Colin and who have been terrorising me are from the Government, aren't you?"

The Alpha Geek shakes his head. "No, I'm not, and I'll deny this conversation ever took place if you go round saying that. I don't want my house firebombing, thank you very much."

There's a pause, and we listen to a whole track off The Prodigy album in complete silence. "Of course, if there are Anti-Aquarians, there are also the Anti-Anti-Aquarians," shouts the Alpha Geek.

I look at him. Surely he just means Aquarians, in that case, but I let it slide. "You mean you?"

He looks horrified again. "No! Not me. But others. One in particular. They say he used to be one of the Anti-Aquarians, but defected to the other side and now he devotes his life to confounding them. He believes that mankind must keep its sense of mystery and its fear of the unknown if it is to survive the tribulations to come. They also say he stole something from the Anti-Aquarians, something special, which he carries around with him the whole time."

I stand and walk to the big window, the music pounding into my head. I can faintly hear one of the neighbours banging on the adjoining wall but I ignore them. Just as I suspected, parked under the streetlight is a silent, anonymous black car. They know he's here.

I turn to the Alpha Geek. "Then I need to meet this guy."

He looks at me from behind the Ray-Bans. "I strongly suspect that you already have. And it is my profound belief, David, that all the answers you are looking for lie inside a certain violin case."

To the intense relief of the neighbours I kill the music. The Alpha Geek consumes another cup of tea and then decides it is time to leave.

"Look, I can't thank you enough," I begin, but he holds up a podgy hand. "No, David, the pleasure has been all mine, believe me. Keep in touch through Agrimony, please. In the meantime, I'll do whatever I can."

The Alpha Geek leaves and as he walks down the two flights of stairs I turn to the window in time to see the black car pull sleekly away from the kerb. Good God, they're going after him. I run to the kitchen, grab a bread-knife and, making a mental note to buy a gun from somewhere, race after the Alpha Geek. He can only be half a minute ahead of me. I get to street level and burst through the doors, almost flattening the guy who lives in the flat below me. He's about to say something then sees the knife and keeps his mouth shut. The street is completely empty in both directions; no black car and no Alpha Geek. I turn to my neighbour and point the knife at him without meaning to. "Did you see a black car a minute ago? Could have been a...a Jag or an Audi or something?"

He shakes his head, not taking his eyes off the bread-knife. "What about a little guy, shades and baseball cap, couldn't have missed him?" Again he shakes his head dumbly.

Shit. Shit. They've got him.

TWENTY-FIVE
WHEN THE GOING GETS WEIRD...

In spite of, or maybe because of, everything that's happened, I'm still trying to desperately cling to the trappings of normality. I go to work, look busy all morning, listen to people mapping out their weekends, huddle behind my computer as Stephen Fucking Doyle prattles on about organising his stag night, willing him not to involve me. But there's no escape. His smug visage pops up over the monitor and he asks me if I'm still joining him on his final soiree as a free man.

"I'm busy up until doomsday," I joke half-heartedly. He nevertheless hands me a printed invitation. I nod dejectedly and stuff it into my top drawer. By the time Stephen and Mags get married, I've no idea where I'll be. A shiver plays up and down my backbone as I realise I don't even know if I'll be alive. Melodramatic? Unfortunately, it's the truth. All I can see in front of me is a great white nothingness, yawning ahead.

Meanwhile, the rest of the day yawns ahead too, similarly empty. George comes over to my desk, chatting to people on the way, and as he passes me murmurs: “Can I see you in my office, Dave? Just a couple of minutes.” I haven’t written a single story all week. It seems he has finally begun to notice.

I give him a moment to walk on towards his small private room, then casually get up and stroll after him. Inside he’s already seated with a stack of newspapers and two plastic cups of coffee in front of him. He motions for me to close the door and sit down, and pushes one cup towards me.

George takes a swig of coffee, grimaces, and peers over his glasses at me. “What are you working on at the moment, Dave?” he asks conversationally. I shrug. “A couple of irons in the fire, you know how it is. Waiting for a few calls to come back, checking one or two things out. You know how it is.”

He nods. “I know how it is. But when one of my top people goes from turning in exclusive after exclusive to doing nothing, I don’t know what *that* is. What is that, Dave?”

He fans out the newspapers on his desk and they are all the editions that I’ve had splashes on in the last couple of weeks. The Crying Boy, the Beast of Shotmoor, Ferdinand Shelley, each headline and paragraph charting my descent into hell. There are other stories that I just can’t tell him. I can’t involve George and risk having his blood on my hands.

I sip my coffee nervously until George breaks into my silence: “I understand that you might be wanting a rest after a good run, Dave, give someone else a chance. Why not just take a holiday, if that’s the case? But you’ve been different these past few days. A little... odd. Is there something going on in your personal life that might be affecting your work?”

I stand up and slam my hands down on George’s desk. “My personal life?” I shout. “My personal life? George, my personal life could fill tomorrow’s paper. My ex-girlfriend, who happens to be Stephen Fucking

Doyle's intended, is pregnant and having an abortion, there are big cats on the moors, my dad's seen a UFO, the landlord of my local has turned into a plant, all my mates think I'm weird, I'm being stalked by a covert quasi-Governmental agency, I need to find a man with a violin case, and I'm seeing a shrink. My personal life? I wouldn't wish it on a scabby dog."

Of course, I don't really say that. I sit there and mumble that everything's okay. There have been a couple of things, my friend died, but I'm all right now. I'm back on track. George doesn't seem convinced. "Dave, if you need any time off... well, you know you've still got a couple of weeks owing to you. Why not take next week as holiday? We can manage without you, we've got quite a few in at the moment. Why not try to get away somewhere?"

Then it hits me like a freight train. Oh my God. They've got to him, they've got to George. He's trying to get me out of the way. I go on holiday for two weeks, then I never come back. I just disappear from sight, someone cleans out my desk, everyone else is told that I've emigrated to Australia or I've gone into hospital. No-one would argue with that, they've all seen that I've been under the weather recently. No, I wouldn't want any visitors, it's best just to leave me and let me get better. I'll be in good hands. Will I be back? Ooh, who knows? Let's wait and see. Good God, I'm sweating like a pig, gripping the arms of the chair until my knuckles have gone white. George looks concerned. "Dave? Dave, are you all right?" It seems like he's in a tunnel, shouting at me from the end of a passageway. Christ, feels like I'm going to faint. Was there something in that coffee? Has

George
given
me
some
"Drugs."

"What?"

The first voice is Stephen Fucking Doyle's, the second one George's. I feel like I'm swimming my way out of a vat of black treacle, rising towards the light. Shit, I must have blacked out. My eyes flicker and George is looming above me. Doyle is trying to force water from a plastic cup between my lips, but it's dribbling all down my shirt and tie.

. Doyle says again: "Drugs, George, if you ask me. You didn't see him at his birthday party. He was off his face on something. It doesn't surprise me."

There's a long pause, then George says gently: "Stephen, stop being such a fucking idiot, will you? I don't expect you to come running in dishing the dirt on your workmates."

"I came running in because I heard you shout when he fell," says Stephen Fucking Doyle sniffily. "And I am the office first aider, after all."

"Well, he's coming round, he's all right now," says George as though talking to a child. "You can run along, now, Stephen. And not a word about this in the newsroom, please."

Doyle leaves me to struggle to my feet. My shirt's soaking, and not just from the water. I'm drenched in my own sweat, but it's cold and clammy. I should have known. It was so blindingly obvious that I can't see now how I missed it. Doyle. He's the one who's been got at, not George. It was Doyle who drugged my coffee. Shit, he probably knows everything, about me and Mags, everything. Then something else occurs to me. Maybe Mags is in on it, too. Maybe they've both been got at. *Maybe* she's not pregnant at all, maybe it's all part of their plan. Christ, I've been a fool.

George helps me to my feet and I slump down in the chair. Doyle has gone. "You gave me a fright there, sunshine, and no mistake. Do you think you should see a doctor?"

I shake my head. "No thanks, George. Look, I'm sorry about that. I just felt light-headed. I'll get back to work."

Concern shows in his eyes, genuine concern. How could I have suspected George? But it's only a matter of time. They'll get to him. I can't really trust George, he has a wife and family and a job he needs to keep, he's a soft target. "If you're sure..."

I nod, thank him, and get back to my desk. Everyone's eyes are on me as I stroll back through the newsroom. That twat has already started his work, turning everyone against me. Geraldine, the young photographer, is chatting to one of the reporters by the photocopier as I pass. "Hey, you okay?" she says. "Stephen Doyle said-"

"I'm fine," I spit through gritted teeth, carrying on past her without looking. I'm grateful to reach the sanctuary of my desk, to hide down behind the monitor and the piles of papers, books and agendas that box me into my own little space. Doyle has his back to me, on the telephone, probably reporting in already. I click on to the Internet search engine and seek out the Knights of Avalon discussion group.

AGRIMONY ON-LINE? I query.

WHO WANTS TO KNOW? Comes back the reply almost instantly. I pause before carrying on. I tap in the net-name I've been using on The Terminus and the Knights of Avalon.

HI ARCADIA. AGRIMONY HERE. I TAKE IT THAT'S WHO I THINK IT IS?

I smile to myself, glad to have an ally. Does that woman never get off the net? Arthur's phone bill must be monstrous. I type: IT CERTAINLY IS, AGRIMONY. DID YOU KNOW I HAD A VISIT FROM THE A.G. LAST NIGHT?

The response comes: WHAT? IN PERSON? THIS IS UNPRECEDENTED. WE MUST TALK.

I type: CAN I COME SEE YOU?

Marianne writes back: COME TONIGHT AFTER EIGHT. A IS AT HIS CLUB AFTER DINNER. THIS IS EXTRAORDINARY.

I write: OKAY, AGRIMONY, SEE YOU TONIGHT.

By way of signing off she sends me :-)

I puzzle over the hieroglyphic until I tilt my head ninety degrees to the left and it all makes sense. That's the nicest thing that anyone's said to me all day.

I decide to take a long lunch. As I walk out of the office into the town centre I almost trip over a vagrant sprawled on the pavement. Under the grime and the rat-tail hair he looks about the same age as me. I dig into my pocket and drop a two pound coin into his Tupperware bowl. He raises a hand and says: "Hey, man, you look like you're having a real salmon day."

I stop and frown. "What?"

"A salmon day. You know, man, spending all day swimming upstream just to get screwed at the end of it. Thanks for the brass."

Christ, he's right. Why the hell am I doing this? What's the point of coming into the office every single day, sitting staring at a blank computer screen, and telling people what they don't really need to know? I used to be full of romantic bullshit about the job, I used to believe that I was fulfilling a public service, entertaining, educating, informing. Now I'm not sure it isn't all partly the media's fault. Maybe we're responsible for the spread of the madness. It's like the Alpha Geek said, he has a thought and seconds later he can send it all over the world. How on Earth can we hope to contain the problem when we've conditioned people to be hungry for their daily fix? We get them addicted to a regular diet of news, events and gossip, and now that it's tainted with the madness it's too late, we can't get them off it. They're all going to go down.

I start to say something to the guy but he's looking for his next pound, hailing one of the advertising reps as she walks out of the automatic double doors from the foyer of the Post building. He's like some ancient holy man, some Boddhisattva, imparting his gem of wisdom and then moving on. When he's managed to panhandle 50p out of his next target I return to him. "Can I buy you lunch?"

He shrugs. "Why the hell not?"

I chase my pasta round my dish while Eric demolishes his second bowl of lasagne. "Man, this is so fucking good," he says through a mouthful of food, breaking off huge chunks of bread and mopping up the sauce with them. The waiters at Benny's nearly went into conniptions when I turned up with Eric, and they gave me my now-usual booth at the back of the brasserie, well out of sight. He pauses mid-swallow and points his fork at me. Enough of my mother's conditioning remains for me to consider this rude, and I cough, embarrassed.

"Hey, did you intend to provide a hot meal for the homeless when you woke up today?" he says suspiciously.

What a ridiculous question. "Of course not," I say, affronted. He resumes his meal. "Good. Random acts of kindness are the only way to turn forward the wheel of dharma. You've got to stop thinking of charity as a word and just practice it as a pure concept without even considering what you're doing is charity if you're going to improve your karma, man."

This amuses me. "What, is my karma in bad shape, then?"

Eric slurps noisily at his Java. "Shit, man, I haven't seen karma like yours since the Eighties. What the hell have you been doing?"

I shrug sadly. "Running, mostly."

He nods. "That's bad. You don't face up to things, they get bigger and more powerful, until you end up meeting them on their terms, on their territory. Always better to turn and fight. You know the ancient Greeks? Their warriors cut their hair short at the front and left it long at the back. That way, an opponent couldn't grab their hair in a fight, and they couldn't turn and be a coward and run away because their enemy could grab them and..." He makes a slicing motion with his knife.

We digest this in silence. I eat a little more of my tagliatelli, but in truth I'm not hungry at all. "So why are you on the streets, Eric?"

He shrugs. "Downsized a couple of years ago, man. Used to be a propellerhead, installing and maintaining computer systems for big companies. My firm didn't bother with Millennium Bug insurance so when they had to start replacing all their chips I was considered surplus to requirements. Collateral damage, man. I was just sitting there, tooling up some new software, when word came down from the adminsphere like a message from the gods. You're in, you're out, you're in, you're out. It was like a fucking massacre. Any more coffee?"

I signal for another cafetiere and abandon my pasta. "Couldn't you get another job?"

"Nah, every other computer consultancy was in the same boat. Ended up doing a bit of cybersitting, you know, teaching basic Internet orienteering to rich kids with big fuck-off systems bought by their parents, but that didn't last. It isn't that hard to find your way round a computer system, the whole thing's just cloaked in mystery and jargon to keep the consultancies in business.

"After that I had a couple of G.O.O.D. jobs working for seagulls, but then the spondulicks ran out, the flat and car were repossessed, and I found myself in nowheresville."

I'm a few sentences behind. "Good jobs for seagulls?" I grasp helplessly.

He gratefully receives the cafetiere from the wrinkle-nosed waiter. "Yeah, G.O.O.D. job - you know,

Get Out Of Debt job, something short term that pays well. But like I said, most of 'em are working for seagulls, the kind of guys who flap in and shit over everyone with as much noise as possible, then flap out again. Bollocks. I'm better off on the streets."

Maybe he's right. I've been running scared, waiting for the shit to hit the fan with my head between my legs and counting down from ten. Perhaps I should be out there, taking things into my own hands. I have friends who can help me. Colin's gone, the Alpha Geek's gone, but I have Agrimony, I have Pete and Tony, I have Emma. I'm not alone.

We part at the foyer to the Post building. Eric shakes my hand and settles down against the wall, producing his Tupperware bowl from inside his thick army jacket.

"Thanks for the scran, man. You need any help finding your way around the streets, you come to me. Ask anyone round here, they all know me. Zen Eric."

I return his thanks and turn to go inside. He shouts: "Hey, your karma's looking better already!"

Inside I exchange a few pleasantries with the reception staff and I'm just about to go through to the newsroom when there's a squeal of protesting brakes and at least two screams from the street. I rush out to where a small crowd has gathered, Zen Eric among them.

I push through to the centre where a big, black, and very dead panther lies in a pool of its own blood on the steps of the Post building. It's as big as a small horse, its muscular rear legs bound by cord, a still-bleeding bullet hole in its skull.

The Beast. Someone's bagged the Beast of Shotmoor, and they didn't stick around for their reward.

I turn wordlessly to Eric. "Man," he says slowly, eyes wide. "This is so heavy. It happened so fast I could barely take it in. This car just pulled up, the back door opened, and someone just hauled a fucking panther right out on to the street."

"What car, Eric," I say fiercely. "*What car*?"

He holds up his hands to ward me off. "Cool your jets, man. It's gone now. Someone threw out the cat and it just sped off. A big car, it was, man, a big, black car."

TWENTY-SIX
...THE WEIRD GET GOING

I sit naked in my silent room and merge with the darkness, willing myself to become invisible, to disappear. The curtains on the big window are wide open, bathing the room in orange streetlight. Zen Eric is right. I can't keep running. I have to turn and fight sometime, and it looks like it's going to be now. There's only one person who can help me, and that's the man with the violin case. I need to find him tonight.

It's almost seven by the luminous hands of the clock in the kitchen. In the darkness I fix myself beans on toast. But how do I find him? Where do I start? I'm due to meet Marianne after eight. I can only hope I was wrong about the Alpha Geek, and they didn't get him last night. Maybe we can contact him at Marianne's. Maybe he can help.

I feel like I should be better prepared than this, but I just don't know how to be. I'm going out into the night with nothing. I get out a small black rucksack but don't know what to put in it. A knife? Maybe a gun, if I had one. I look at my book collection. The Bible?

Crowley's Magick in Theory and Practice? Bukowski's Tales of Ordinary Madness? No-one else has been through anything which can prepare me for tonight. I'm the one who's writing the plot now. I just wish I had an ending in mind.

In the bathroom I look at my reflection. Christ, I've changed. I never knew I was so thin, so pale. My eyes are black, dead, like sharks' eyes. I remember what Zen Eric said about the Ancient Greeks, and take up the scissors I brought with me from the kitchen along with the two sharpest knives in the flat. The steel feels cold against my forehead as I slice along my fringe, cutting a jagged line from ear to ear. There. No turning around now.

I walk around my flat, touching things, feeling their strangeness. The stereo system, the television, so much money spent on the messengers of my downfall, the machines that beamed the words and the pictures of the fever into my home and into my head. My fingers trail along the racks of uniform CDs, bursting with the potential energy of words and discordant clashings, full of sound and fury and signifying, I realise now, nothing. I brush with my fingertips pointless little trinkets and ornaments from faraway places. Did I really visit these countries in the far-flung reaches of the world, or did I merely dream them? It doesn't seem to matter much, now.

I stop at the wardrobe, shirts and tops and jumpers crammed together, bought purely for the labels that marked them with a perversely individual uniformity. I select my clothes for the evening. I'm dressing for the night now, black jeans, black polo-necked sweater, boots, leather jacket. I clothe myself in the darkness, all the better to merge with it, to fight it where it least expects. I'm part of it, now.

I pick up the mobile, then decide against taking it. Too many people know the number now; they could use it to get at me. I take it to the kitchen and drop it in the pedal bin.

I take a last look around my flat before I leave, I believe, for ever. Memories sit silently like dusty ghosts. Not my memories, not any more. That was then. This is now.

I walk the streets of my town, but it's not the town I thought I knew. Scraps of black polythene flutter in the wind, hanging scarecrow-ragged on rusty, barbed wire that's forgotten whether it's supposed to keep people in or out. A lamp-post buzzes furiously as I walk past, the electric whine almost telling me to turn back. But I walk on along the rain-sheened streets, past the bastard raven-crows that chatter on telephone wires and fall suddenly silent as I stride past. A wet dog with bright eyes sniffs the air from a darkened doorway, its way home obliterated by storms. It's not the town I knew, but all this seems strangely familiar, as though it was all here all the time, and just occasionally I glimpsed the world under the surface, when my guard was down.

It occurs to me that it's a hell of a walk to Marianne's. Somehow the car didn't seem right, too visible. I cut through a darkened ginnel and emerge near the bypass, in time to see a double-decker in the distance. It's ages since I caught a bus. I fumble around in my jeans for change and jog the hundred yards to the grafitti'd shelter in time to stick my hand out and signal for it to stop.

I'd almost forgotten what day it was. The bus is full of Friday night people, the girls, the boys, the couples, the bingo pensioners. I squeeze into the only free seat and try to stare out of the window, but have to content myself with my reflection. The occupants of the back seat, a bunch of billykids coming up on their first pill of the night, bounce up as soon as the bus stops near an out-of-town club and jostle me as they fight their way to the door. A shaved head looms in front of my face and sneers: "Sorry, mate," in the sort of voice which suggests he's not sorry and I'm not his mate. I turn back to the window and try to stare past my mirror image into the night.

I clutch my bag close to me on my knees. In the end I brought the two knives, the scissors, a battery torch and the Bible. Don't know why. I've never really been a Christian. Never really been much of anything. In fact, I think it was my dad's old Bible from when he was a kid and it just got lumped with my things when I moved out of home. What good I think it will do, I don't know, but for some reason it feels vaguely reassuring as I brush my fingers over its soft leather inside the bag, which suddenly is wrenched from my grasp as I stare absently through the window.

"What've you got in here, then? Mucky books?"

The girl can barely be old enough to go into pubs. Her skirt just about covers her backside and her legs are blue and mottled in the cold. There are three other clones giggling behind her. "Give it back," I say quietly.

With a childish grin to her friends she digs into the bag and pulls out the book. "It's a Bible. Here, are you one of the God Squad, then? One of the doomers? Come to tell us it's all a sin, and we're all going to burn on Judgement Day? It's only a Friday night out, you soft shite. What else have you got in here?"

She reaches in again and withdraws with a small cry, blood colouring her pale fingers. "Fucking hell," she screams, to the tutting disapproval of the pensioners. "It's full of knives! He's a fucking serial killer!"

My face burning, I lurch to the front of the bus, abandoning the bag. "Stop, please," I urge the driver. He ignores me. "Please?" I try again. Eventually he looks at me. "Not until the designated stop, mate."

"Just fucking stop!" I yell, and the bus goes quiet. "Nutter," says a deep, menacing voice. "Ooh," says one of the girls, and giggles. The driver looks shaken and pulls up sharply at the kerb, and I tumble off, to catcalls and jeers from the bus. It pulls away as a gang of blokes bangs on the windows and someone shouts "wanker!"

I watch the bus rattle off into the distance until I'm alone on a strange street. A rain spot hits me square on the nose, but no more falls. A downpour is threatening. It's holding off for now, but I can feel the pressure bearing down. It's going to be a heavy night.

I don't recognise the area but I set off walking in the direction that the bus took. Dark, soot-grimed brick walls rear up on either side of a wide road, impassive mills now given over to fly-by-night business cocooned in prefabricated cells within. Closed circuit television cameras wearing necklaces of barbed wire are perched high on the buildings like modern gargoyles. A ripped poster has been pasted on one wall: "Watch therefore, for ye know neither the day nor the hour which the son of man cometh." The Alpha Geek? Or the work of one of a thousand members of a thousand doomsday cults? I don't care any more.

I leap a good six inches in the air as two metal dustbins clank together sharply and a cat screams like a baby as I pass a dark alley. Shit. My heart's beating like fuck. I feel in my pocket and pull out one of three tight joints I rolled before leaving the flat. As I drag the first breath of sweet smoke down deep I can feel the tension easing. Christ.

I'm still miles from Marianne's, with a nasty part of town to cross first, if I've got my geography right. Ahead of me the quiet street opens on to a harshly-lit and busy ring road. Maybe I can get a taxi there.

On the corner is a pub and after trying in vain to flag down two or three passing cabs I decide to dive in, phone a taxi firm, and maybe have a pint while I wait. Big mistake. As soon as I push open the door to the lounge I realise that. It's one of those pubs you know you shouldn't be in, in that no man's land between the town centre and the estates, the sort of place where you wouldn't go in a million years unless the landlord knew the name of your father and his father before him. It would be an exaggeration to say everyone goes quiet and looks at me when I walk in, but only just. It's not the kind of place where you look too closely at people, so I keep my head down and head straight for the bar. The woman standing behind it is blonde and blousy, her breasts forced together like unwilling dancers, her face powdered and painted like a whore. She stares at me dispassionately, as though through me she can see the long night stretching ahead. When she says: "Yes, love?" it's in a bored monotone.

"Pint. Lager." I say quietly, dumbing down my accent to what seems like an acceptable grunt, all the time casting around for the payphone. As she pushes the pint on to the drip-tray and I drop the coins into her hand, I spot the phone behind a trio of fleece-clad lads watching the football on the satellite TV.

"'Scuse, mate," I grunt, squeezing past them to the phone. The biggest one raises an eyebrow but they say nothing. There's one business card pinned above the phone with a taxi number on it, and three for escorts. I dial and book a cab. As I give Marianne's address, one of the lads behind me says none too quietly: "He's a bit far from home, innee?"

Fifteen minutes to the taxi. I sip my pint, trying to concentrate on the football. "Nice fucking haircut," comments another. Shit. I get that adrenaline rush that signals trouble. I wish I had my bag and my knives. I sneak a look and realise with dismay that they're the group of lads from the bus, the ones who shouted wanker at me. The big one clocks me looking at them and leers: "Got a fucking problem, *mate*?"

"I think he's queer," pipes up the one who mentioned my hair.

The big one, obviously the spokesman of the group, pushes his cologned face closer. "You fucking *queer*, then? That why you got a stupid fucking *haircut*, then?"

Obviously, these aren't questions which demand answers. When the big one pushes me hard on the shoulder, the rest of the pub clientele avert their collective eyes. When the first punch lands home in my gut, I briefly meet the gaze of the barmaid, but she just closes her eyes and shakes her head, as though it's all my fault.

"In't you going to *hit* me, you fucking puff?" roars the big one, just before his forehead finds mine. As my legs crumple, I hear a growing cheer, and wonder what sort of people they are, before I realise it's coming from the TV. "Goal," says the big one, taking a long draught from his pint. "What a fucking result."

Thirty seconds later a booted foot propels my arse on to the pavement just as a red Citroen glides to the kerbside. The fat guy behind the wheel looks at me pityingly. "You must be my nine o'clock," he sighs. "Where to, sunshine?"

It finally starts to rain as I reach Marianne's. The house is in darkness as I pad up the drive to the elaborate double door and ring the chiming bell. The doors are yanked open almost immediately, but to my dismay not by Marianne. A short, balding man with an unkind face glares at me. "Um," is all I can think of to say.

He turns and shouts into the hall: "Is this the one? Congratulations, you bloody slut. He's younger than I thought he would be." He turns back to me and shouts: "Have you been fucking my wife?"

This, then, must be Arthur. I start to back off. He's nothing special, but he's angry and I'm still smarting from the last kicking I had. Behind him I can see Marianne, her cheeks puffy from crying. She looks like she could be nursing a black eye, or it could just be the mascara. Arthur advances on me as I retreat.

"I don't know what sort of bullshit you've been filling her head with, but it stops now," he hisses at me, jabbing me in my shoulder with his forefinger. "Christ, she's been having treatment for three years now and the doctor reckons it might all be for nothing, because of you."

I keep staggering backwards until I reach the gate, and look beyond Arthur to where Marianne hides in the shadow of the doorway. "I need help!" I shout over his shoulder. "They're after me! I think they got the Alpha Geek. Marianne!"

As Arthur pushes me off his property and slams the wrought iron gate shut, he says quietly: "You sound madder than she does, son. I feel sorry for you, more than anything. I'm sorry, but as of now, Agrimony is well and truly off-line."

The clouds let loose their burden as I stand in Marianne's cul-de-sac. I could panic now, but I won't. I've lost Marianne, and with her any chance of finding out what happened to the Alpha Geek, but it isn't quite the end of the world. There are others. I jog through the rain to the end of the street and head off for the main road and, I hope, a telephone box. Half an hour later my taxi draws up outside Emma's house.

Emma opens the door to my insistent ringing. "Christ, Dave, I've been trying to find you all day," she whines. "You're soaking. Come in."

I gratefully sip the sugary tea she's made for me. Over the fireplace in her lounge there's a big poster of Gustav Klimt's The Kiss. "We're alone," she says, unnecessarily. "Everyone went out but I stayed in trying to get hold of you. Dave, it's nearly ten o'clock-"

"I know, I'm sorry," I cut in. Christ, this is the last thing I need. "Emma, listen, they've got to the Alpha

Geek and somehow they've got to Marianne as well. I need to find the man with the violin case tonight. You've got to help me."

"Marianne?" she says sharply. "Who's Marianne?"

"Marianne. Agrimony. I'm sure I told you. Anyway, this isn't important. Are any of your housemates connected to the Internet?"

Then, incredibly, she starts to cry, just sits there with her hands tangled in her lap and starts to cry. "Dave, what's happening to you?" she sobs. I put the tea down on the floor. She isn't going to be any use to me.

Emma's hands claw at my leather jacket as I try to leave. "Dave, you need help," she screams. "Please, let me come with you. Let's go to Steam, talk to people, come on, Dave, *please*!"

Before I leave, I turn to her. "Look, when all this is over, I'll call you." I give her a chaste kiss on the cheek and leave her sobbing in the doorway as I press on through the rain.

I'm running out of allies, and fast. It's Friday night, I can only guess where Pete and Tony are. The Green Man's out, of course and we don't go to the Cross Keys on a weekend. Chances are they haven't gone on to a club yet, so that leaves a shortlist of about three possibles for this time of night. After striking out on the first one I make Mad Paddy's at ten to eleven. The bouncers give me a quizzical look but can't be bothered to hassle me so late in the evening. I push through the crowds thronging the bar for last orders, scanning the shirts and mini-dresses for any sign of Pete and Tony. Eventually I spot them chatting to two blonde girls who could be sisters and squeeze my way over.

Pete greets me with a beery grin. "Dave! Thought you'd fucking died! Meet, ah..."

"Sonya," grins one of the girls. "Tanya," says the other, more sulkily. I'm not surprised, really, as she's got Tony and he's probably boring her with the relative merits of super unleaded petrol. He was never a knockout with the ladies.

"They're twins," says Pete, and if he intends the wink that accompanies the statement to be surreptitious, he doesn't make a very good job of it. I nod at both the girls and then take Pete by his elbow. "Listen," I whisper. "I need help. I'm in trouble."

Pete takes in my dishevelled appearance and blackened eye for the first time, and squints into the crowd behind me. "Have you been scrapping? Where are they?"

I shake my head as Tony joins us. "No, not that. I'm..." Suddenly, I'm lost for words. How do I explain to Pete and Tony what's going on? How much use are two pissed up lads going to be to me anyway? I start to tell them it's okay, but it doesn't matter. They're puffing out their chests and preening their feathers ready to see off two interlopers with their eyes on the twins. Leaning on a cigarette machine is never a good idea if you want to pull successfully without potential rivals butting in. Without another word I quietly withdraw into the crowd and make my way out of the pub.

By now I've almost resigned myself to facing this on my own. Perhaps that's as it should be. One more chance, but as I find a telephone box and dial the numbers, I know it is so slim as to be almost non-existent. By a fifty-to-one chance, Mags answers instead of Stephen. "Hi," I say quietly.

She knows who it is. "Hi. What are you doing calling me at home?" Christ, she sounds so cold.

"Mags, I need help, I-"

She cuts right in, emotion cracking her voice. "I needed help today, Dave. I needed help when I drove to that private clinic and booked myself in for the afternoon. I so wanted someone to hold my hand when they sucked that bloody mess from inside me, Dave. There were nuns demonstrating outside with placards, for Christ's sake. And when they let me out there was a big truck marked clinical waste parked up to collect it all." She degenerates into strangled sobbing and then hangs up. I stare numbly at the handset for some moments, then replace it. I know better than to call again.

So, that's it. I don't really know anyone else. I'm no closer to my goal, yet in a way I've come so far tonight. But there's still a long way to go, and somehow I'm sure that one way or another, I'll have answers by the morning. I leave the main square and head for the quieter streets, walking past the shuttered department stores and the homeless huddled in doorways. I need to find him tonight, the man with the violin case, but I've not the faintest idea where to start looking. I don't even know what I'm going to do when I find him, whether he'll have the answers I need. I walk past the market hall towards the Post offices, with vague notions of getting on the Internet. But that's a pointless exercise. I know deep down the Alpha Geek's been taken, and Agrimony is beyond me now. Besides, the man with the violin case isn't hiding on the World Wide Web, he's here somewhere. I need a guide to the streets. I stand before the darkened foyer, pondering my next move, when a voice hails me from a darkened doorway:

"Looking lost, man. Need help?"

Zen Eric.

TWENTY-SEVEN
PARADISE REGAINED

The rain-wet streets are my uncharted territory, Zen Eric my guide. I really thought I knew this town like the back of my hand. Only someone's chopped off my hands, and I've lost my way. It's as though I've been walking around in sunglasses for a quarter of a century and I've suddenly taken them off. Now I'm blinded by the things I never saw before.

Zen Eric seems singularly unsurprised to see me. "I knew you'd be back," he nods, taking a deep drag from a tight joint and handing it over.

"So, what do we do now?" I ask, sucking in the hot smoke. Eric lets the smoke trail from his mouth and shrugs: "A journey of a thousand miles begins with the first joint." We laugh like old friends. We're off.

Our first stop is a caravan which doles out soup to the homeless in a side street off the market square. I gratefully accept a Styrofoam cup of watery minestrone, digging in my pocket for change but the volunteer worker has already moved on to the next one, just as I seem to have moved seamlessly into another world. Despite its tepidity, the soup is warming, and serves to remind me that I can't remember the last time I ate properly. At the end of the alley the Friday night world goes by, gangs of lads, groups of girls, couples. The street people weave unseen between them. Here in the darkness of the alley, fed by well-meaning charity workers, I could be watching my old life flash by on a television. Not so long ago I would have been out there on a Friday night, chartering a meandering course from pub to bar to club. I'm half sure I've spotted this soup caravan before, but it's always been on the periphery of my vision, out there in the hinterland.

We move away from the disparate group huddling around the stark light of the caravan. As we finish our soup I take out one of my two remaining joints and light it with the Zippo. "You're looking displaced," says Zen Eric. "I felt the same way when I first took to the streets. Like you've stepped sideways and no-one can see you any more."

I nod wordlessly. He goes on: "There's an old story out of the teachings of Buddha. A king gathers together three blind men, takes them to an elephant, and asks each of them to tell him what an elephant is like. The first touches a tusk and tells the king an elephant must be like a giant carrot. Another feels an ear and describes the elephant as being like a huge fan. The third, right, the third touches its tail and says the animal's like a huge rope.

"That's like life, man. If we only experience one aspect of it we might as well be blind men. Start feeling your way around a bit, you're going to get more of an idea of the big picture."

We contemplate his words silently, passing the joint between us. As Zen Eric grinds the roach under his boot, he says: "It's time for us to find what you're looking for, man."

I look at him seriously. "Have you ever come across a man with a violin case?"

If I'm expecting some momentous epiphany, a drawing of breath, a flicker of recognition, even, I'm disappointed. Zen Eric looks at me blankly. "Is he on the street?"

"I don't know. I haven't a clue where he is. But I've got to find him, Eric, and tonight."

He doesn't ask me why, and for that I'm thankful. I feel that if I start going into why I need the man with the violin case, even Eric will think I'm crackers. He nods. "Fair enough. I haven't been on the streets that long, so it doesn't mean much that I haven't met this guy. But there are others who've been here longer. They might know."

At the edge of the alley, the brightly-lit market square ahead of us, Zen Eric pulls me back into the shadows. "This is a mission, isn't it?" he hisses.

I shrug. "I suppose so."

He digs into his bag and pulls out a small plastic bag, the kind banks use for change. From the bag he takes out two garishly-decorated tiny cardboard squares. "I never do a mission without these, man."

"Acid, Eric? I don't think so."

He tosses one of the cardboard tabs onto his tongue and gulps it down. "This is a mission, man. Don't tackle it on the terms of your old life, you'll never survive. The acid'll help you strip away the filters, get a better view of the elephant, man."

What the hell. Things can't get any worse. I take the tab and chew its bitterness before swallowing the pulp. I run a hand through my hair. I'm a true Ancient Greek, now.

No turning back.

We stride up the main drag, past a number of ragged figures huddled in shop doorways. I call for Eric to stop. "Shouldn't we be asking these people?"

Eric shakes his head. “Think of the streets as an onion, man. Different layers. This is just the top, the surface, they don’t know shit about what you want. We’ve got to go deeper. Can you handle it?”

I nod. The acid is coming up, uncurling at the base of my skull like an awakening serpent, the hairs on my head feel itchy. Christ, is it coming up. We move on.

Eric leads us out of the town centre, towards suburbs I don’t recognise in the dark. Fly posters advertise happenings in venues I’ve never heard of, featuring bands and DJs I’ve never come across. Sometimes I have to look twice at the street names and shop signs, as though they aren’t written in quite the correct English. We avoid people, which is fine by me.

I begin to lose my sense of time. I’m not sure whether it’s ten minutes since I ran into Eric, or two hours. Sensing my agitation, he lays a calming hand on my shoulder as we walk. “Nearly there, man,” he assures me quietly.

“Where?” I ask, trying to keep the hysteria from cracking my voice as Eric steers me into a dark alley blown with papers and rubble. We stop by a darkened doorway. It all seems horribly familiar. Eric looks up and down the alley then raps once on the door. A panel slides back and a pair of eyes peer at us. Christ, I don’t believe it. A pair of eyes, one blue, one green. Arcadia, at last.

The eyes regard us for a moment, then the hatch slams closed. Painstaking seconds later the door swings open and Eric steps in, nodding to the hulking bouncer. “Cheers, Otto. Come on, man, let’s get a drink. You’re buying.”

We push through the purple smoke into the club, discordant jagged sounds squalling at us from the DJ booth. I catch up to Eric and shout into his ear: “Eric, what is this place? This is where it all started to go wrong, I’m sure of it.”

He stops and stares at me. "You've been here before?" he shouts. "I'm impressed. Straights can't normally find this place, much less get past Otto. It takes me all my time to remember where it is. Best policy is to *not* try to get here, and you tend to just stumble across it."

I nod and we continue to the bar. I remember the first time I was here. "I'll get them, Eric. I know the password."

Eric grins at me. "It's one of the worst-kept best-kept secrets on the street. Anybody who's nobody knows the Arcadia password." To prove his point he nods at the bored looking girl who was behind the bar the first time I came and shouts: "Two Red Mists, Angie. *Et In Arcadia, Ego.*"

We get the drinks and lean on the bar. "That's typical of Arcadia," Eric shouts. "You don't need a password to get in, but you need one to get a drink. That cracks me up."

Arcadia's full of its usual weird crowd. The transvestite Pete was trying to pull is sandwiched between two besuited young thrusters, being plied with drinks. Lola's certainly got something that keeps the boys coming back for more. By the door, Otto whiles away the time between new arrivals by reading an Enid Blyton paperback. In the corner some lucky bastard's getting a blow job. "It's a bit weird," I mutter.

Eric hears me. "If you think this is weird, wait until we get downstairs."

"What then? Do we ask questions?"

"Not unless we want our throats opened with a straight-razor," shouts Eric. "No, what we do is wait until we get an audience with Miss Marbles."

We wait, and while we wait, we drink. Eric sits on his stool, nodding his head in time to the music, waving at people he knows and briefly chatting as they pass. I sit silently beside him, struggling to control the acid that's making me want to run screaming into the street and keep running until I get back to normality. But it's too late for that, and I know it.

"Eric, how did you find this place?" I ask him.

He wipes his nose on the back of his sleeve. "Not sure. Just stumbled across it. What about you?"

I think back to that night which seems so very long ago. Me, Pete and Tony in Arcadia, fish out of water. They managed to shrug it off and forget about it, so why not me? "We were brought here by a cab. Well, a guy in a car, anyway."

Eric nods. "One of the scouts."

"Scouts?"

"A lot of people find their own way to Arcadia, but occasionally some of them have to be brought here. There are scouts, looking for them. I guess one found you."

"Brought here? But for what?"

Then the doorman, Otto, lumbers over to us and whispers into Eric's ear. Eric drains his Red Mist and leans in close to me, shouting: "It's time. Miss Marbles will see us now."

I follow Eric on a zigzagging path across the dance floor to the back of the club where a man who can only be Otto's twin brother stands sentry by a doorway shielded by strings of metal beads. He pauses, then nods us through, and Eric shouts: "Cheers, Otto." I don't ask. Inside the doorway is a steep staircase that descends into a darkness tinged with red. The gateway to hell if ever an LSD-soaked mind saw it. Bass-heavy music thumps up to greet us as we cautiously follow the stairs, me fumbling for the rail as we go. The stairs end at a blank door and Eric raps on it sharply. Otto opens the door and lets us into a room at least as large as the club above us, bathed in red light and hung with thick velvet drapes. To the left is a DJ booth, a dark figure in a bulky fur coat spinning heavy, thudding tracks a tad short on melody. Still, the denizens of

Arcadia's basement seem to like it. Zen Eric forges ahead, pushing through the drapes, and I follow him meekly, trying not to look at the masked woman flagellating a fat, middle aged man with a cat o'nine tails. As we negotiate a knot of leather-clad dancers gyrating to the noise, a tall man wearing stockings and suspenders grabs me by the shoulder and looks into my frightened rabbit eyes with what he must believe to be a meaningful stare. A similarly dressed woman pushes his hand away, winks at me from beneath her domino mask, plants a light kiss on my lips, and leads the man back into the dancing. Eric is disappearing ahead of me into the red smoke. I dash after him, dragging him to a halt. "Eric," I shout into his ear. "What the hell is this place? It's like a bad fucking Rocky Horror Show nightmare. Do you really think anyone is going to be able to help us here?"

"Not *anyone*," he calls back. "Someone. Specifically, her." I follow Eric's outstretched hand to where the fattest, oldest woman I have ever seen in a nightclub reclines on a huge mountain of bean bags and cushions, surrounded by attendants in S&M gear. She must be seventy if she's a day, the wrinkled canyons of her saggy face cemented with thick foundation and lipstick. A young man of barely twenty is on his knees in front of her, massaging her monstrous thighs through the diaphanous dress that covers her like a tent. I have a sick feeling he is about to perform oral sex on her, something I don't think I could stomach right now in my delicate state. Oblivious to what he might be interrupting, Eric blunders ahead, dragging me with him. The enormous woman turns her heavily khol'd eyes, like two fat beetles, towards us and they light up with recognition.

"Zen Eric!" she cries. "Darling, it's been so long!"

Eric inclines his head and kisses the podgy, ringed fingers proffered to him. "Miss Marbles, still looking as beautiful as ever," he says, without any trace of irony whatsoever.

She looks past him and sizes me up like a lioness checking out a gazelle at a watering hole. "Who's your friend, Eric?"

Remembering his manners, Eric turns and introduces us. "Miss Marbles, this is David."

She pushes the kneeling boy away from her and beckons me forward. I take a couple of uncertain steps and she indicates I should sit. I glance at Eric who gives me the minutest of shrugs and then I squat awkwardly by her feet. She lays a thick hand on my head and ruffles my hair. "It's strong in you," she whispers, almost to herself. "So, what do you want, David?" she says kindly.

"We're looking-" begins Eric but she silences him with a sharp wave of her hand. I sit mesmerised by the folds of fat on her arm as they ripple with the sudden movement.

"Let him speak," she chides, turning her eyes on me.

"I'm looking for someone," I say falteringly, the drug making my hair stand up on end. "A man..."

"Darling, we're *all* looking for a man!" says Miss Marbles, and her entourage laugh easily.

I blush furiously and blurt out: "A man with a violin case!"

There's shock, then, in those beetley eyes. She blinks twice, then claps her hands. "Leave us!" she commands. The attendants melt into the drapes. "You too, Zen Eric."

"No!" I shout, then more calmly: "No, Eric stays."

Miss Marbles looks at him levelly, then back at me. "No. Do not implicate others more than necessary. It is better that Eric knows as little as possible about what follows. Leave us, Eric."

Then we are alone, it seems, in the basement of Arcadia. All around us the music thuds dully, deadened by the heavy velvet drapes. I know Eric and the others are but feet away, but it feels for all the world like Miss Marbles and myself are alone in the drifting red smoke. She steeples two fat fingers in front of her clumsily made-up lips for a moment in silent contemplation, then speaks in a measured tone. "The man with the violin case. Where did you learn of him?"

"I've met him, at least twice. Seen him another time. I've *dreamed* of him."

Surprise registers on Miss Marbles' rouged face. "He has shown himself to you in reality and in dreams," she nods to herself. "Have you heard others speak of him?"

I tell her what the Alpha Geek told me of the Anti-Aquarians, of the defector who stole something secret and special from them, which he carries around in his violin case.

Miss Marbles laughs richly. "That sounds like one of the Alpha Geek's, all right."

This time it is my turn for the disbelief. "You know him?" I ask.

Miss Marbles nods. "There are few who walk these paths who don't, David. He is a little... excitable, and his theories are often tinged with hysteria, but in the main he has a sound grasp of the truth."

"I think they may have taken him," I say glumly.

She smiles again. "I doubt it. He's a slippery character, and isn't often taken unless he wants to be."

"What about the man with the violin case?" I ask. "Have you ever met him?"

Miss Marbles takes a moment before nodding. "Yes, long ago. Before I was who I am now."

"Before you were Miss Marbles? Before you ran Arcadia? Who were you?"

She sighs, as though the memories are buried too deep to fish out. "A wife, a mother. A good woman. Then I realised the world wasn't quite the place I had always believed it to be, so I left it." She pauses for a moment, as though lost in a dream, then snaps back to the here and now. "But that is, perhaps, a story for another time. That was then."

"And now?"

"Now I sit here with others like me who have seen beyond the thin veneer of life, and wait."

"Wait for what?"

She smiles. "Ah, that we don't know, but not too long to wait now, I think. Not too long to wait." There's another long pause, then Miss Marbles evidently comes to some kind of decision. "I think we can help you find what you're looking for David, but first you must do something for us."

"A test?"

"If you like. I want you to find someone. Two lost souls, two who belong here. Bring them to me, and I will give you what you want."

I'm frustrated at further delays, and it obviously shows on my face. Miss Marbles ruffles my hair affectionately. "Ah, David, do not fear. Your old life is over, you know. *This* is your life, now. It's not a big thing, I ask, is it?"

"I suppose not," I sigh. "Okay, I'll find your two lost souls. Who are they?"

Miss Marbles smiles enigmatically. "You already know, if you're the person I think you are. The answer is practically in your hand. As you said, David: a test. Find them, bring them here, and you'll make an old woman very happy."

Zen Eric is waiting for me as I navigate the heavy drapes. "Well, man?"

I shrug. "More fucking riddles, Eric. More mysteries. I've got an errand to run for Miss Marbles. You coming?"

He shakes his head. "Better not, man. This is your mission. Good luck, eh?"

Otto lets me out of Arcadia into the silent street. What the fuck do I do now? I don't even know my way out of this weird fucking place. Annoyed, the acid levelling out and leaving me gutted and empty, I ram my fists into my pockets and march off down the alley. As I do so, my fingers brush something in my pocket.

It's a crinkled old press cutting, headlined "Fears grow for pregnant woman". I stare at it blankly, then remember. The island on the duck pond, the twin sisters clumsily working Jepson Street. Miss Marbles' words echo in my head: *"The answer is practically in your hand."*

Heh.

TWENTY-EIGHT
THE LOST WOMEN FOUND

Two lost souls. The twin sisters of Jepson Street. So that's my mission, then. Jepson Street is clear across town, and I've got to get there, persuade the girls to come with me, and bring them back to Arcadia. No problem. We're off.

Finding the cutting has kick-started the acid again, sending little shivers racing up and down my spine. How the hell do I get to Jepson Street from here? I check my watch, but the hands of the fake Tag Heuer don't seem to give me a clear reading, as though time doesn't really matter for me any more. It must be a little after one, I figure. I could get a taxi, I suppose. I fish out my wallet and pull out a wad of notes, staring at them blankly. They don't seem to register for me; they don't seem to have any meaning. What was it Miss Marbles said? This is my life now. I don't move in a world where I take taxis and carry money any more. I stuff the wallet back into my jacket pocket and head off down the alleyway, back the way me and Zen Eric came, or at least what I think is the way. It's difficult to get my bearings around here.

I emerge on to anonymous, deserted, wind-blown streets. I'm lost, but it's a good kind of lost, an expectant, exciting kind of lost. Choosing a direction at random I forge ahead, along gloomy, red-brick rows, shuttered shops, derelict tenements. I need to avoid the town centre, need to avoid people, on my route to Jepson Street. Not that I think that anyone would notice me. I've passed over, changed sides, drawn a veil over my life and stepped through it to otherness. No-one can see me, no-one wants to see me.

No-one, except them.

The sight of the big, black car chokes me. It's there, silent and dead on a street corner maybe two hundred yards ahead of me. Clothed in black I push myself into the grimy grill of a dark shop doorway, absorbing myself into the shadows. Involuntarily, I whisper a word: "Skidoo." It hangs limp and useless and impossibly loud in the dead air. The car seems to shift, as though waking up or solidifying. They know I'm here. The car, though still and quiet, nevertheless seems to cast about like a living thing, sniffing the air, trying to pinpoint my presence. I try to shut down my systems, feeling the cold metal of the grill seeping into my back through my jacket and jumper, becoming one with it. The reinforced wiring is all, merging with my body, molecules slotting seamlessly together until I'm sure that anyone looking at me would be unable to tell me apart from the shop doorway. I try not to react as the car roars loudly into life, its headlights like yellow eyes awakening and sweeping the street as it executes a turn in the middle of the road. Bright light fills my clenched eyelids and then it is dark again, the high beam of the headlights fading from my retinas as the car purrs away, and all is silent once more. I allow myself to open one eye; the car is gone.

They want me, they want me badly. They know I'm near to bringing this to closure, to slipping from their grasp forever. When I bring back the twins, Miss Marbles will tell me where the man with the violin case is hiding, and then it will be over. I will have my answers, and one way or another it will all be over.

I do wonder if I'm just insane, you know, if all this isn't real. But how could it not be? How could I have imagined it all? The Alpha Geek, Zen Eric, Arcadia, Miss Marbles, the man with the violin case... I've met these people, been to these places. Now, to me, it is my *old* life that feels unreal. Getting up every morning, going to work, mindless banter with people I don't really know, drinking in the evenings with Tony and Pete, going to Steam with Emma and Fi and Kex, stolen moments with Mags... this now seems like a fantasy. Having taken a step back from it all, my old life looks so... *pointless*, I suppose. I feel like I've woken up, like some kind of reverse-Dorothy in the Wizard of Oz. I've pulled back the curtain to see who's pulling the levers and turning the wheels that maintain the facade of everyday existence. Instead of the Wizard, there's a man with a violin case, and once I've uncovered him he's making no attempt to hide or help me continue the drama. There's no "ignore that man behind the curtain". He wants to be seen, wants me to know that life is just canvas and greasepaint and wobbly scenery. I've been roughly shaken awake from a deep sleep, and the dream is over. Welcome to the real world.

I've been walking without aim, letting my feet guide me through the maze of badly painted backdrops until I see things I recognise, remember from my dreams. Buildings, shops, pubs, the intricately-assembled pixels of my virtual reality. Advertising hoardings scream their true messages at me now, the garish images stripped away until only the essence remains: EAT OUR FOOD AND LOSE WEIGHT....DRINK OUR BEER AND HAVE FRIENDS....SMOKE OUR

CIGARETTES AND BE SEXY....WEAR OUR CLOTHES AND BE SOPHISTICATED....PLAY OUR CD AND FEEL YOUNG....DRIVE THIS CAR AND FUCK WOMEN....READ MY BOOK AND BE ENLIGHTENED....

And still everyone falls for it, even though they know exactly what messages hide behind the clever slogans and pretty faces. People are willing architects of their own deception, because what's the alternative? The alternative is to be me, skulking through the streets in the early hours of the morning, unseen, unremembered, unmourned.

And finally, finally, I arrive at Jepson Street. It's busy, cars cruising slowly along the kerb, stopping occasionally to carry out small transactions of flesh and money. I move among the streetwalkers and johns, unbothered and unnoticed. An unmarked police car sits quietly at the top of Jepson Street, just keeping an eye on things, but those inside pay me no heed as I wander along, just another lonely soul, just another desperate man.

I pause for a moment outside Cheryl's building. Dare I try to see her again? Is there any point? I hesitate, and the decision is made for me. A new card has been inserted alongside the bell for flat four: Jade. Cheryl's gone, if she was ever here at all. Maybe she's just joined the growing ranks of phantoms which haunt my madness.

I'll know. I'll know soon enough. If the twin sisters aren't here, if no-one's ever heard of them, then I'll know. If I try to go back to Arcadia with my news, and I can't find it, it isn't there, and no-one on the street's ever heard of anyone called Zen Eric, I'll know. I'll know.

"What you looking for, darling?"

The woman is distant, perhaps off in some dreamy reverie of a sun-washed foreign island she is saving up to visit but which only exists in her head, her voice monotone, reciting the lines she has been given in this vast production.

"I'm looking for two girls... sisters, I think..."

She sighs. "Oh, them. Try the top of the street, love. The rest of the girls drove them off the main drag. Bad for business with all that shouting and stuff. Sure I can't tempt you with something a bit more classy? I've got a room..."

I make my apologies and head to the far end of Jepson Street, where the punters and whores thin out somewhat, and the lights are dimmer. And I see them.

They're huddled in a doorway, one with her arms around the other, seemingly talking and soothing her sister quietly. They're filthy, their long hair dull and matted, dressed in rags and cast-off shoes. They see me approach and their eyes flash from the darkness, their teeth bared like animals. The slightly taller, more confident of the two takes a step forward, brandishing a length of iron pipe. "No more!" she screams at me. "We no do more tonight! Okay?"

I lift my arms in appeasement, trying to coax them out with tender whispers. "Hey, hey. Wait. It's okay. I'm not going to hurt you."

The same girl takes another step, holding the pipe up feebly. "She already hurt. Man hurt her. Did it to her and wouldn't give money. Hurt her. No more tonight."

I hold up my hands again and back off slightly. "Hey, it's okay. I've been sent to get you. Take you off the streets, where it's warm and safe. You know Miss Marbles?"

"Miss Marbles? Know no Miss Marbles. You go away now, okay?" She's looking unsure now, but still suspicious. I push my advantage.

"Miss Marbles knows you. Sent me to get you. She wants me to take you home."

The girl lowers the pipe now, and her sister emerges from the shadows, pressing into her side. "Home? He take us home?"

"No," says the girl with the pipe firmly. "We have home. No know no Miss Marbles."

"Home," says the other girl wistfully. "Home. Warm. Safe."

They look at each other. The girl with the pipe looks at me curiously, hope shining in her black eyes. "Home? You promise? Safe?"

"Home," I smile. "Where it's warm and safe. I promise."

They both take a step towards me and the girl gratefully hands me the pipe.

Then all hell breaks loose.

There's a roar of an engine and the three of us are suddenly bathed in the bright white light of headlamps on full beam as a vehicle screeches around the corner. The girls take one look and melt into the darkness. Shit. Shit.

I stand alone, deserted, helpless in the glare of the headlights. I can't see the vehicle beyond the lamps, but I don't need to. There's nowhere to go now, nowhere to run. It's all over.

I hear doors click open and feet step out on to the street. I idly wonder what they're going to do to me. Take me away somewhere? Torture me? Re-programme me to fit back into the game? Or just kill me here and now?

One of the figures steps into the light. "Dave? Oh Jesus, thank God we found you."

It's Emma.

She's joined by Pete and Tony, then Mark kills the engine and the lights on his BMW, and him and Fi climb out of the car as well. Emma's still talking: "After you came round to the house I just didn't know what to do. I phoned Fi and she got Mark and Mick together. Mick and Kex have gone to your flat. Then I managed to get Pete on his mobile. We looked everywhere you might be, and then they said you might be here. I mean, Jepson Street, for fuck's sake, Dave..."

"Thought you were joking about coming here, lad," says Pete kindly.

I stand there and say nothing, but I'm boiling with rage. What the fuck do they think they're doing? I had the girls, had them in my hand, and now they've fled. Emma's holding out a hand to me. "Come on, Dave, come back with us. To Steam. It's going to be all right, baby."

"You have no fucking idea what you've done, you stupid bitch," I manage to spit through gritted teeth.

Emma looks upset and Pete takes a step forward. "Now hang on a minute, Dave," he says warningly. "If it wasn't for Emma here we would never have found you. Try to be a bit grateful, eh?"

"Grateful?" I sneer at him. "Did it ever cross your tiny, pissed minds that I might not want to be found? Get the fuck out of here. You've ruined everything."

Mark and Fi exchange worried glances. Emma appeals to me again: "Please, Dave. Just come with us. Everything will be all right."

I laugh loudly and humourlessly at that. Tony takes a step forward to me, putting a hand on my shoulder. "Come on, mate," he says softly. "We'll sort you out."

"You dozy cunt," I say quietly, and then raise my right hand, the one holding the length of iron pipe, and bring it down sharply across Tony's head. Quiet, easy-going, wouldn't-hurt-a-fly Tony. I just pull back my hand and let rip, smacking him across the temple, indifferently watching the blood gout from his wound. The others stand stunned, shocked, frozen to the spot. Then Tony goes down like a bag of shit, and Pete whispers: "You fucking bastard..."

Then I'm running, flinging the pipe towards Mark's car and hurling myself into the darkness, half of me wanting to laugh and the other half wanting to sob. At the end of the street I risk a glance over my shoulder, but they aren't following me, they're gathered around Tony's crumpled form, Fi on her mobile undoubtedly calling an ambulance. I close my eyes and give myself completely to the darkness.

I sit on a park bench, sucking nervously on a joint. Jesus. No amount of madness or acid can explain away the fact that I just crocked one of my best friends with an iron pipe. I finish the joint and flick it away, staring out into the darkness at the duck pond. This is where they'll be, the lost women. I remember it all now. The young girl who escaped from a mental hospital and gave birth to her twin babies on the island in the middle of the pond in the park, bringing them up on scraps and clothing them in rags. It's a miracle they survived, but they did. And when their mum died, they just carried on living, stealing from bins and thriving on leftovers, until one day someone visited the island, and forever corrupted the twins' idyll. And then it happened again, and he told his friends, and they told their friends, and eventually half the town's men were out here on moonless nights, desperately fucking a pair of feral girls and then leaving a couple of quid before going back to the wife. A veil of secrecy built up around this place, became a tangible thing, until the shame became so strong that the men who did visit the girls genuinely did forget about it as soon as they left the island. Fucking hell.

The night is a few degrees warmer than the last time I visited the park, so the unseasonable, early ice has thawed completely. I stand in the mud on the bank of the duck pond, quietly regarding the black mass of the island in the centre. A quick hunt through the undergrowth turns up a rotten but fairly watertight little rowing boat. Heh. I wonder how many men have pushed this little dinghy into the black waters in the dead of night, aflame with lust, and then slinked away dripping with shame. Who were these men? Builders, bankers, mill-workers and shopkeepers? My dad, for Christ's sake? Who knows? Not them, even, the grimy magic they unwittingly wrought about this place affording them blissful ignorance.

The little boat grinds against the bank of the island close to where another patched-up boat lies in the mud. Makes sense they would have more than one. I tether the dinghy to a naked tree before pushing on unafraid through the dark undergrowth. As I approach the den there's a scratching sound inside, and I cautiously draw back the curtain. My eyes have adjusted to the dark, and I can make out the two girls crouched over a candle, desperately trying to strike wet matches on a worn-out box of Swan Vestas. They look up at me in terror, but I just take out my Zippo and quietly light their candle, watching their faces soften as they recognise me from Jepson Street.

"It's okay," I whisper soothingly, "No-one's going to hurt you now."

"Mister?" says the smaller, quieter of the girls. "You said you take us home."

I hold out my hands, and tentatively they sit up and take one each. "That's right," I smile in the darkness. "We're going home."

TWENTY-NINE
THE MAN WITH THE VIOLIN CASE

I thought I'd have trouble finding Arcadia again, but having the lost women with me seems to act like some kind of charm, a homing device, a passport through the confusion. We walk the streets from the park, sometimes me leading the way, sometimes them, not speaking at all, ignored by the one or two club stragglers and vagrants we meet on the paths. Eventually we fetch up in the dark alley, the door to Arcadia solid and impassive. I knock loudly and wait until Otto slides open the little spy-hole. His different coloured eyes betray no emotion as he opens up the heavy door and lets us in.

Arcadia is still crowded. To be honest, I don't think these people ever go home. The normal rules don't apply here, time doesn't exist. Somehow, I feel it is always night in Arcadia, always party-time. The girls look frightened, holding each others' hands as I lead them through the throng towards the stairs that lead to the underworld. The crowd quietens and watches us as we pass by, as though they know full well of my mission. We push through to the beaded doorway, where Otto waits, quietly listening to Zen Eric.

"Man, you did it!" exclaims Eric. "Shit, I didn't think I'd see you again. Are these...?"

For what seems like the first time, I look at the girls properly. I don't know who the hell they are, is the truth. Ragged and dirty and scared, they've been plucked off the streets by a stranger on some mad mission. God knows what I've brought them to. I'm probably guilty to half a dozen criminal offences here. I shrug at Zen Eric. "The lost women. I've brought them home."

Otto takes me, the girls and Zen Eric down to the other Arcadia, bathed in red light, the drapes dulling the thud of the music. More so than upstairs, the denizens of Arcadia stop and stare as we pass, whispering to each other and pointing at me and the girls. Zen Eric is loving the attention, smiling and waving at people. Otto comes to an abrupt halt and holds aside a heavy drape for us to pass through. We've arrived at Miss Marbles' inner sanctum.

I'm not sure what reaction I'm expecting from Miss Marbles when I step forward with the twins, but it probably isn't this. The vast matriarch of Arcadia is reclining on her bed of cushions and bean bags, while one of her bondage-gear-dressed coterie feeds her *petit fours* and another massages her feet. Otto coughs to announce our presence, and as soon as she spies us her kohl'd eyes light up and she shoos her attendants away. "Oh, David," she cries softly. "You did it. You did it."

She half-rises from the pillows and throws her fleshy arms wide, smiling at the lost women. "My girls, my girls," she sighs. They take a hesitant step forward glancing nervously at each other and back at me. "Come to me, my girls," says Miss Marbles happily. "Come to grandma."

Later, I'm sitting on the floor at Miss Marbles' feet,

while she encloses one of the lost women in each of her vast arms. They seem agreeable to the situation, especially as Miss Marbles has had them cleaned up, dressed and fed. They look quite presentable now, pretty even, and lounge contentedly on either side of Arcadia's queen, sipping at brightly-coloured cordial through straws. Zen Eric has wandered off somewhere, and apart from the lost women, we are alone in the drapes, the red mist rolling lazily around us, the thud of the music seemingly miles away. Miss Marbles regards me levelly.

"You have done well, David," she says quietly. "Extremely well. I did not expect you to return so quickly. You are an adept pupil of this mysterious way of life we lead."

Well, it hasn't been without its cost. I think glumly of Tony, his head split open by the iron piping. I hope he's okay. Miss Marbles says: "Earlier you asked who I was before I became Miss Marbles, before I ran Arcadia. The truth is, I don't run Arcadia. No-one does. It has been here for a long time, far longer than any of its patrons, longer than me, even. There are those who claim it has always been here, in some form or other, a refuge for the lost and lonely and newly-awakened."

"But why here? Why this town?"

Miss Marbles pauses, and smiles. "That's the odd thing, David. Arcadia doesn't seem to be just in this town. Ask someone at random where they are from, and you might be surprised at the answer. People from all over the country tend to find their way into Arcadia, just by taking a wrong turn or getting lost in a strange part of their own town or city. It's almost as if Arcadia exists in its own little..." She searches for the appropriate word.

"Hinterland?" I offer.

She smiles again and nods. "Yes, I like that. Hinterland. On the edge, undiscovered, unmapped. The hinterland. Of course, people in Arcadia say a lot of things, David, much of it undoubtedly clap-trap. But it gives you something to think about, no?"

We pause while Miss Marbles signals to an unseen attendant to bring us fresh drinks. When they arrive and her servant has melted into the drapes once more, Miss Marbles continues. "I was a very normal woman once, David. I kept a good house, had my husband's dinner on the table for him at six-forty-five sharp every night, and doted on my children. My world was clean, and ordered, and smelled of beeswax. My world was nice. I was happy." She sighs, lost in a reverie of times long, long gone. Then her face darkens, and she goes on: "But then I found out that my world was not as perfect as I thought, David. I had a daughter, Elsie, a good girl who was eighteen and worked in a factory sewing jackets that were sold in boutiques in Carnaby Street. She was a little slow, Elsie, a little... uncomplicated. But a good girl, a good girl who did exactly as her parents told her to do.

"She was a little too obedient, unfortunately. On Thursdays I used to play bridge with friends across town. One night one of our number was taken ill and we had to abandon the game after only an hour, and I returned home by taxi, returned home to my normal, uncomplicated, clean, ordered life. My nice life. Do you know what I found there?"

I shake my head. She tells me. "I found my husband fucking my daughter, David. On the settee. With the curtains closed and the lights off, and the television turned down. He was lying on top of her, fucking her like an animal. She was eighteen years old. He had been having sex with her since she was twelve, and the poor girl was too stupid to know that what he was doing was wrong."

I realise I'm holding my breath. I let it out slowly, and whisper: "What did you do?"

She closes her eyes, as though the memories are painful. "At first they didn't see me, standing in the doorway of the kitchen. I had come in by the back door. I watched them for some moments, then calmly went into the kitchen, took my largest knife from my well ordered drawer, and stabbed my husband in the back thirteen times as he had sex with my daughter."

"Jesus..." I breathe.

Miss Marbles nods wryly. "Yes, I used to believe in Jesus. Not then. Not after that. My husband died in agony, rolling off Elsie and falling on to the floor. I idly wondered how I would get blood out of the hearth rug when I realised Elsie wasn't screaming as I would have expected her to be. She was just sitting, staring, not uttering a sound. In fact, she never spoke another word as long as she lived, as far as I know."

"As far as you know?" I say, accepting another drink from one of Miss Marbles' coterie.

She sips her cocktail and shrugs. "Shortly afterwards I was convicted of murder and sentenced to prison. Elsie was put into St Helena's mental hospital. Her mind had shut down. Hardly surprising. Then they discovered she was pregnant."

Then I'm scrabbling in my jacket pocket for the yellowed old newspaper cutting. "Pregnant... Christ. Elsie Peters. Your daughter. Then these..."

Miss Marbles gives the two lost women a squeeze. "Yes. Elsie's children. My granddaughters. While I was in prison, Elsie fled from St Helena's, had her twin children, and died. You can probably fill in the gaps for me, now. I knew these girls were out there somewhere. When I was released from prison, I was told that Elsie had probably been expecting twins, and it was unlikely either she or they would have survived a birth in the open. But I knew better." She hugs the girls again.

"But what about the man with the violin case?" I ask.

Miss Marbles nods. "After I was released from prison, I knew that my world was not the ordered, kind place I thought it to be. I had woken up, very much like you must have done, and it was then that he found me. He told me things, things I won't repeat to anyone, not even you, and showed me the world as it is."

"Is it true what the Alpha Geek told me?" I say. "About the Anti-Aquarians? That he was one of them, and stole their big secret, and carries it around in his violin case? That they want us to lose our sense of mystery? Is it all true?"

Miss Marbles holds up a hand. "I have had my answers from the man with the violin case, and they are for me. You must get your own. He found me, and not long after that, I found Arcadia, and I have been here ever since. And now my little family is complete."

Miss Marbles hugs the girls again for long minutes, and it seems like she has forgotten I am here at all. I fidget for a moment, and I almost think my audience is at an end, when Miss Marbles says: "Why do you seek the man with the violin case, David? What do you think he can give you?"

That's a question I've been trying to answer since my life went down the tubes. I shrug. "The truth, or at least a version of it I'm happy with."

Miss Marbles laughs lightly. "A regular little Boddhisattva-in-training, eh? Well, David, we'll help you here at Arcadia as much as we can. Just remember, when this is all over, there will be a place for you here. I think you'd fit in fine." She claps her hands and suddenly Otto - or one of the Ottos - is looming over us. I struggle to my feet. "Otto will take you to the door, from then on you're on your own."

"But I still don't know where he is!"

"Use your instincts, David. He's there, if you know where to look. Don't make it too complicated for yourself. Sometimes the most well-hidden things are right there in front of us."

The door shuts behind me and I'm well and truly alone in the pitch-dark alley, just me and a head full of strong acid. There was no sign of Zen Eric in the club as Otto marched me out. Still, I'm sure he'll be fine. I can't remember which way we came into the alley, but I'm fairly sure it was from the left, so I strike out to the right, towards a well-lit street. I emerge on to a quiet road intersected by another, red-brick shops and businesses standing silent. It all looks terribly familiar. There's an old-fashioned red telephone box on the corner and I jog towards it, yanking open the door to the piss-stinking cubicle to read the location sticker inside: This British Telecom Call Box is located at the junction of Fugue Street and Lethe Lane. Ah. Full circle.

So this is where he hides, the man with the violin case, this forgotten corner of town, this place on the fold of the map that no-one can quite remember properly, this perpetually twilit world known only to the lost and the lonely, the dispossessed, the street people, the dogs who have lost their way home.

Rubbish blows in the wind, a Daily Sketch bill flutters outside a boarded-up newsagents. I stand in the road, roaring at the top of my lungs. "Where are you, you bastard? Show yourself!" No-one wakes, no lights go on in flats above shops. I doubt if there is anyone here to wake. Then my eyes light on a rusty sign on the cross-roads, white with a familiar red logo and a single word. Station. Miss Marbles' words come drifting back: "Sometimes the most well-hidden things are right in front of you." Hiding in plain sight, it's a ninja trick, the Japanese have a name for it. I remember that train journey home after the visit to Emma's therapist, stopping alongside that Beeching'd station, overgrown and forgotten, in full view yet completely ignored. The streets beyond it were these streets, out on a limb, the hinterland. The forgotten station. That's where he'll be, the man with the violin case.

Everything forgotten is in these streets. As I walk to the station, I pass Ford Cortinas and Morris Minors parked by the kerbs. A rusty bicycle with a shopping basket on the handlebars and the peeling branding of some long-forgotten children's TV show lies propped against a concrete lamppost. Litter blows past, crushed Woodbine packets, empty cans of Cresta, wrappers from Black Jack and Fruit Salad and Bazooka Joe. A shuttered off-licence advertises Watney's Party Four and four-packs of Long Life. Maybe if I stay here long enough I'll be forgotten, too. People will slowly stop remembering that someone used to sit at my desk at work, the neighbours will find it hard to recall who lived in my flat. I'll be just a dull pain in the stomach for Mags and a dull pain in the heart for Emma. Maybe that wouldn't be such a bad idea.

I have to climb a wire fence razored with barbed wire to get on to the boarded up station platform. Even in its heyday it wasn't much, two concrete slabs on either side of the track with one waiting room. Bushes and weeds have choked the life out of the place now. I kick away rubbish blocking my path to the waiting room and there's a chattering and squealing of rats. I was scared of rats, once.

The flaking wooden door hangs off its hinges, once padlocked up but burst apart by glue sniffers or teenage shaggers. I push the door back, squinting into the darkness of the dusty waiting room, making out broken benches and, in the far corner, a table and a shadowy figure.

"Welcome," says a rich, modulated voice from deep inside the room. "I've been expecting you."

THIRTY
WEIRD SHIT'S HAPPENED

In a dark, dark town, there's a dark, dark street. In that dark, dark street, there's a dark, dark house. In that dark, dark house, there's a dark, dark stair. Up that dark, dark stair, there's a dark, dark room. In that dark, dark room...

In that dark, dark room, there was always a ghost, or a spider, or some amalgam of movie monsters and childhood nightmares. That was a favourite when we were kids, a staple, a standby for when the real ghost stories ran dry. Huddled around a flickering torch in a tent borrowed from an older brother of someone's, after the fire had burned down to dull embers, no-one brave enough to venture out into the blackness for more wood. Someone might suggest turning in and there'd be a scramble for the tent, none of us wanting to be the last one in, none wanting to feel phantom fingers raking their back. Then we'd collapse laughing, burrowing into our sleeping bags, six or more of us wriggling like blind puppies until we interlocked as comfortably as possible in the four-man tent. It was always better to be in the middle. If you were unlucky enough to be on the outside you would be the first target of the mad slasher. The mad slasher who never came, at least for us. When did he start to come, the mad slasher? He was an issue only for us, the mad slasher, never for our parents, or if he was they never really voiced their fears. I don't think kids go camping these days. If they do, they stay in their front gardens, and even then the mad slasher still gets them. Where did he come from, the mad slasher? Did we birth him in the dead of night? Did our stories give him form? Did our nervous giggling breathe murderous life into him?

Worse still, did we become him? Did we grow up believing in him so much that when we found he wasn't real we put on his clothes and picked up his knife, running its keen edge along our thumb, acting out surreptitiously-snatched video nasty moments with blood-red clarity?

No. No, I can't believe that. He's always been there in the shadows, the moors not far from here testify to that. Like everyone else, the mad slasher got the fever. As the clock ticked on towards a million doomsdays, he slid from the shadows more and more frequently, until he no longer needed the protection of the night. I hope to God that when all this is over children will be able to go camping in the woods again and tell each other scary stories.

Another of our favourites was the one about the couple who ran out of petrol on a lonely road. He goes off for fuel while she nervously waits, turning on the radio for music to take her mind off the heavy darkness pressing down on the car. She hears a newsflash: a dangerous psychopath has escaped from the local high-security mental hospital. She moans in terror, praying for her boyfriend to return. She almost leaps out of her skin when something thuds wetly on the roof of the car above her. Then again. Again. Again. She is almost out of her mind in terror when suddenly lights flash on, surrounding the car. A megaphoned voice booms out: "Ma'am, please get out of the car. This is the police. Everything is under control. Please get out of the car and walk towards us. Do not look back, I repeat, *do not look back*!"

Shuddering, mute with fear, she stumbles out of the car and towards the blinding lights. Behind her, the slapping, thudding sound rings in her ears.

"Do not look back!" urges the police chief, but she can't stop herself, whimpering with the inevitable knowledge of what she will find as she turns around...

You know what she sees, but you carry on reading anyway. The psychopath is on top of the car, bouncing her boyfriend's severed head on the roof, cackling maniacally. The story is always the same. Yet we listen anyway, rapt, terrified, right up to the anticipated denouement. Always, the psychopath bouncing the boyfriend's head on the roof of the car. Every time, the dark, dark room yields... a ghost.

Those tall tales told around the flashlight were the direct descendent of protean world views grunted out by the first men. Little has changed. We still hug the light, fear the darkness. But as scary as the darkness is, do we really want bright headlights shining into every corner, dissipating every shadow?

I had to get out, you know? I took the last of my money and put down a deposit on this place. I don't expect to be here long enough to pay next month's rent. I probably could have bought a one-way ticket somewhere, somewhere warm, but I don't really see the point. They'll find me. At least here I'm close to the place where it all began. I may be on the outer strand of the web, but at least I'm linked to its centre, here in the hinterland.

I haven't seen myself for some days now, and I'm not

about to make much effort to search out a mirror. I can feel at least a week's worth of growth on my chin, and I never did bear whiskers gracefully. I'm wearing a white T-shirt that's yellowing under the armpits, underneath a creased shirt. The bottoms of my jeans are caked in dried mud. These clothes used to mean so much to me, once.

I brought a cardboard box containing fourteen tins of beans, a can opener, three one-litre bottles of Coke, and about a half-pound of speed with me when I moved in. I've been eating one tin of beans a day, the speed keeping my appetite under control. I've been pissing in the sink in the corner of the room and sleeping in my clothes, my head on the squashed cardboard box.

They call this part of town Dodge City. The main road through it is the only old part of town, pre-war housing converted into flats and boarding houses, one or two shops hiding behind security shutters and blank-eyed closed-circuit television cameras. Behind this facade that aspires to some kind of half-remembered respectability sprawls a housing estate, the Frankenstein's monster of some jittery town planner, intended for good but gone rotten and stunted, gangs of lost boys roaming its streets, buying, selling, stealing, taking, giving what nobody asked for.

It's life on the edge. Not just because of the acned youths glowering from darkened doorways, the jumpy crack addicts, the joy riders tearing up the council's lame attempts to brighten up the estate with flower beds. All that's like a flaking layer of anaglypta, barely covering the cracks underneath; the howling dogs and the streetlights that buzz harshly and flicker off as you walk past, the skittering things that scrabble on wet stones in black alleys. I used to be scared that they were rats. Now I pray that's all they are.

He's been expecting me. I walk into the waiting room,

fear and acid making my heart pound like the music in Arcadia. He's sitting at the table, the violin case in front of him. He's been expecting me. Of course he has. I'd telegraphed my movements to anyone who cared to listen. *They* knew where I was, what I was doing, so why not him? A man with a violin case is slightly less obtrusive than a big, black car, after all.

We don't speak for a very long time. He stares at me impassively from under his tombstone brow, I stand there, clothed in night, my eyes adjusting to the darkness. Finally I feel the need to say something, anything, to break the silence bearing down on us. "I've found you."

"You have indeed," he says in his dry, graveyard voice. "But have you found what you were looking for?"

"I don't know," I admit, sitting heavily on one of the broken benches. "I'm not really sure what I was looking for in the first place."

He pushes the violin case forward an inch or two on the table. "This, perhaps?"

I stand again and approach him in the darkness. "That's what you stole from them, isn't it?" I sense a brief nod of assent. "The secret of the Anti-Aquarians."

"Call them what you will," he says.

"Then it's true," I breathe, my legs feeling like jelly. I have to sit again. "It's all true. If we just sit here and let the future wash over us, let them take away our thirst for the unknown, then we've lost, haven't we?"

Silence.

"*Haven't we?*"

In answer, he pushes the violin case an inch further towards me.

And then I know. I know what he stole from the Anti-Aquarians. Like Prometheus stealing fire from the heavens, he whispered away the mysteries they had been hoarding and then began to redistribute them, Robin Hood-like, to the rest of us.

I reach for the case, unclip the locks, and lift the vinyl lid quietly, knowing all the while what's in there.

Nothing.

Nothing. And now I know. So now I sit in my little room, miles from anyone I know and love, and wait. And wait.

And wait.

Days have passed, I don't know how many, any more. They've found me. I've seen the black car twice now, patrolling the street outside my room in the night. They even came to the door, but they were clever, oh yes. They used Emma's voice the first time, pleading with me to open up, saying she'd been trying to find me for days. But I'm cleverer than they are. I said nothing, just sat there with tears streaming down my face until they went away. The next time they used Emma's voice again, and Pete's and Tony's, and they tried to break down the door, but I was ready for that, and I'd pushed all the furniture I could find against it. They said that Tony was okay, that it was just a flesh wound, that it didn't matter. I'd like to think that was true, but I know how cruel they can be.

That was just an hour ago, and I know they'll be back. They're getting desperate now. But it won't matter. When they come back, I won't be here. I know I'm weakening, and I might just let them in next time, if they use the right voice, if they talk to me as my mother, or Mags, or Helen, God forbid.

I wait until nightfall, then I slip silently out on to the street. The car is there, of course, silent and dead-looking, on the other side of the street. I melt into the shadows, willing myself to become invisible. It isn't hard. In a way, I've been invisible for days. I'm the person you pass on the street and ignore, either because you genuinely don't see me or because you don't want to. With an ease and fluidity that is new to me, yet oddly enough seems always to have been there, I slide and swim through darkness and dusk, evading their all-seeing eyes and slipping quietly away.

I'm calmer now than I've ever been. They've made their move, now I'm making mine. I wasn't sure what I was meant to do until I found the man with the violin case. I thought they had to get me then, that it was inevitable. Now I realise I still have choices. If I'm going to wait and hide, I might as well do it with others, at a place where I'll fit in just fine.

Like Zen Eric said, these streets are like an onion. I used to live on the top surface, never even considering that there was more underneath my feet. Now I strip away the layers with ease, tearing through the levels, getting deeper. Helen said it wasn't her fault, she wasn't responsible for all this weirdness. She was right. I think I've always been like this, I think maybe we're *all* like this, it's just that we're so scared of the dark we push the weirdness into a tiny, locked Pandora's boxes in the darkest corners of our mind, and forget about it. Sometimes, though, we're handed the keys to unlock the box, and it all comes flying out. The keys can take different forms, like seeing lights in the sky that may be visitors from distant stars, or hearing voices in your head, or just standing on a hillside and watching the unbelievable bulge of land ahead of you, merging into a deafening sky, and feeling insignificant before the weight of creation. Sometimes the box is unlocked by more mundane things, perhaps watching a loved one die with a steering column jacked into their gut, eyes wet and mouth soft with blood.

Like Pandora, sometimes we have hope left inside, and we can get better. Like me, there sometimes isn't any hope at all. And when that happens, there's only one place you can go.

I've grown to feel comfortable only in the dark. I can't really imagine standing in a street in bright, blazing sunshine any more, visible and vulnerable, every line and pore of my flesh naked to whoever cares to glance in my direction. Better to soak yourself in the night, let your colours drain away until only the shadows and textures of the darkness remain, half-glimpsed and wondered about. As I walk an unerring path, people huddle in doorways, dead eyes long past pleading for help. A mad woman dances in a deserted supermarket car park, pirouetting and curtsying to a shining shopping trolley, for one night only her chivalrous paramour, and hers alone. Dogs nod agreeably at me, sniffing undetected pheromones or receiving squalling transmissions that mark me out as one of the touched. And all the while I weave in and out of you, unseen, each step taking me deeper and deeper into the onion. Although my body walks the same pavements as you and pauses at the same traffic lights, my self is sinking below the crust of normality, through previously unacceptable strata of being, until my mind's eye is sufficiently skewed enough to take me where I want to go.

I find it easier than I thought I would. Remembering that acid-soaked feeling of alienation, I try to latch on to it again, calling up the chemical memory of the LSD trip, re-aligning my brain, clenching my muscles, until I can feel the hairs prickle on the back of my neck and the shivery feeling at the base of my spine. Then I follow Zen Eric's advice and *don't* look for it, just wander around until I find myself in a litter-blown alley and in front of a big wooden door.

I pause for a moment, looking left and right up the alleyway. There are no black cars nosing through the quiet streets like sleek sharks. No men in black or Government agents or horsemen of the apocalypse. I'm alone.

I rap smartly on the door and the eye-level panel slides open. I recognise the face on the other side.

"Zen Eric!"

He opens the door to let me in, the warmth and music billowing out from behind him. "Yeah, man, it's Otto's night off. I figured, hey, it's getting colder, might as well get off the streets until things seem a bit more... sorted out."

"You too, then?"

Eric nods. He holds the door wide open for me. I remember Cheryl's words from long ago: "Even in paradise, things are not always perfect. Even in Arcadia, there is death." And for a moment I look back at the world I thought I knew, and see the death of the life I thought I had, and then accept his invitation and step across the threshold into something new. It's almost a kind of rebirth. Things may not be perfect in Arcadia, but I'll take my chances. Quietly I whisper three *skiddoos*, not to ward off the madness this time, but as a kind of goodbye to my old life.

"*Et In Arcadia Ego*," Eric says as he lets me in and shuts the door behind me for the last time. "And in paradise, I am."

Printed in the United States
95122LV00002B/28/A

9 781904 853190